second chances

by Bill Beaman

Cover photography by Lisa Hurd.

Cover design by Jill Schaben.
www.jillschaben.com

Printed in the USA by
Morris Publishing®
3212 E. Hwy 30
Kearney, NE 68847
www.morrispublishing.com

ISBN 978-0-9838968-0-7

To order more copies:
www.theiowafarmer.com

For Mary.

CHAPTER

No twelve-year-old boy should have witnessed what Henny witnessed on that dark October night in an Iowa cornfield. It was not at all what Henny had been looking for when he'd snuck out the back door of the dilapidated house that lay on the outskirts of a proud rural town with very few houses in as much disrepair as his.

Make no mistake about it; Henny was looking for adventure. He'd been planning this trip for days. Having skipped school that day, Henny had slept in so that he would be rested and could travel swiftly through the cool, dark night. The tires of his secondhand mountain bike had been inflated to just the right pressure at the gas station. He'd even washed the bike and had oiled the wheels to make them run more quietly. He'd filled his water bottle with Mountain Dew, stuck a few Snickers and some dog biscuits into his tote bag, tied a full roll of duct tape to his bike, and left the house quietly, precisely at 10:00 P.M. Henny tiptoed out of the house, not wanting to wake his mother, but fat chance that would happen. The woman was so stoned on whatever she'd been able to get her hands on that week, that she could have watched him go out the door and not given a damn.

Henny knew the route to take. He'd head down the back streets that were darker and avoid the one patrol car that casually cruised around Pigmy at night. The officer would be especially alert this time of year with Halloween just around the corner. A lot of townsfolk became upset when they found busted pumpkins on Main Street and kids caught wandering around after curfew were quickly detained and hauled home.

Henny was out of town in less than five minutes and headed for Dead End Road, just outside of Pigmy, where he would meet up with his partner. A quick trip down the gravel road to the Chambers' farm and there was his buddy, a half-grown border collie pup, that Henny knew would follow him on his bike. He did every time Henny peddled down this road, and sure enough, right on cue, Tippy came sprinting out on the road with his tongue hanging out in a big smile, giving two quiet little barks.

Henny quietly turned his bike around and peddled back up the road a couple hundred yards with the little dog sprinting alongside, easily keeping pace. He stopped the bike, got off, and gave the dog a hug. He teased Tippy's ears a little, rolled the pup around on the ground, both boy and dog happy to be together. Henny talked to the pup a little bit, but as always, felt odd doing it because this was a typical small community and everybody knew everything about everybody, including the fact that this little border collie that Jamie Chambers owned was completely deaf.

Still, as if by fate, Henny had discovered this little dog on other nighttime adventures the past summer, and they had become friends. In fact, Tippy was the best friend that Henny had, actually the only friend Henny had. Two quick swigs of Mountain Dew, a doggy treat for Tippy from his bag, and they were on their way.

When they reached the intersection where Dead End Road began, the duo turned and headed east. Henny knew it was just a little over two miles to the Gunther Farm, their destination. Old Man Gunther had a nice pen of feeder pigs in his lot behind the barn, and Henny needed a boar pig for the little farm he was building behind his house in town. It was a joke at the feed store in town that Old Man Gunther never got his boar pigs castrated until they were too old, and that was just fine with Henny. He needed an intact boar pig to put with the three gilt pigs he'd stolen earlier this fall. He dreamed of raising spotted piglets in the

2

makeshift pen he had created in the dump behind his house.

Tippy playfully nipped at the front wheel of Henny's bike as it rolled down the hard gravel road. The bright Iowa moonlight flooded the landscape, giving them the illumination they needed to travel quickly. Henny, in turn, teasingly kicked a foot out at Tippy, having no desire or intention at all of actually hitting the small dog. Tippy would be of no use whatsoever in stealing a pig, but he loved the little pup, and the dark roads sure seemed a lot less scary when you had a friend.

Almost to the Gunther farm, Henny stopped the bike, got off, and laid it out of sight in the tall grass alongside the road. He unfastened the roll of duct tape, again worrying how difficult it was going to be to catch and hog-tie a boar pig. He whispered to the pup to be quiet, hoping the little dog saw something in the gesture, because he darn sure didn't hear anything.

The partners crept through the wooded pasture behind Gunther's buildings along a predetermined and scouted route. Henny pulled out the Chuck Norris Junior Commando flashlight he'd shoplifted from the Big Mart and turned it on, being careful to keep the light pointed straight down. Twice he got slapped in the face by low hanging branches and darned if a mosquito hadn't found the tiny hole in the seat of his pants where he'd snagged them crawling through a barbed wire fence on a prior trip. He scratched at the irritation as it itched and swelled, and cussed quietly to himself.

Henny could smell the pigpen now and heard a steel feeder lid bang shut, reminding him that pigs don't necessarily sleep at night and that this wasn't going to be a cakewalk. He'd have to catch a boar pig, tie it up with duct tape, pull it up and over the main frame of his bicycle, and walk the whole contraption back to town. He planned to stop every couple-hundred yards and lay the bike down so he could let the pig relax a little and check to make sure it was still breathing. He didn't want to kill it.

The trip would be a tough one, but he'd pulled off this stunt three times already this summer, and tonight should be the last step in putting together his little herd of swine. As he got close to the gate, Henny heard an odd sound and froze. An engine had started nearby. It was probably a tractor, but where? He turned off his flashlight, dropped to the ground, and held Tippy close to him, partly to keep the small dog quiet and partly to help control his fear.

Listening intently, Henny gauged that the sound was coming,

not from Old Man Gunther's farm, but from somewhere west of there, across the cornfield on the neighboring property. He could tell it was not some combine running late at night harvesting corn. Growing up in a farming community he knew that sight and sound. No, this was something else. The engine was working in one place, laboring in cycles. Henny should have ignored the sound, should have stayed with his mission, but Henny, being Henny, had to know what machine was causing that sound and what it was doing on this dark October night out in the middle of someone's cornfield.

So, with Tippy in tow, the two of them began making their way across the wide cornfield, most of the time zigzagging through row after row of eight-foot tall cornstalks, spaced about ten inches apart. With the leaves slapping at his face, Henny would sometimes find a spot where he could scurry down end-rows and make better time. And of course, the sound of the machine they were stalking, like a lot of sounds heard on a clear, cool night, was farther away than he had at first thought. It took nearly fifteen minutes for the boy and dog to reach their destination.

When they did, Henny realized that the noise was coming from a large, yellow backhoe with powerful lights. He could see it digging a sizable hole. He wondered why. Why in the darkness of night, and why out here? Henny dropped down to the ground and crawled on his belly for a better position, all the while keeping track of Tippy. The little pooch appeared to be thoroughly enjoying himself, also crawling on his belly and stalking along with Henny, loving the game.

As the backhoe labored away digging a deep hole, the pile of displaced dirt kept growing higher. Henny saw an opportunity to sneak beyond the standing corn, in which they were hiding, into a position behind the dirt pile in order to get a better look at what was going on. He proceeded to belly-crawl toward the pile of dirt and got so close that he could actually feel small clods of dirt bounce down over his body as the machine dumped more of it on the pile.

Then, without warning, the digging stopped and the engine fell silent, but the bright lights remained. Henny heard the door open and close on the cab of the backhoe. Then he heard a car door open and the motor start. Henny wondered if the person was leaving. If so, why leave the backhoe's lights on?

But the car didn't leave. Henny heard it moving about and couldn't take the suspense any longer. He just had to crawl up to the top of the dirt pile to peek over and see what was going on. So, inch-by-inch,

4

he quietly worked his way to the top, all the while keeping a firm grip on Tippy's collar. Slowly Henny raised his head just high enough to peer over.

He watched as the car's lights reached to within a few feet of the hole. The engine stopped, the trunk's latch unlocked, the driver's door opened, and out stepped an obscure figure. There was plenty of light directed at the hole and the surface nearby, but anything a few feet above ground level was nearly impossible to distinguish. What Henny did see next, however, took his breath away.

Whoever was on the other side of the deep hole was dragging a body, by the legs, around the car between the headlights and the hole. The dark figure dropped the legs, braced against the grill of the car, took a deep breath, and with both feet, rolled the body into the hole. Henny heard it hit the bottom with a sickening thud. Scared to death by what he had just witnessed, he put his hand over his mouth to stifle the scream of terror that wanted to escape. Shaking, he fought the urge to vomit as he slid back down the dirt pile as quickly and quietly as possible. Tippy, smelling something he didn't like, started growling softly, and Henny froze. He hugged the small dog to himself, and as calmly as he could, considering the situation, worked on soothing the irritated pup.

Suddenly, all movement stopped on the other side of the dirt pile. Henny's heart started racing as he thought about the hole, the body down in it, and what would happen if the monster doing all that—found him. The seconds of silence seemed to go on and on, and then Henny heard a familiar noise—a cigarette lighter igniting. The smell of smoke drifted into his nostrils. Thankfully, Tippy seemed to sense his buddy's fear and remained still on Henny's lap.

After moments that seemed like hours, Henny could hear the door of the backhoe open and close and its engine start up. He knew what was going to happen next, and under the cover of the laboring engine, he stood up, grabbed Tippy by the collar, and ran back into the cornfield, not dodging stalks now but crashing through them, tripping again and again, but doing anything to get away from that sound.

CHAPTER

2

Jamie Chambers was doing her early morning thing, not really a prayer, not really meditation, but somewhat like both. She sat quietly by herself on her front porch in the earliest part of a brand new October day, while the sun tried to get out of bed but the rest of her world still slept. Sipping coffee, inhaling long slow breaths, and feeling the gentle fall breeze whisper across her face, Jamie listened to the quiet sounds of her farm waking up: the bleat of a lamb, a bark from her pup, and other animals in the pastures harvesting grass.

She sipped her coffee, took a deep breath, and closed her eyes to clear her thoughts. She then started listing the things in her life that were good, taking each one and rolling it around in her mind a little, making sure she felt it. Her first efforts were somewhat contorted in her mind. Problems and unresolved issues wanted to rush in, set her heart to beating . . . clouding her thoughts, but slowly she pushed them away and settled into a deep feeling of appreciation for her life. It had not been an easy one.

Her husband, Bud, had committed suicide, hanging himself in

their barn not even three years ago, and the scars from that loss still lingered. Holding onto the farm after Bud's death, while taking care of their small daughter, Andrea, had been an almost insurmountable task. Then, having a banker murdered just down the road from her farm three months earlier, and being caught up in that mess, had almost undone her again. She still thought of the incident as bizarre, and, at times, wondered if it had been a dream, but it hadn't.

Of course there was her beautiful daughter to take care of, all the farm animals, and the sustainability of her farm to maintain. She could quit like Bud did, or she could get back up and go on. She'd chosen to go on.

There had been some gifts along the way to go with the pain. She loved her life, her daughter, and her farm. The murder investigation after the banker's death had ironically brought new friends, especially Adam Hawkett. There was a bit of confusion in her thoughts as she wondered . . . was thinking of Adam purely being thankful, or was she letting feelings of insecurity slip into her thoughts? Another sip of coffee and another slow intake and release of air. No, she thought, it was okay. Maybe he brought some of both, but he'd been the best thing to come into her life since the birth of Andrea.

Adam Hawkett, whom she'd first met as a detective with the Iowa Department of Criminal Investigation, was a man a little older than her, but not by much. He'd been through a divorce and was what many would have described as a burnt-out homicide detective with a pretty severe drinking problem. However, Hawk, as his friends called him, hadn't had a drink in over a hundred days. He was still recuperating from the vicious blow to the head he'd sustained during the climax of the investigation into the banker's death the previous August. Thankfully, he was growing stronger every day. He was developing good muscle tone, and . . . well, she thought, he just looked good enough to . . . what? What should she do about her feelings for him, their unusual relationship?

He was asleep in his own bedroom inside her farmhouse, where he'd lived since resigning from the DCI shortly after solving the banker's murder. He willingly gave up that career in order to throw his efforts into helping her run the farm. They were going to get married, hinted at it, talked about when, but he'd not actually proposed yet. A mystery yet unresolved she thought, smiling to herself.

And although they worked together now every day, shared life like husband and wife, hugged often, they'd not yet been intimate. Alright, she thought, they'd not gone all the way. That day would come, but not until he took that last step, proposed to her, and they became man and wife in the eyes of their family, the law, and God. That time would come.

Well . . . so when would it come? Negative thoughts began slipping into her head once again. Another sip of coffee, a deep breath, and here we go again she thought, smiling to herself. Well, if he wanted to be her husband and the father of Andrea, then the call was up to him. She'd been through far too much to push something faster than it needed pushing.

Feeling somewhat blue, and wanting to start her day on a positive note, she took a deep breath, inhaled the sweet fragrance of her flowerbeds and searched her thoughts for more good things in her life. Back to new friends. Again the word bizarre came to mind, that Hawkett and his older partner, Benjamin Willoughby, had come into her life, both involved in the murder investigation. And, that at the end of it, both men had retired from the Iowa Department of Criminal Investigation.

Benjamin had taken the job of sheriff in her county following the resignation of the former one. He, like her, was unmarried. After two amicable divorces, he seemed happy as a bachelor and appeared to be a man who could always be happy with his lot in life, wherever he found himself.

Her body language was right. She could feel it. She felt quiet, calm and at peace with her world. Yeah, that was where she wanted to be. No guilt here, just a body recharging itself to take on the world in a fair and dignified manner. She collected her thoughts, staying right there in that peaceful mode.

From out by the barn, a loud crowing could be heard as her rooster, Ed, announced the official beginning to a new day. She opened her eyes, catching just a touch of sunlight from the morning sun peeping over the horizon. Standing up, she set her coffee cup on the porch rail, stretched some muscles, and walked out into the farmyard to meet her animals and begin another day.

Hawkett, hearing that damned rooster making racket, awoke as well, thinking he could use another couple of hours of sleep but that wasn't going to happen around this place. He got up and glanced at the clock. It wasn't even seven o'clock yet. He pulled on his jeans, his favorite flannel shirt, and his socks. He brushed a hand through his hair, rubbed the stubble of his beard, stretched, and went off in search of his old chore cap and work boots. It was time to go help chore. He'd grown up in the city, had hardly ever been near an animal in his entire life, and here he was, starting every day with a good two hours of physical toil, taking care of animals.

Hawkett walked to the coffee pot in the kitchen and poured himself a cup, then opened the fridge and grabbed a cinnamon roll from yesterday's batch. A few quick bites and the roll was history. He took two more swigs from his cup, and then headed out the door, picking up the stainless steel milk pail on the way. It was time to milk Flossie. He looked toward the north pasture and could see Jamie moving the sheep to a new paddock. He knew after that, she'd do the same with the yearling beef steers, then come back and take care of the chickens.

Milking the cow was his first chore of the morning. A loud "moo" of urgency came from behind the barn as Hawkett walked in. He went to the feed bin, and scooped up some grain to pour into the feeder hanging on the barn wall. He opened the door and in marched Flossie, heading straight for her feed trough. And, as he usually did, Hawkett remembered that he'd forgotten to bring water to wash the cow's udder before milking.

So, he went back to the porch to retrieve some warm water and a clean rag. Before milking the cow, he tethered her by clasping the hook on the end of a rope attached to the barn wall to the ring on the collar she wore around her neck. Securing her like this seemed somewhat silly since Flossie usually stood still and ate the entire time he milked, but there had been a couple of times when she'd been "in a mood" and had taken off, knocking over a nearly full pail of milk. And that did not make the senior management around this place happy at all.

Having secured the cow, Hawkett turned his cap around so that the bill wouldn't get in the way. He sat down on a small stool, right next to the cow's flank, reached in and began washing her teats thoroughly with the warm water. Then he placed the clean bucket under her udder and began the arduous task of gently squeezing the milk into it. The rhythmic music of the milk streaming into the pail became a familiar tune as the volume of rich, white, foamy liquid climbed in the silver bucket.

9

He really didn't care much for this job, but damn if it wasn't always kind of a satisfying way to start the day. It did pretty much loosen every muscle in his body, and walking into the house carrying a full pail of fresh milk gave Hawkett a feeling of making a real contribution to the farm.

The milk was strained through a filter, put into gallon jars, and placed in the porch refrigerator to cool. He always enjoyed watching Jamie ladle the cream off the top after the milk had settled. The milk and cream that the cow produced was converted into milk for them to drink, butter, cheese, ice cream, and, if any was left over, was mixed with oats and fed to the feeder pigs, who just loved that treat. After every milking Hawkett turned Flossie back out to pasture where she was given access to the best grass on the farm.

Currently her calf was weaned, but there would be a time next spring, after Flossie's short winter vacation from milking, when she'd give birth to a new calf. Then, for the next several months, half of the cow's milk would be carried to the house and the other half would be fed to the calf for its growth and development. It was such a neat system. Well, "sustainable" was the term Jamie liked to use. She really liked telling him how she was making the whole farm sustainable, from pasture to table, right in one system.

Having completed the milking, filtering the milk through the strainer, and placing it in the fridge, he finished washing up the equipment and then headed back outside. He met up with Jamie who was balancing on the fence by the pigpen trying to count her weaned pigs, and he had the same familiar feeling go through him every time he saw her. She was just plain beautiful, dressed in bib overalls, over a plaid flannel shirt and wearing muck boots. Darned if she didn't look about as sexy as he could imagine. He smiled and called out, "Aren't you getting tired of counting those pigs every morning?"

She turned and smiled at him, "Well, good morning to you too, Mr. Hawkett. I know I'm hyper over such a small thing, but I'd still like to know where those three pigs that disappeared earlier, went to. I mean, they're too big for a varmint to get them, and if a pig gets out, it hangs around, it doesn't head off into the wild." She shook her head, climbed down off the fence, and smiled at her daughter who was petting Tippy.

Hawkett playfully hugged little Andrea, a five-year-old mini-version of her mother. Looking down at her pup, he said, "That mutt doesn't seem to put on much weight. I've seen you sneaking treats to him, and we keep his food bowl full all the time. I wonder what the deal on him is?"

Jamie frowned a little as she observed the dog, "I know what you mean. He's been wormed and vaccinated and seems to have a good appetite. The little stinker sleeps away nearly half of every day. I don't know why he won't fatten up a little more. Maybe it's just in his genes." As she spoke, she thought to herself that being thin was the least of the pup's problems.

Tippy had been a gift to replace their previous herd dog, but after receiving him, they'd discovered he was deaf, and trying to train a deaf puppy to respond to livestock herding commands was nearly impossible. She'd tried using different hand signals to get Tippy to perform different tasks, but, so far, had gotten nowhere. She didn't know what to do with a pet her daughter dearly loved but which appeared to be quite useless for livestock herding purposes. Getting another pup to train would be tough while the original one ran loose.

Secondly her neighbors, Thelma and Pearl Oldham, had observed the pup running up and down the road at night. What the heck was the little bugger up to? A dog that didn't stay home was a dog heading for trouble. Oh well, she thought, not big problems, but still, problems that would have to be resolved.

"Who's hungry? I know I am! Let's go in and have some eggs and bacon." And that's just what they did. It would be a long day with plenty of work to do on the farm, and they needed to make a trip to town later. A good breakfast would be just the fuel to power the team.

CHAPTER

3

Benjamin Willoughby turned and looked into the mirror hanging on the back of the closet door in his two-room apartment. Not bad. He was all decked out in his new "Sheriff of Taylor County" attire with khaki pants and shirt, black leather belt, and shoes so shiny he could almost see his reflection in them. The fifteen pounds he'd lost since Jamie put him on her 'Farmer's Diet' had certainly made the pants fit better. He sucked in his gut, turned, squared his shoulders and took stock of the 55-year-old man who had made the biggest career change in his life. Was it going to work out? Well, what did he have to lose?

He'd been with the Iowa Division of Criminal Investigation for almost thirty years, specializing in homicide investigation, and he'd been good, damn good, he didn't mind thinking. Oh, not a spotless career. There had been a few problems along the way, and he'd had a pretty poor record getting along with the upper brass, but still, never a day unemployed in all those years, holding a job in a pretty stressful occupation. He'd held up well.

He'd shot four men during his career, two fatally, but that didn't drag Benjamin down, it was just part of his job. He'd never lost sleep over them, never regretted the shots, and never had any doubts. And, thinking to himself, he could do it again in this job if he had to. No, he wasn't a hothead or a gun-nut, he had no desire to shoot at anyone, it brought him no thrill. He'd just grown used to the fact that there were a lot of vicious criminals running around, with absolutely no consciences, who committed horrible acts against their fellow human beings. Some were just better off dead and if they put him into a position to kill them, it was part of his job, period, end of subject.

Benjamin was certain that none of these ugly memories were necessary today and maybe never would be again with his new job. Leaving the DCI to work in a quiet southwestern Iowa town was going to be a nice change. He pulled on his light tan jacket that matched the rest of his attire. It had the words *TAYLOR COUNTY SHERIFF*, in large, dark-green letters, imprinted across the back. He pushed his brand new Beretta into the holster hooked to his belt, put a fully-charged cell phone into his front shirt pocket, turned, and caught a sideways view of himself in the mirror once again before leaving his apartment.

It was a mere two blocks walk to his office in the basement of the courthouse, and it was a beautiful fall October morning, but the car was there at the apartment and it needed to be at the courthouse, so he slipped into it. He switched on the radio, backed out of the parking spot, and leisurely drove the two blocks through the county-seat town of Pigmy, waving at six different pedestrians along the way. His brand new Crown Vic had only forty-two miles on it. It carried the fragrance of a new car and seemed to be a fitting vehicle for a man starting a new career, trying to get off on the right foot with the rural public of Taylor County, Iowa.

On his arrival at the sheriff's office, his one deputy/office assistant, Jan Tenton, would have the coffee made, the mail organized, his phone messages compiled, and the computer on and set for him to visit his new emails of the day . . . all with a smile on her face.

The former sheriff, who had since retired and moved to sunny Arizona, had employed three deputies on his staff at the time when Benjamin had landed in this part of the state to investigate the murder. One of the deputies had been killed in an unrelated car chase during the time of the investigation, and Benjamin had fired the other one immediately upon being chosen as the new interim sheriff. The deputy he fired had been under-qualified for the position and didn't seem to have any inclination of putting forth the effort for further training, so Benjamin got it over with quickly. Besides, the board of supervisors had been clear that budget cuts had to be made. However, he was still short one deputy and that problem would have to be resolved soon.

For now, he was getting along, taking care of this rural county of nearly sixty-four hundred residents spread over approximately five-hundred thirty square miles, living on farms and in small towns amidst the rolling hills of a county that butted up against Missouri, with just one assistant and one night-time dispatcher. Benjamin had served thirty days as interim sheriff and, just last week, had been officially hired by the Taylor County Board of Supervisors as the new sheriff.

Things had gone pretty well during the probationary period. All the usual problems: road violations, an accident now and then, some petty theft, but all in all he had coped pretty well. It was certainly a big change compared to the plodding investigative work that had occupied most of his life, trying to chase down murder suspects working for the DCI.

Getting along with the supervisors was a constant challenge, but they were fair-minded people who wanted to do the "right thing" and that went a long way with Benjamin compared to some of the bureau-cratic jackasses he'd had to deal with in his former occupation. Anyway, things so far seemed to be a lot less stressful. And why not, he thought? These southern Iowa people were basically a laid back lot with, almost always, smiles on their faces. Every person you met driving down the road waved at you. No it wasn't retirement, but for the first month it'd gone pretty damned well as far as Benjamin was concerned.

Jan spent half of her time in the office and half the time patrol-ling in the department's other car—a 2005 Crown Vic with over two hundred thousand miles and a brand new set of tires. She carried a short-barreled Remington Police Special in the car when on patrol. It was her only gun, although she was qualified to shoot handguns as well and was pretty darned good at the gun range with Benjamin's Beretta. Jan was a topnotch employee dedicated to her job and to Benjamin. They liked and respected each other and had developed a deep personal friendship, which Benjamin knew could be a problem in this line of work. Jan was divorced, had one grown daughter, and was a loyal and trusted employee with a good head on her shoulders, everything Benjamin could wish for in a deputy. To top it off, she seemed happy with her job.

The only other employee was Cindy Jacobs, who worked Tuesday through Saturday nights as a radio dispatcher . . . not a perfect employee but Benjamin was working with her and there were some signs that he could transform her into an adequate employee. He still cringed when he thought of the incident that had occurred the week prior. Someone, he was pretty sure it was one of the old retired guys who frequented the coffee shop, had phoned Cindy to report that one of his neighbors was doing over twenty-five miles per hour on his exercise bike, which didn't even have a license on it, and he "just wanted to report the incident." He had probably made the call in front of a bunch of his cronies, all having a good haw-haw at early morning coffee, trying to fill in another boring day of retirement. Of course poor, naive Cindy had taken the entire report down and forwarded it to his desk.

As Benjamin walked into the office, Jan met him with a smile. "Well, look at you, Sheriff. Very spiffy! Makes me feel like I ought to go home and put on something a little flashier."

"Well, Jan, I know you've heard this speech before, but I believe, I really believe, that how the public perceives us, their respect and trust, can inadvertently enhance their support and cooperation, sort of like having an invisible deputy so to speak. So, Jan, I intend to always present my office and my position in the most impeccable and professional manner as possible. That covers my attire and yours, and our vehicles, which should always be washed and waxed. Things like this office, which I believe you do an excellent job with, our press releases, public education events, court procedure, well, everything we do that the public can see must have the most professional image to it. Jan, image is everything. So as I proceed out today, my first official day as sheriff of this county, I want them to see a sheriff who dresses professionally, acts professionally and who, in turn, receives the respect and cooperation of our constituents. That could be our motto, Jan. Always remember that."

So, on that fine October day, finding no really pressing issues, he left the office in Jan's care, slipped down to June's Restaurant for her Heart Healthy Platter of poached eggs, ham, and toast. After downing two cups of excellent black coffee he had officially started his week. Lord, how he missed the cigars he used to enjoy so much. Only Jamie could have convinced him to quit smoking. It was pretty hard to turn that lady down, but boy, did he miss those stogies.

June filled up his official SHERIFF coffee cup as he paid his bill. With his stomach pleasantly satisfied, and his caffeine level at full, Benjamin stepped through the swinging door out onto the sidewalk. Bam! A

15

speeding bicycle, ridden by an elderly woman, blindsided him causing the coffee to douse his front side, with most of it saturating the front of his pants. The bicycle careened off of Willoughby's body, merely missing a fire hydrant, and crashed directly into the front fender of his new Crown Vic, hurling the woman across the hood of the car where she landed with a thud on the opposite side.

After regaining his composure, Benjamin grabbed the two-way radio from his belt and summoned Jan, telling her to get the rescue crew on its way as he hustled around the car to inspect the woman. She lay motionless in a pool of blood. No, not blood. It was oil, he discovered, which must have leaked from some automobile and was now leaving oily stains on the knees of his pants as he knelt down to help the old gal.

Pearl Oldham! He'd thought it was her at the moment of impact. Why was that old woman speeding a bike down the sidewalk like that? Irritating questions were racing through his mind as he knelt down beside her to check for a pulse, all the while remembering nasty confrontations he'd had with this tough little woman in the past. Damn, he was angry with her, but still . . . Yes, he thought, she's just knocked out cold, but she did hit that car hard.

He could hear the rescue sirens down the street, and anxious people started gathering around. Someone handed him a blanket, and he spread it over her, trying to tuck just a little of it under her head. Someone else handed Benjamin a pair of broken glasses. As people gathered, questions and advice were coming from all directions. Still she was breathing. Good.

The ambulance pulled up with sirens blaring and lights flashing although they'd only driven half a block. Three volunteer EMTs piled out making Benjamin wonder if they couldn't have walked there faster than riding in the van, but still, protocol he supposed.

Benjamin stepped back and surveyed the situation while the medical professionals went to work. He felt dampness on the front of his pants and looked down to see that the coffee had left a distinct ring of moisture around the area of his crotch. And just that quickly, he heard a small child's voice in the crowd ask, "Did the sheriff pee his pants, Mommy?" The little child's statement produced some nervous chuckles from the crowd and then more questions ensued.

"Is she dead?"

"What did he hit her with?"

16

Oh man! Benjamin could feel his anger building. He reached around to pick up his handheld radio once again but discovered two small children were playing with it, and just that quickly, in a bit of a tug of war, they snapped the antenna right off the top. A nervous parent retrieved both pieces of the radio and handed them to Benjamin. And this time, angry with everybody, he yelled at Jan over the radio, "Get over here, will ya?" putting just a little more impatience into it than he'd meant to.

Thankfully, it appeared that Pearl was stirring. The young EMT who was kneeling at her side placed his stethoscope on her chest while another technician prepared a mild sedative injection to help calm and stabilize Pearl.

Suddenly she awoke, and typical of old Pearl, she was madder than a wet hen. That was when things really got exciting. She grabbed the end of the stethoscope and the EMT reared back in surprise. Then she let go of it, and the metal bell catapulted right into the young man's Adam's apple, causing him to lurch backwards crashing into the other EMT, who was holding a loaded syringe. She promptly lost her balance, stumbled and drove the needle into Benjamin's left thigh. He let out an incredibly loud cry of pain, and the entire crowd was momentarily stunned and silent, except for Pearl. She was cussing everyone out and trying to get up. Seeing Benjamin, and remembering he'd been involved in her wreck, Pearl turned his direction and kicked him in the shin with the point of her boot, causing him to let out another embarrassing yell.

All right! He'd had it!

"Get hold of her and get her in the damn ambulance, and do it now!" he bellowed. Then louder, and in a higher-pitched voice than he'd intended, he spoke to the crowd.

"Number one: Pearl ran into me, I did not run into her. I did not hit her with anything. Number two: She is not dead, hopefully not hurt badly, and if you'll get the hell out of the way, these people can wrestle her into the ambulance. And number three: I did not pee my pants. I spilled coffee on them. Okay?"

The crowd went dead silent, for only a moment, then someone started clapping and the entire group of people joined in giving Benjamin a hearty round of applause, just as the editor of the Pigmy Gazette snapped a picture of the disheveled Benjamin holding the radio with its antenna dangling, his knees stained in oil, and an embarrassing wet spot on the front of his pants.

Benjamin looked over at Jan who was staring at him with an amused look on her face, just waiting for her to make a crack about the "invisible deputy."

Yeah, the public's perception was everything, he thought glumly.

CHAPTER
4

Pretty much stressed out and angry at everybody, including himself, for the way the silly run-in with Pearl Oldham and her bicycle had turned into such an embarrassing fiasco, especially on his first official day as sheriff, Benjamin felt he needed a smoke. He'd quit two months earlier at the prodding of Jamie and her daughter, who seemed to have a genuine concern for his health and well being, and quite frankly that touched him deeply.

Benjamin had no family. He'd been married twice, but had no children, so Jamie, Andrea, and his former partner from the DCI, Adam Hawkett, were the only family Benjamin had. Apparently they meant a lot to him because he'd abandoned a thirty-two year smoking habit out of concern from them and had been true to his goal for over sixty days. But the desire for a smoke never completely went away, and he really, really wanted a good smoke and a good think to calm himself. So, into the local convenience store he strode, picked out one of his favorite brands, paid for it, and with just a little bit of guilt on his conscience, left the store heading for his car.

And, consistent with how the rest of his day had gone so far, Benjamin ran right into Jamie and Andrea. Both of them were staring at the half-opened cigar pack he carried, and real guilt traveled right through his thoughts.

"Having a bad day are we? I heard about your run-in with Pearl." Jamie wasn't giving him a chance to speak, but was giving him a frank, deliberate stare. "When did you start smoking again?" She let the question hang right there, making him feel even worse.

"Uh . . . well actually I haven't started again." Feeling foolish as he said it, with everyone looking at the cigars he held. The mother and daughter looked an awful lot alike with matching brown hair and brown eyes. Both of them wore faded blue jeans and matching sweatshirts with the slogan, BUY LOCAL, printed on them. They continued to stare at him and Benjamin felt the need to explain. "It's just that this has been a really rotten day so far, and it's not the way I wanted to start out with the people in this community, and I felt really stressed so . . ." He could see this ship was not going to float.

Andrea marched forward and held out her hands. He did the only thing he could under the circumstances. He guiltily handed her the package of cigars, and she immediately marched over to the closest garbage can where she slam dunked them, then rubbed her hands together seemingly to convey she'd just finished some dirty business.

And that was that. Jamie smiled, Benjamin felt awkward, and she took over the conversation as if nothing had happened.

"Well big guy, we heard you had a bad run-in with Pearl this morning, but the story is, she isn't hurt all that badly. She's more angry than anything else, and everybody knows that's just Pearl, so I think you need to put that embarrassing incident behind you. Although it does look like you could use a change of clothes. What in the heck happened that you got that dirty?"

Talking about the incident helped him a lot. It was a chance to release a little of his frustration and anger, telling her what had transpired, and the need for a cigar was long gone.

"Well, you have to admit," she said, "the whole incident does sound a little bit humorous, especially since nobody was seriously injured. Actually, I almost wish we'd been there." She stopped with that line of thinking, seeing as it would only make the situation worse, and switched gears. "Well anyway, we saw your patrol car parked here and thought we'd stop in and invite you out for supper Sunday night. What do you think?"

He didn't have to think; he knew right away. "Hey, set another plate for me. You know how much I love your home-cooked meals. Can I bring anything?" he asked, already knowing the answer to that question, but still throwing it out there, feeling a little guilty at the generous way she always treated him.

"No. Be there around six and, if we have the chores done, we'll eat then. Could be a little later, you know how things go out on the farm."

Benjamin nodded. He did know . . . now. He hadn't known much about farms and farming until arriving in her neighborhood the previous August with Hawkett, to investigate the murder of a banker just down the road from Jamie's farm. During that investigation, and during his tenure as temporary sheriff of Taylor County, he'd gained an immense knowledge about farming, but he knew he had a long way to go.

"Hey, unless I get caught up in something here at work, I'll be there at six o'clock sharp with a good appetite," he smiled as he said it.

"Great, we'll see you then." The two females proceeded on down the street to complete their errands. Fortunately his craving for a smoke had been vanquished. He felt a lot better and decided he should probably touch base with Jan, go get some clean clothes at his apartment, and get back to being sheriff.

His radio crackled just as he was walking down the sidewalk to retrieve his car. He spoke into it telling Jan he was going to drive over to his apartment and get a clean change of clothes.

About a half hour later, entering his office, Benjamin noted a heavyset woman, probably in her early sixties, with graying hair, sitting in a chair next to Jan's desk, clutching her purse in her lap, with a worried look on her face. Something was wrong here Benjamin guessed, wondering if the day was going to continue to spiral downward.

He nodded his head as Jan introduced the lady as Emily Smith, wife of Carl Smith. "Carl is a farmer. They live about three miles south of town, and Emily says he's gone missing." Jan was always good about getting to the point, never much idle chitchat. Benjamin pulled up a chair near the desk and shook Emily's hand as he introduced himself.

"Well, first questions, Emily. How long has your husband Carl been gone, and is this something he's done in the past?" While asking these questions Benjamin was thinking that nine out of ten missing person incidents ended with some noncriminal mischief: a wandering spouse, a runaway teenager, a confused senior citizen. But still, he was taking the matter seriously.

"Oh no, Sheriff. Carl always stays in touch with me. We work together out on the farm, and we talk all the time on these cells." Emily held up the small black cell phone as she spoke, as if to confirm her point. "He was combining corn over at the Davis farm last night, running real late you know. Anyway, he told me to go home, he'd fill the wagons and the semi, and then head home. Nothing surprising about that, the same way most nights end during harvest. Carl runs a lot of nights 'til around midnight. Anyway, I went home, had a bite to eat, cleaned up, and went to bed. I was exhausted. This damn harvest wears me out. When I woke up around six, Carl wasn't in bed and I couldn't see his pickup out in the yard, so I tried calling him, but the calls kept going right to his voice-mail. So I threw some clothes on and headed over to the Davis farm. His pickup was there and some of the wagons hadn't been filled and neither had the semi, so I assumed he'd broken down, but I just can't find hide nor hair of him, and I'm beginning to really get worried." Her voice was breaking as she said it, and then tears started finding their way down her cheeks.

Benjamin noted, with a feeling of satisfaction, that Jan was jotting down every word spoken in a notebook.

"His pickup was still there, nothing else he could have driven off in? No other tractors or trucks he could have left in, delivering grain somewhere?" Benjamin was still thinking that this was going to be some sort of failure to communicate by a tired farmer trying to get his crop out.

"No, the machinery is all there, just no Carl." She started crying softly, took a deep breath, and accepted the tissue Jan passed her way.

Benjamin was thinking this could be serious though, remembering stories of farmers caught in their combines, limbs ripped off, or worse yet, drawn completely into the powerful machines and chewed to death in the process. He also remembered hearing reports of farmers suffocating under grain in their wagons or bins. Things could have gone very wrong here, and he'd better go take a look.

"All right, Emily. Why don't I follow you with my car and we'll take a look around out there. I'm sure we'll locate Carl somewhere, probably just some miscommunication on his part, but still, let's go take a look."

The trip out to the Davis farm was uneventful and even rather enjoyable Benjamin thought, as he drove along the country roads, admiring the picturesque fall scenery with the colorful array of leaves that were getting ready to call it quits for the year. Both vehicles came to a quick halt at one point as three does and a huge buck crossed the road in front of Emily's SUV.

Arriving at the farm, they found three men milling around and examining the machinery. Benjamin knew why they were there. Bad news, well all news, traveled quickly in a small community, and already neighbors were coming to help search for Carl. Each man introduced himself in turn, and gave some comment or question about where Carl might be or what might have happened, but none had a plausible explanation. One thing Benjamin learned was that they had already inspected the combine and all the other corn hauling equipment, and no one had seen anything out of the ordinary, including no body lodged inside the combine anywhere. That was good. These men would know what to look for. The decision was made to haul the three loaded wagons to the auger parked by the semi and unload each of them carefully, just to make sure Carl had not somehow become buried in any of the wagons loaded with corn. The three farmers got to the task immediately as more people showed up to join in the search.

Carl had not been in any of the wagons; he wasn't in any of the ditches, behind any trees, or lying out in the unpicked corn. By noon, a group of twenty-two volunteers had come to the conclusion that Carl was not on the Davis farm. The search then moved to the home farm. By noon, the local Methodist church women's group had stepped into action and had prepared a meal for the search party, now numbering thirty.

After the meal, Benjamin climbed up on a hayrack in order to give a short lecture on what to look for and how to look. He thanked the people on behalf of the Smiths and on behalf of his department. He ended up his short speech with the true heartfelt statement that it was so impressive the way neighbors took care of neighbors in the country. But, even through all this effort, he still believed that there would be a plausible explanation and that Carl would turn up alive and well.

He continued to convey that message to Jan confidentially on his cell phone. He also continued to resist gentle requests by Mrs. Smith to step up the search and officially declare Carl a "missing person" and to appeal for more statewide assistance in the search. He would later regret his reluctance.

23

CHAPTER
5

Roydel Nuxton stepped out onto the new deck alongside his trailer house, a deck he had recently fabricated using wooden pallets and lumber stolen from the Pigmy Lumberyard. It was a little shaky but a nice place to sit and drink a cold beer early in the evening. The trailer house was a 1957 blue and white Comfy King, abandoned by his uncle, Paul Nuxton, who was currently spending time at the Fort Madison Penitentiary, doing fifteen to twenty years for armed robbery. The trailer house was old, but didn't leak a drop, had plenty of room, and with the stolen satellite dish and air conditioning unit he'd added, it was just pretty damn "comfy." Set out in the country, well south of Pigmy, the building site provided everything Roydel needed: privacy, good hunting, and great fishing.

Up the lane a ways was an older, two-story white farmhouse in an advanced state of decay. It was where his father and mother had once lived. Poor Ma had died of lung cancer, God rest her soul, at the ripe old age of 44. Just too many unfiltered cigarettes, Roydel figured, which was why he chose to smoke the ones with the gold filters. He didn't want that poisonous tar down his lungs.

Roydel's father, Pete, was alive and well, but like Uncle Paul, was also serving time. Daddy's crime was bootlegging shine and marijuana. This was his third offense, and he had really torqued the federal judge off when he'd shown up for trial high on sweet weed. Old Judge Carter slammed his gavel down and gave Daddy twenty years with parole at ten for good behavior. It was the "good behavior" part that got Papa Pete in trouble. All the Nuxtons had a short temper and felt most disputes needed to be solved with fists rather than with words, and it looked like Pete was probably going to serve the entire twenty.

It could be said that Roydel had inherited the family business, so to speak, and was currently doing quite well. He was not a big man physically, only five foot, seven inches, and weighed one-hundred fifty pounds soaking wet, but he'd gotten serious on the weights during his short stay in prison for grand larceny car theft and was pretty well muscled up. He had a neo-Nazi haircut and some badass tattoos to go with the look.

Roydel had been out of prison for almost a half a year after telling the parole board he'd learned his lesson. Damn right he learned his lesson . . . don't get caught. Roydel had learned in small business classes at the penitentiary that successful businessmen always found their marketing niche and Roydel had followed this sage advice. He purchased meth, only in "eight balls" and resold them to a high-flying businessman who took them into the cities for redistribution. Sure he gave up a lot of the profit, but Roydel wanted nothing to do with operating those stinking meth labs, and quite frankly the thought of leaving deep farm country to deal with urbanites and city folks with bad habits just didn't appeal to him.

So he bought the meth, drove it up out of the labs hidden in the hills, always in a clean four-door car, licensed and insured, with his seat belt fastened, sober as a church choir director and took cash from his upline contact. It was good living—bringing in nearly a thousand a week—with little or no overhead. Yes, it was a successful niche he was quite proud of.

Living in this abandoned trailer house basically provided him with free housing. He did have to pay an electric bill, but it wasn't prohibitive. He stole a lot of what he needed and ate a lot of excellent deer, turkey, rabbit and squirrel, some of which he'd shot right off of this very

25

deck in the nearby wooded area. Yes, Roydel thought, life was good.

Three cars had driven past his place in the last ten minutes, so when another one crept by this caught Roydel's interest. He wondered, why all the traffic, when hardly anyone ever drives by this place. He thought to himself that the last car looked like one he remembered from high school. It had belonged to a guy he hated. He couldn't recall the guy's name but he remembered the guy always referring to Roydel as Numbnuts . . . Numbnuts Nuxton to be exact. Boy did that piss him off. It had happened back at a time when he didn't know how to deal with such bullshit or how to even the score. Roydel had suffered at the mercy of numerous bullies in his growing up years. He'd been called that ab-horrent nickname all through junior high and in the two years he'd attended high school. It still made him boiling mad.

Let some son-of-a-bitch call me that today and we'll just see . . . yeah, we'll just see, thought Roydel as he pulled a cold Blatz beer out of the ice chest setting on a round table located nearby. He was sitting in the one good lawn chair of the set he'd picked up from the dump. It was held together by duct tape. Roydel was proud of his craftsmanship.

An hour earlier Roydel had placed a freshly-taken cottontail on the homemade spit above the grill he'd stolen from a display in front of the True Value in Bigsby. The roasting meat gave off an excellent aroma, and his mouth watered anticipating the feast he would later consume, adding a few taters and some onions to the grill. Shit, it just didn't get any better than this, Roydel thought.

On second thought, it could be better, he thought grimly. It could be if Erlene was still here and was sitting on his lap wearing her cutoffs and Nascar tank top, the red one with Junior's number printed and stretched across the front. But, she'd left. He shouldn't have slapped her, he knew that and regretted it immensely. But, feeling his temper re-ignite, he recalled that Erlene had clearly not been faultless herself in the matter. She should not have been dancing with that sons-a-bitchin' truck driver down at the Truckstop Tap. She knew better, her ma had raised her right, but you get a little tequila in Erlene, and there was no tellin' what she'd do.

Well she was gone now, showed him all right, climbed up in that big rig and headed west, to who knows where, and he just waved bye-bye. He reckoned she'd be back, this had happened twice before. She was a woman who liked to be taken care of in style, and hell, thought Roydel, what woman wouldn't want this little piece of paradise he lived on. Yeah, she'd be back.

Hell, he offered to marry her, make her an honest woman, but wincing, he remembered his proposal and how that event had turned sour. He'd bought a damn nice engagement ring. Okay, maybe it was hot, stolen from a jewelry store in Kansas City by one of his buds, but still a nice ring. Roydel tied it onto the collar of Erlene's little beagle, thinking it'd be cute if the beagle carried the ring over to Erlene, make her appreciate his romantic side. Problem was, her other beagle snatched the ring right off of the first beagle's collar and devoured it. And then of course, Erlene had to keep a close eye on that beagle, waiting to officially get her ring when it passed through the dog out in her yard, and somehow that just took the shine off his big idea. Still, he'd tried. Didn't that count for anything?

Roydel enjoyed his meal of rabbit and taters, drank another cold Blatz, and leaned back in the lawn chair. He closed his eyes and listened to nature's music while smoking a couple Gold Tips, resting up a little and letting his meal settle before starting off on the night's work. He'd slip down south a few miles, cross the Missouri border, and go visit one of his "production specialists" hoping to hell they hadn't used up all their meth produced that day. He hoped that the damn space heads had remembered that he only took eight balls and always paid in cash. He never smoked any of it, and most importantly, he did not want to sit around and chew the fat with those tooth-decayed methers who looked thirty years older than they should. Shit, he thought, what a horrible, horrible drug. He had never touched the stuff and had no intentions of starting. That would take him down and take down his business. What in the hell got into people, a little shine or weed wasn't enough to get you floating high? No, they just had to have somethin' better. Had to prove they had nothin' but shit floatin' around in that space between their ears. Well, they provided his livelihood he guessed, so more power to 'em.

CHAPTER

Out at the farm, Jamie, Andrea, and Hawkett had just finished a delicious meal of pork roast with potatoes and carrots from their fall garden. Fresh produce was getting harder and harder to find as the growing season came to an end. They also enjoyed cold cider, squeezed from apples picked in Jamie's orchard the previous week. There would be fresh apple pie to eat later in the day, and, Hawkett was thinking, they had no trouble meeting the "an apple a day keeps the doctor away" adage around this place. Having put in a good six hours of physical toil already that day, the two adults dozed off in comfortable chairs on the front porch while Andrea occupied herself with Tippy.

After a short snooze, Jamie stood up and stretched, and Hawkett, sensing her movement, tried to force himself to come alive from a very satisfying nap. It never ceased to amaze him how easy it was to relax out on the farm. How odd it seemed that everybody else in the world seemed to rush to an eight-hour job, then rush home, and try to fill the hours in between with whatever was important in his or her lives. Here on the farm, they worked hard, rested, worked some more, maybe played a little in the evenings, but still always had the work ethic. Like Jamie had said to him before, "There are a lot of things to be done around here and nobody else is going to come in on the next shift and do them."

"What's on tap for this afternoon? Finish up that garden, or what?" Hawkett asked.

Jamie looked over the farmstead, "Well, we'd better start putting together a load for the Farmers' Market in Des Moines tomorrow, maybe even take a trailer load of firewood to drop off on the way. I have a customer between here and Des Moines who keeps after me, worrying about his supply of firewood for this coming winter, so that would be one thing I guess." She was always a little uncomfortable being the boss. Still, Hawkett seemed okay with it, and, to be honest, it was her farm, her business, and she knew better than him. He'd only been here about three months and had learned a lot. He was always a good worker, never complained, had a good attitude, and almost no temper.

They got along well and he seemed happy, so she assumed he was happy. Still the fact that they were still not officially husband and wife troubled her. That needed to be resolved. They'd come together in a bizarre set of circumstances, and the conclusion of those had led to where they were today. Still this just wasn't natural, living as a man and woman . . . as what . . . partners? What was the next step? Well, Adam should say to her, "Will you marry me?" Then they would visit with her pastor, set a date, and do the right thing, but he just hadn't asked her.

She was pretty sure he was a normal heterosexual, so she would continue to wait, and they would continue to work together and enjoy life as partners. Still it wasn't what she wanted. Maybe she should blame his former wife, Ann. He claimed she'd destroyed any faith he had in matrimony. Well, she thought, why waste time worrying—do something positive.

On that note, she asked Hawkett to start loading a cord of split firewood onto the trailer while she and Andrea got busy harvesting pumpkins, Indian corn, popcorn, and squash from their fall garden. Frost had pretty much put an end to growing fresh produce and this would probably be their last trip to the Farmers' Market this fall.

Back in his office, and trying to decide what the next step in this missing farmer problem would be, Benjamin was surprised to see Thelma Oldham, sister-in-law of Pearl Oldham, walk in. He was wondering, oh boy, what now?

Thelma was not like Pearl; in fact the two ladies were almost exact opposites. Pearl, a widow, was short tempered and foulmouthed, while Thelma, who had never married, was quiet, somewhat shy, and chose each word carefully, always quite cautious of saying anything the least bit offensive.

"Thelma, have a chair." Benjamin said, "How's Pearl?"

"Fine I think." Clearing her voice, she added, "Maybe a little bit worked up, you know, using some vile language that I don't care to hear, but you know, that's just Pearl." Boy did he know. He'd had more than one run in with Pearl. She was a very tough character for a woman well into her seventies.

"Anyway." Clearing her voice again and nervously trying to maintain a little eye contact with Benjamin, she went on. "Anyway, I was wondering, Sheriff, if you could find it in your heart to, you know . . ." Again with nervous hesitation, clearing her voice, and repositioning her purse. "I was wondering if you could find it in your heart to apologize to Pearl for wrecking her bicycle this morning, and buy another one for her to ride," speeding up her message as she said it, wanting to get the dreaded words out.

Benjamin frowned. He almost swore at her, but then he took a deep breath, calmed himself a little, and regained his composure. "Why in sam heck would I apologize to Pearl? She was clearly in the wrong. It's a violation of city ordinances to be riding your bicycle on the sidewalks. Heck! I warned her about it a couple of times the last month. That's why we have these laws, so an incident like what transpired this morning doesn't happen."

"I know, I know. I try to reason with her, but she's so darn stubborn."

"Tell me this, Thelma, why doesn't your sister-in-law drive a car like everybody else. I mean, man, it's got to be hard on her, a woman her age, pedaling a bike up and down the road. Why isn't she driving a car? You have a car. Do you allow her to drive it? Is there some problem between you two?"

Thelma got just a little bit of a frown on her face and from past experience Benjamin knew she was getting just a little bit worked up as well. That was probably about as much anger as she could show.

"No, Sheriff, she could drive my car, though I don't much care for her driving ability, but that's not the issue. The problem is that she

30

lost her drivers license a couple of years ago, then they canceled her insurance, which by the way I was paying . . . "

Thelma stopped momentarily, digesting another issue that didn't set well with her at all, and then continued, "She got three speeding tickets within a year and that just did it. The magistrate took away her license. So now she either walks or mostly rides her bike, and she says you've wrecked her bike, and I'm caught in the middle."

"Speeding tickets! She's what…75…76 years old? Where did she get her speeding tickets? In town?"

"No. All three tickets were outside of the city limits I believe," Thelma paused. She seemed to be trying to sort things out. "I can't really remember, I do know there were over $400 worth of fines, and I had to pay them all."

She let that statement set there a little bit then went on. "I do remember the last one she got, she was trying to get home from a chicken dinner over at the Methodist church in Clarinda. She was afraid she was going to miss *Wrestle Mania* on TV that night. You know how much Pearl loves her darn wrestling shows. Can't stand that sort of thing myself, but still, when you live with someone there has to be some give and take, and I tolerate her watching that nonsense. It does seem to calm her down a little. Anyway, the patrolman said she was doing eighty-seven in a fifty-five zone and she got a little lippy with him and well, that was that. They took away her license and she's not gotten it back since." Thelma shrugged, end of story.

Eighty-seven miles per hour? Benjamin couldn't believe it. That little old woman? He wondered how good her eyesight was and how hard it was for her to see over the steering wheel of the 1978 Oldsmobile, a fairly large vehicle. No wonder they'd yanked her license. Thank goodness, he thought, she's not been involved in an accident. No . . . not with the car but look what she'd done this morning. Benjamin was thinking of his embarrassment in front of the general public and the nice dent in the left front fender of the new patrol car.

Benjamin had had a long day and this nonsense was really wearing on him. He had a possible "missing person" to get busy on and here he sat wasting time with this issue. "Well, Thelma, I'm truly thankful that Pearl was miraculously uninjured this morning. I mean, how a woman takes a collision like that and appears unharmed, especially given her age, is indeed a miracle, but she was clearly in the wrong, and I've no intention of giving her one penny towards her bicycle damage. Please make that clear to her, okay?"

"I know, I know Sheriff, but you know how Pearl is. She says her bike is wrecked and you're the reason. She keeps yelling she's going to sue you and I just think that's a bad idea, but if I go back home telling her what you just told me, then she's going to be yelling at me and . . . "

Benjamin had had enough of this nonsense. He held up his hand interrupting her plea, "Here, let me be more specific. I'll send a message along for you to deliver to Pearl." Careful to control his anger, he pulled a book from his desk drawer and filled out a citation for Pearl, fining her twenty-five dollars for violating county ordinance #442A: Driving a bicycle on public sidewalks. He knew the ordinance. He had looked it up after past complaints about Pearl driving on Pigmy's sidewalks.

He gently tore the ticket out of the book, handed it to Thelma and politely added, "Thank you, Thelma. Have a good day." He got up, walked into the back room by the jail area, got himself a cup of coffee, and busied himself with other matters.

Thelma picked up the ticket and held it like it was a bomb about to go off. Gently, ever so gently, she deposited it in her purse then quietly left the Sheriff's Office with dread and anger written all over her face. Pearl was not going to be happy about this.

CHAPTER 7

Peeking out from the backroom, Benjamin deduced that Thelma had gone and was thankful for that. He needed to deal with the more serious issue of the missing farmer. He got on his cell phone and called Jan, who had replaced him at the scene of the search.

"Hey, anything new?"

"No, Sheriff. There must be over forty people out here. I mean they're actually almost tripping over each other. We've had three short organized searches, but I mean there's no sign of that man."

"How's the uh . . . Emily, holding up?"

"Well, given the circumstances, I guess pretty good. Thankfully she's got relatives in this neck of the woods and several people are with her. Or maybe it's depressing, depending how you look at it."

"What do you mean by that?"

"Well, it's like he's dead you know? All these people stopping in, bringing food, offering condolences. It's exactly what they'd do if there was a pending funeral."

"Yeah, I see what you mean. Well let's hope that's not the case.

No vehicles missing, nothing we can put an APB out on is there?"

"No, his pickup is there. Every vehicle that they own is setting somewhere right around here."

"I suppose I should get on the phone and notify the law offices in the adjoining counties, just in case."

"I've already done that Sheriff . . . got all their numbers on my cell . . . covered that base in Missouri, too."

"Well, good for you," Benjamin replied, and he meant it. There was just a moment of silence over the phone as the two of them thought. "Okay, Jan, I guess I'd better hunt up some more help. I'll call the DCI and get it on their radar. Hopefully, we won't get the FBI in here but being so close to the Missouri border, if there is any foul play and it crosses the state line . . . "

He let that hang knowing she knew what he meant. "And I know, dammit, I just know this is not going to turn into something sinister, you know? There's no theft, no wayward lovers, no accident, no crime scene, just nothing."

"I know, I know," she replied. "Doesn't seem to make any sense does it?"

More contemplative silence, then, "Okay, stay out there 'til about five, then I'll call you and we'll figure out a new plan just in case Carl doesn't turn up one way or the other."

"Sure, Sheriff. Talk to you later."

Having completed his call with Jan, Benjamin picked up the phone again and dialed the DCI office in Des Moines, deciding to keep this conversation low key. He didn't want to have to call back and tell them they'd found Carl asleep out back somewhere, but on the other hand, if foul play became apparent, he wanted his track record to show he was moving through the channels. When the receptionist answered he asked to talk to somebody on the second floor. That's where his section had been, where Benjamin had reported to work just a few months earlier, before retiring and taking this job.

"DCI, Stephanie speaking, how may I help you?"

"Hey, it's me. How are you doing?"

"Benjamin!" she responded. The fact that she had recognized his voice gave him a warm feeling, almost like calling the relatives back home. "Benjamin Willoughby, don't tell me you're calling to ask for your old job back. I knew you couldn't stay away from us."

"No, Stephanie, I've got an honest occupation now."

34

"Oh yeah, I forgot, it's Sheriff Willoughby. So how's that going?"

They exchanged chitchat and kidded each other for a few minutes, and then he got down to business. "Hey, I've got a missing person down here and it looks for real, meaning it probably isn't going to be your typical 'they turned up later at the malt shop' missing person deal."

"Uh-oh, I hate those. You probably want to talk to somebody, huh? Get some help from your old friends?" Still kidding him and enjoying it. "I'll put you through to Brightwall."

Benjamin sighed. Brightwall was his old boss, and they never, ever got along. That was one of the reasons this career switch had been easier—leaving the DCI before Brightwall forced him out. They were on different teams now. Maybe they could get along. Well, he thought, they had to get along.

Brightwall finally came on the line and acknowledged Benjamin with some routine conversation. Benjamin told him why he had called, being very careful to give clear-cut facts about the case and all the while wondering to himself if it was really going to be a case. He told Brightwall all the steps that had been taken so far and the results.

"Well it doesn't sound good, but we know how these missing person deals go about ninety percent of the time. Anyway, give it twenty-four hours and if this Smith doesn't turn up, one way or the other, get back to me and we'll send some people down to help you."

Benjamin was surprised at how smoothly the whole exchange of information had gone, given their past history, but never-the-less he felt good about it, and was about to say thank you and goodbye when Brightwall interjected. "I've been going to call you about another matter. We had a meeting yesterday with our drug task enforcement team and an issue that came up directly affects you. We have some pretty good informants that are reporting a fairly steady stream of drugs coming out of Taylor County and being distributed here in Des Moines. Any ideas on that?"

Well, hells bells, thought Benjamin, caught off guard. "No, I haven't heard anything down here. Actually not one word. What? Marijuana? Meth?"

"Meth. We don't know how much, but it seems to be regular, pretty sharp crew. We aren't getting much to go on, just know it's coming from there and ending up here."

"Well, I'll ask around, but I don't have that many contacts with the underworld down here, you know what I mean? I'll have to check with some of the locals, neighboring law, get some leads I guess."

"Don't waste everybody's time. Go talk to Roydel. It's that simple." Brightwall was coming at him with that rude condescending tone he so hated.

"Roy who?"

"Roydel Nuxton, Benjamin. Do your homework. Surely you've heard of the Nuxton family. Regular little crime machine . . . half of them in jail right now I think."

"Why do you suspect this Roy . . . this Nuxton? Somebody finger him?"

"No Benjamin," again with that tone. "This isn't New York City. When we have crime activity, it's usually the same people just repeating past sins. The Nuxtons have always been dirty, and young Roydel is just carrying on with his family's tradition. I'll bet you if there are drugs coming out of your backyard, Roydel's your boy. Check up on him, will you?"

"Sure, what . . . " Click the line went dead. Another Brightwall stunt that always irritated the heck out of Benjamin. Gets done talking and just drops the receiver down.

Sitting there, trying to digest this latest bit of bad news and determine how he would have to deal with it, Benjamin was interrupted by his cell phone ringing. It was Jan.

"Please tell me you found Carl Smith alive and healthy, and are headed back into town."

"Sorry, no luck there. But I do have some more information and it probably isn't anything, but . . . well you never know."

"What?"

"There's a gal out here, a mom, who said that when her kids got off of the school bus they were chatting about the big story at school. Seems a sixth grader named Henny Henderson is telling people he saw a body being dumped in a hole last night. I should tell you that I know this Henny and the kid is a bit of a character. He lives down there in that dump, out at the end of Vine Street, with his mother who is next to worthless. It could very well be that Henny heard there's a missing person everybody's looking for, so he just concocted a story to get attention. Anyway, it's out there, and I thought I'd report that little bit of information to you for whatever it's worth."

36

"Well, I guess we should check into it. Like you say, kids talking . . . " He left it at that. "Come back in will you? If you could watch the office until Cindy gets here, I'll go try to run this kid down. Better yet, if you know where he is, could you try to pick him up? Probably should bring his mother in too if we're going to be asking him questions. Sixth grader did you say? What . . . twelve years old?"

"Yes, he's a sixth grader, but knowing Henny, he was probably held back a year. Anyway, I'll try to track him down. Talk to you later."

In a sequence of events that happened fairly quickly, Jan found Henny and got him into her patrol car. She tried to pick up his mother as well, but the woman was just too intoxicated. Jan was hardly even able to wake her as she lay on the couch. After a short interview with Henny, Benjamin and Jan took him to the location the little guy said he'd seen the body being buried, and sure enough there was a pile of fresh dirt there with tire tracks everywhere. Organizing volunteers and locating a backhoe took almost two hours, but given the gravity of the situation, everyone was quite willing to help. Under the illumination of powerful lights, powered by portable generators, the group uncovered Carl Smith's body at around nine o'clock that evening.

CHAPTER

It was just getting dark when he slipped down the lane in his '08 maroon, four-door Chevrolet Impala. He always kept the car clean, especially the license plate, and kept all the lights in perfect working order. He always drove the speed limit, and never drove if he was nodding off. Roydel thought the large AARP sticker in the back window and the Support Your Local Law Enforcement bumper sticker added a nice touch. He just didn't want some trooper to pull him over to check a faulty license plate light, then casually mention, "You care if I look over the inside of the car, just, you know, standard protocol?" Yeah shit, standard protocol.

The only thing that could get Roydel in trouble, big trouble, was the slit in the front of the seat just under where he sat. In that slit, with some effort, he could force both his current supply of meth for delivery and his prized Glock 35/.40 caliber. If he got stopped, and if he had to get out, the Glock would come with him. In his young life, Roydel had already killed two men, and he would not hesitate to kill any police officer wanting to search his car. That was part of his successful business plan.

Roydel drove up the dirt lane from his trailer house to the gravel road, headed west for three miles, and then turned onto Highway 48. He flicked on his headlights and drove south, holding his speed under the limit, driving cautiously, actually more worried about hitting a deer than running afoul with the law. Twenty minutes later and well into the state of Missouri, he left the highway and started weaving down a series of gravel and dirt roads through a heavily wooded area where nearly every old farm-building site had been abandoned or bulldozed away.

Twice he stopped, backed into lanes where he could be hidden from the road, turned off his car and sat quietly, always wary of being followed, thinking how could anybody not know these brainless idiots were out here making meth? And as always, nobody seemed to use this road but him, and so he drove to the driveway with a cattle guard across it entering what looked like just another Missouri cow pasture and eventually came to the dump. Well it looked like a dump to him. Man-oh-man, what a mess he thought as he drove through the abandoned vehicles among the weeds, wild hemp growing up through the cars' bodies, Roydel considering the irony.

He stopped his vehicle, turned off the engine and sat quietly. It was always the same protocol but still it made him nervous, sitting there in the dark. He reached down and pulled the pistol out from the front of his seat, giving him some feeling of confidence. He reached over to his glove compartment and pulled out the envelope with five, one hundred dollar bills in it.

After about ten minutes, a thin woman, sickeningly thin and gaunt in the face and wearing a dirty dress, ambled silently toward him. He could barely make her out in the dark, and even though she was always the one, it still made his skin crawl. Through the window of the car, she handed him a package, and he in turn handed her the envelope. She opened it, counted five, one-hundred dollar bills, and smiled at him. Oh, how he wished the woman wouldn't smile, having lost most of her teeth to meth decay.

But that was how it always worked, and he started his car, shoved the gun back into the seat, turned on his headlights, and backed around carefully to get out of there, wanting to hurry up, being a little spooked like always. He was feeling real relief as he started down the driveway, then was forced to hit the brakes, yelling, "Damn!" as two children sprinted in front of his car, through his headlight beam, and raced off into the weeds.

Man, he thought. All this hell, and kids living here. Some things were tough even for a hardened con to imagine. He should start going to church again he thought. After visiting this hole he had no doubt that there was a hell, and the devil was at work close by.

Jamie leaned over to kiss Andrea on her forehead, turned off her light, picked up some stray clothes destined for the hamper, and as she left the room, the little girl was sleeping soundly. It had been a long, hard day and Jamie was just bone tired, but it had been a very productive day, and they were prepared and ready to roll very early the next morning. All the many things needed for the farmers' market were loaded and secured in her pickup. Hawkett was out hooking the trailer loaded with split firewood to the truck. The firewood would be dropped off at a customer's house on their way to Des Moines.

She took a quick shower, dried off, and threw on more clothes than she wanted, a necessary precaution with a strange man around the house. Well no, darn it, not strange she thought to herself, just not my husband. Why was she thinking so much about that lately? Well, what had seemed a logical move when he moved in three months ago did not seem so logical now. The next step hadn't been taken and . . . there I go again, she thought, looking at herself in the mirror.

She heard the screen door open and Hawkett started to say something but she shushed him, not wanting to wake her sleeping daughter. He nodded his head in understanding and started talking again more quietly, but she found herself spacing him out and thinking about how much better he looked than when he'd first shown up on this farm. He was more tan and muscular now, and . . . she must be tired, for her thoughts were wandering to places they didn't need to go.

"Well?"

"I'm sorry, my mind was elsewhere. What did you say?" feeling foolish as she spoke the words.

"I said, how long will it take to unload that firewood we're dropping off?"

"Oh, no, don't worry about that. I sold it with the understanding that we'd leave the loaded trailer there and they would unload it while we're in Des Moines."

"Hey, that's good. It could be another very long day tomorrow. One less job to worry about." As he said it, he picked up the scent of soap or shampoo or something on Jamie and boy, she not only looked good, but smelled good, and he felt that urge coming over him big time.

There were just a few seconds of silence as the two adults stood looking at each other, and then Hawkett stepped closer, put his arms around her and hugged her firmly, not wanting to let go for awhile, but then it happened like it always happened. She gently pulled away and smiled at him, looking up into his eyes. Looking for what, he wondered?

"Big day tomorrow, Adam. We'd best get some sleep. Have to leave here around four . . . four-thirty to get there and set up."

She gave him what could have been considered a sheepish smile, then turned and slipped into her bedroom, closing the door quietly behind her and leaving Hawkett thinking about what might have been.

Roydel woke with a start and spent a little time remembering where he was and why he had such a bad headache. It was the shine. He probably shouldn't have polished off a full jar of it earlier, but damn if that guy hadn't pissed him off. At a rest area on Interstate 35 where they'd been meeting, always at two in the morning, this last deal hadn't gone at all like the preceding ones. Always before, the guy would pull up beside him, Roydel would hand a sack full of eight balls over and the man would hand him twenty fifty-dollar bills held together with two rubber bands. Most times, nobody said a word, and he liked that. He'd get his money, get the hell out of there, and head for home.

Such a sweet system—but not last night. There'd been a bit of a glitch. The man said he was having problems moving product up-line. Said he'd take the product, but the wad of bills felt light and only turned out to be five hundred dollars. Roydel didn't believe there was any let up in the market for meth. He believed he was being screwed. He was thinking this morning, while lying in the back of his trailer house, maybe he should have gotten out, put a gun in the man's mouth, and straightened things out right there.

Still, he should keep his cool, that was the ticket, and try to not let his temper get the best of him. He'd use some good sense and stay out of the "big house" so as not to end up in a family reunion with his dad and uncle, serving time for stupidity. Still, it'd better not happen again.

Roydel stepped out onto the deck of his trailer house, aimed his .22 rifle at the chatty squirrel whose racket had awakened him, and fired. Roydel was a good shot, and the squirrel's life came to an end as it tumbled down out of the tree. Roydel picked up the squirrel and prepared it for the grill. He would enjoy a fine breakfast, then head for the timber later. He'd been watching a huge buck from time to time and he had a hankering to put an arrow in it. So he would sit up in the tree-stand he had, up on the hill by the pond, and relax until dark, and then maybe put some venison in the freezer before the end of day.

CHAPTER

Benjamin was up early, but not nearly as early as Hawkett, Jamie, and Andrea. The three of them had left Taylor County around 4:30 that morning and were now setting up their stand at the Des Moines Farmers' Market. Still, the day had begun early for Benjamin because all of a sudden this quiet little 'semi-retirement' job had taken on huge responsibilities. A dead farmer was found buried in one of his own cornfields, he'd received news that a major drug runner was working out of his jurisdiction, and he had to deal with this small boy, Henny, and whatever the heck his role was in all of this. Benjamin was thinking he needed more assistance. Well, one thing at a time he thought.

He spent an hour at the office catching up on paperwork he didn't really want to do, then slipped over to June's for his morning breakfast. The early morning crowd was there and all of them were pestering him, wanting to know what he knew about the murdered farmer, but he shrugged off their questions. And quite frankly, he thought to himself, there wasn't much to tell anyway. He sure as hell had no idea what had happened. The body of Carl Smith was scheduled to receive an autopsy later that day in Des Moines, but there probably wasn't much to be learned. He had a bullet hole right through his chest. Carl's wife of course was very upset at the thought of her husband's lifeless body being dissected in another city, as opposed to being prepared for his funeral, but there was nothing Benjamin could do about that.

He left the cafe, being careful to look both up and down the sidewalk as he did, vividly recalling the fiasco with Pearl's bike just twenty-four hours earlier. He pondered what he knew, and what to do next, as he walked back to his office. Once again, he thought, what he knew wasn't much. Carl Smith had been murdered and then buried on a farm he rented.

It apparently happened sometime around ten or eleven o'clock the previous Thursday night, given the story from this lad, Henny Henderson. Benjamin wondered about the boy, too. That strange name, was it really his name? Cocky little kid, full of bravado, telling how he witnessed the corpse being kicked into the hole, claiming he'd picked up a rock and thrown it at the presumed killer. That, and some of the other parts of the sketchy story they'd gotten out of the initial interviews with Henny, didn't really add up, and he suspected the boy was a bit of a storyteller. Well, they'd talk again and sort through all of that, maybe even stumble onto some important information.

He'd called the DCI just before midnight and reported the status of things to some staff member and felt that base was covered. Now what? He guessed he'd communicate with Jan to make sure the office and calls were being covered. That would probably mean some overtime for Cindy, but they had to have someone in the office answering potential calls for help.

Even though it was supposed to be her day off, Jan was there, working on a cup of coffee and looking at a Taylor County plat map, making notes. "Good morning, Sheriff. Get any sleep?"

"No, not much, probably catch up with me later today. What've you got there, a map that you're going to use to explain to me what the hell has happened to our local farmer?"

"No just trying to figure out why he was buried where he was buried. We know from talking to the neighbors that the farm Carl was buried on was a farm he rented, which by the way is referred to as the Dickenson farm, a two hundred and forty acre parcel according to this plat book. It says here, it's owned by a guy from California that we know owns several thousand acres around here. He's an investor who buys a lot of land, turns the management of it over to a professional farm management company, and never actually comes near his farms. Anyway, that's what the guys at the coffee shop tell me. I wish I had money to burn like that," she said shaking her head back and forth. "I was just figuring out, this guy, or rather his corporation owns three thousand, two hundred, forty-five acres in this county alone, according to this plat book."

"So let me see if I understand. A corporation from California bought thousands of acres of land, and Carl Smith rented one of those farms. Did you say two hundred forty acres, and the farm is managed locally by who?"

"Well, according to the scuttlebutt, it's managed by Iowa Land-Co, a farm and ranch management outfit out of Council Bluffs. They assign a farm manager to work between the owners and tenants, and the farm management firm gets a percentage of the gross from the farm's income. Don't ask me to explain that, because it was just what I was told by an area farmer last night. One of the things we're probably going to have to follow up on, huh?"

"Yeah, I'm afraid one of the many things we're going to have to check up on. Sounds like we won't get much help from the DCI until Monday, other than the autopsy. Hell, we can go back out to the crime scene, but man, all those people and machinery digging a body up out of a hole it's just been buried in. Can't be any tracks worth noting. And the damn backhoe, parked not 500 feet from the body."

"Well . . . probably the backhoe Henny saw. Going to be pretty coincidental if it isn't. We're going to have to find out who that thing belongs to, if it is stolen or what. Suppose we need to worry about contamination of evidence on the backhoe?"

"Well," Benjamin sighed, "that probably happened before we found out about it. However, before everybody left last night, I placed a KEEP OFF sign on it and put some of my crime scene tape around it. Would have been nice to have left a deputy out there to guard it, but hey, there's just you and me, right? This isn't the big city."

"Yes, wait for the DCI lab folks, huh?"

Benjamin paused before speaking and finally replied, "Yes, wait for the DCI," thinking how odd that sounded, thinking of his past experience with them, how they would react to this. "All right, first steps today. Would you work out a schedule with Cindy—make sure someone is here to cover the telephone at all times? We'll allocate whatever overtime is needed. Secondly, please talk to your farmer friends and find out who manages the farm where we found the body. Thirdly, sometime before the day is out I want to have another sit-down interview with this young lad Henny. Be sure to get his mother to come this time, okay?"

Jan shook her head back and forth in disgust, "I think I can get the boy, but his mother—man, she's a real piece of work. Let's just hope she's sober enough to come in."

Benjamin met Hal Dallis, Farm Manager for Iowa LandCo, at the Cubby's Truck Plaza/Deli in Red Oak, another farming community town located about fifty miles northwest of Pigmy. A couple of mid-morning phone calls had led to the agreement to meet in Red Oak for a late lunch. Hal was fifteen minutes late, but that didn't upset Benjamin too much. He was glad that the guy took time off on a Saturday to meet with him. Of course, thought Benjamin, one of Hal's tenants had been murdered on a farm owned by one of his clients, so Hal darn sure ought to make time to help law enforcement.

Benjamin spotted Hal's pickup pulling into the parking lot, magnetic Iowa LandCo signs affixed to both sides. He observed that Hal was a stocky built guy, probably about fifty, smoking a cigarette as he came across the parking lot, and obviously wearing a toupee. Hal stopped, dropped what was left of his smoke, did the casual foot squish that smokers do with the burning embers, and walked on into the restaurant. He didn't have any trouble picking out Benjamin, given the uniform. The two men shook hands and made small talk about the weather, both ordering the special of the day, and then they got down to business.

"So, the lady who called me said you found Carl Smith buried on the Dickenson Farm. Is that right? What's the story?"

"Carl was reported missing by his wife Friday morning. He'd been combining corn on another farm and didn't come home the previous night. To make a long story short—a search was organized, and, after receiving a tip, we located his body in a freshly dug hole on the Dickenson farm, which I think is about two miles from where he was supposed to be combining corn. There's not much more I want to say about it—ongoing investigation you know," said Benjamin as he shrugged his shoulders apologetically.

"So you don't know what happened to him, who killed him,

46

none of those things?"

"Well, we're trying to piece things together, that's why I asked you here—get some information."

"Okay, what can I tell you? I manage the Dickenson farm for an investment group out of California, who, by the way, would be very, very sensitive to having their names mentioned with any kind of scandal like this. You know what I mean?"

Benjamin didn't reply to that. Actually he could care less about what some investment firm in California worried about, but he wanted to keep the information coming and not offend this Hal right away.

"Did Carl farm any other farms that you manage?"

"Hell, Carl farmed most of the farms in that area. He farms . . . er . . . farmed almost four thousand acres. He farmed all of the farms owned by the California investors. Had been for almost four years now."

"Tell me, Hal, how does it work? How do you choose your tenants? Interviews, applications, references, what?"

Hal snorted, almost choking on the drink of coffee he'd taken. "They come to us, we don't go to them. There's no shortage of farmers willing to farm, believe me. What it boils down to is how much cash rent they're willing to offer, plain and simple. The guy who pays top dollar gets to farm the land. That's what my clients want—top dollar."

Well, Benjamin could understand that pretty clearly. "What's top dollar mean, I mean per tillable acre or what?"

"Oh yeah, and it's gotten pretty pricey the last few years. I don't have a single grain farm that I rent for less than two hundred dollars per acre."

A waitress bringing them their meals interrupted them. She topped off their coffee as well while the two men sat quietly in thought.

Benjamin suddenly got a look of disbelief on his face as he did the math. "If Carl farmed four thousand acres and paid two hundred dollars per acre that would equal what? Nearly a million dollars?"

"Well, that would equal around eight hundred thousand if he rented all of it for that much. I'm pretty sure Carl has some land already paid for of his own that he inherited from his wife's folks. But still, I know he pays us, Iowa LandCo, over half a million, and remember that's just for rent. You can easily double that amount when you add in his crop inputs, fuel, insurance, repairs, those kinds of things."

"Wow, I had no idea it took that kind of money to farm. Boy, think of the risk!"

"Carl was like most of the other high rollers. He carried the maximum amount of government revenue insurance. Really slashes the risk exposure. Something most of the lending institutions require."

Benjamin nodded. He was taking this all in, but it would probably take the whole trip home to digest it and figure out what other questions he should be asking. In between bites he asked, "When was the last time you saw Carl? You guys meet regularly or what?"

"We generally meet twice per year. Once late in the summer to renegotiate next year's leases and once in the winter assuming all payments have been made on time. Carl had always been good about making his payments. I sure as hell wouldn't try to do what he's doing, but that's why I'm a farm manager and not a farmer, I guess." Hal gave him a wry smile as he made this last statement.

"So, no problems, no enemies, nothing you can give me to suspect why somebody would have killed Carl and buried him on this . . . uh . . . Dickenson farm?"

"Well, no. Well there was a little controversy about that particular farm. Nothing unusual, but it did get a little nasty. See, this is actually the first crop that Carl was taking off the Dickenson farm. For three years previously it'd been rented to a younger guy named Josh Flora. You might know him. He's another farmer in your county. Anyway, when Iowa LandCo took over management of that particular farm, we of course wanted to receive the top cash rent bid we could get, and, quite frankly, Flora just wouldn't ante up the kind of money we wanted, so I ended up kicking him off and renting it to Carl Smith instead. Flora got pretty vocal. I can tell you he called Carl and me some pretty nasty names. Actually threatened to 'kick the shit' out of both of us."

"I don't know Josh Flora. I'm new to the county. Just threats, nothing else? Why would he get so worked up? Hell, there must be all kinds of farms out there, can't he just rent another one?"

"Well, it's tougher for a younger guy like Josh. He only rented about six hundred acres to begin with, so when he lost that two hundred forty acres to Carl it took away a significant portion of his business, and he knew he probably wouldn't be able to cash flow his operation. You don't have to be a farmer to know that any business that doesn't cash flow is a business in trouble. And yes to your second question, there are all kinds of farms to rent, if you can afford to pay more than anybody else, and there's the rub. Generally most farmers are already sticking their necks way out, so if you outbid your neighbor—see what I mean? Josh's trouble was, this farming business doesn't have much use for smaller beginning farmers, you see? If they want to play, they've got to pay, and that's the name of the business."

"So generally, you and your investors don't rent to beginning farmers . . . "

Hal interrupted him, "Sheriff, we don't give a damn who we rent to just as long as they can pay one dollar more than the next highest bid."

The two men finished their meal, and Benjamin questioned Hal some more but didn't learn much of value. Hal handed him a business card, and the two parted ways with Benjamin thinking he didn't much care for this Hal Dallis and his farm management company with its far off investors, and he was damn sure glad he wasn't trying to farm for a living.

CHAPTER
10

She was tired, but the smile wouldn't leave her face, and why not? Next to hugging her daughter and well . . . yeah . . . Hawkett, nothing brought her quite the rush that dealing face to face with her customers did. And the Des Moines Farmers' Market crowd was buying! It'd been slow going when they first set up in the chilly October morning air, but as the temperature warmed up, it developed into an absolutely beautiful Iowa fall day, and the crowd grew and grew. Though hundreds strolled past their booth, Jamie was surprisingly able to recognize dozens of regular customers—people who always bought from her on her treks to the market. And this wasn't the Big Mart crowd looking to find everything you had to sell at the absolute "rock bottom" prices. No, this group wanted quality food and they wanted to know who raised their food, and Jamie was proud to be their provider.

She handled customer after customer, enjoying the questions and friendly banter as they cleaned out her inventory of frozen chickens, eggs, nearly one hundred pounds of ground beef, and every one of her gourds, bags of popcorn, and ears of Indian corn. She took a breath and stepped out of her booth during a short lull in business. She looked up and down the street, just amazed at the variety of vendors, customers, sights, smells and sounds this wonderful event brought, thinking as she did . . . wouldn't it be wonderful if all farmers had this type of venue to market all their products.

She glanced back at Hawkett, in some sort of serious conversation with Andrea, no doubt pulling her leg. He loved to do that and she loved to be teased. For just a second she thought of the injustice that Andrea had really never known her father, Bud, who'd taken his own life when their daughter was just an infant. Now at five years of age, she had begun to stretch up a little and was beginning to show what kind of young lady she would grow into. She had begun to ask pointed questions about her real father, questions about Hawkett now being her father, although of course he wasn't—not even a stepfather. Jamie could feel the shadow of depression sneaking up on her, and being determined not to let that happen anymore, she took a deep breath, looked up and down the street and hustled back to her post to wait on yet another customer.

As late afternoon approached the crowd began to dwindle just a bit, and, given what little she had left to sell, Jamie thought that was probably a good thing. She did hate to have a customer come up and want something and then have to tell that person they were sold out. Jamie straightened up from stacking empty coolers, starting to think about calling it quits for the day, when she spotted a woman stopped about twenty feet from their booth with her eyes locked on them. She wasn't a regular customer, and Jamie hoped she wanted a pumpkin, because that's all they had left—two of them. She'd make her a deal—two for the price of one—and they'd go home celebrating selling every item they'd brought to Des Moines.

The woman started walking toward them looking somewhat mystified, and now, really had Jamie's attention. She was quite attractive, with blond hair flowing down over tan shoulders, wearing a sleeveless knit top and tight-fitting designer jeans tucked into high-heeled, black boots. The way her makeup was applied and her hair fixed, she looked as if she was all set for a photo shoot for the cover of Vogue. Smiling, she started walking toward Jamie, stopped, shook her head as if amazed, and then took another couple of steps. Jamie had this strange feeling she should know the woman, the way she was walking toward them acting gaga, but she couldn't begin to think who the woman was.

Not knowing what to do, she just fell into business mode, gave

51

a smile and said, "Good afternoon. Can I help you? We're just about sold out of everything unless you're needing a couple of good pumpkins for Halloween." But her words went unheard. The woman, now at their booth, carrying the fragrance of expensive perfume and setting a Gucci handbag down on their countertop, was not interested in Jamie. She was looking at Hawkett.

"Adam, I can't believe this. Running into you here! I mean, what are you doing . . . well or whom are you doing? No, I mean . . . " she laughed. "I'm sorry." And having said that she walked around the corner of Jamie's display table, stepped up to Hawkett, and wrapped her arms around him. She placed her head against his chest, then kissed him quickly on the cheek and backed away, looking up into his face. "Well say something, silly," she said, now sensing that Jamie and Andrea were staring at her with stunned expressions. "Oh, is this your new girlfriend?" looking at Jamie with a look that seemed to Jamie as if it had just a little bit of distaste behind it.

Hawkett, clearly caught off guard and embarrassed, turned to Jamie, "Uh . . . this . . . this is Ann Mora, my wife. I mean . . . " laughing nervously, "my former wife. She . . . uh . . . lives here in Des Moines and works as a news reporter. I guess you still do, right?"

This was not news to Jamie. She'd known that Hawkett had been married, was now divorced, had no children, and that his former wife was a television news reporter. What he'd failed to mention to her was that the woman was stunningly beautiful and knew it. Dressed like that, Jamie was wondering if maybe Ann wasn't a little chilled wearing so little, even on this warm October day.

Hawkett, still doing a poor job of it, introduced her to them, "This is Jamie Chambers, a farmer from southern Iowa, and this is her daughter Andrea." He tried to think of something witty to say about them, something to say about what he was doing at a farmers' market in Des Moines with them. He knew why he was there and what he should be saying, but the words just weren't flowing. Jamie saved him—sort of.

"Well hello, Ann," sticking her hand out to offer it for a shake and noticing that she had some sort of pumpkin vine particle clinging to her shirt sleeve. Suddenly she was self-conscious, maybe more self-conscious than she'd been in years over her appearance, standing there in blue jeans and a faded cotton shirt. And it didn't help to note that Ann was not nearly as elated to meet her, as she'd been to grope Hawkett.

No, grope was not the word. Pull yourself together here Chambers, Jamie thought. But still, Ann seemed to have a distinct look of distaste as she gingerly shook hands with Jamie and then held her hand at her side. Jamie could just swear she was looking around for a towel, something to use to wipe her hand.

So suddenly, a beautiful fall day in Iowa had turned into a very awkward moment in the history of Jamie and Hawkett's relationship. Jamie ran her fingers through her hair, not wanting to feel the way she was feeling. She attempted to save the situation with small talk by asking Ann about herself, her career. The problem was, that every time Ann answered a question she would turn and bump into Hawkett with that beautiful body, while he just stood there with a dumb, bewildered smile on his face, and Andrea, her big brown eyes glaring, sat in the corner with a wry look on her face and said nothing.

There was some respite from the situation as an elderly man came walking up to their booth asking what she would take for a pumpkin, and she did in fact give him the last two for the price of one. That really seemed to make the old boy's day until Jamie, distracted with more of the bumping going on out the corner of her eye, miscounted his change. He pointed it out, and she had to correct her mistake with apologies.

Then thankfully Ann left after borrowing Jamie's pen and one of her order forms to jot down her cell number for Hawkett. Jamie was thinking, what the hell did he need her number for, but was trying not to show her anger. Ann sauntered away with those long legs filling out those designer jeans, and Jamie suddenly was wishing that she had a good ripe tomato she could throw.

"Hey, I'm sorry about that. I had no idea she'd be here today. Ann's just . . . well . . . well, she's just Ann. Comes on a little strong I guess."

"Hey, glad to meet her," Jamie lied. "Get to know a little more about your history, huh?"

"Yeah, my history," he chuckled nervously watching Ann walk down the street.

So the day at the farmers' market ended on a bit of a somber note with everyone working together to pack up and head for home but being none too polite about it, even little Andrea. Gone was their normal playful attitude, sharing the happiness of a bountiful day together. They didn't even stop for ice cream on the way home—something that had become a bit of a ritual on market days. Everyone remained quiet, and there didn't seem to be a way to get Ann out of his or her respective minds.

They did stop to pick up the trailer, and, true to his promise, the buyer had unloaded it. The bad news was that it had a flat tire, and by the time they got the tire off, found a station that would repair it, got it back on, and traveled the distance home, it was dark. Everybody was tired and chores still had to be done. Hawkett went out to check the stock, while Jamie gently forced her daughter to take a quick bath and got her into bed, hoping the snacks she'd eaten at the farmers' market would carry her over until morning.

Jamie then grabbed a flashlight to go out and check on Hawkett. She heard him yelling obscenities somewhere in the dark, only to discover that the cows had gotten into the alfalfa while they'd been gone, and he was trying to chase them out. The cows were finally driven back into their pasture and the fence fixed, allowing Jamie and Hawkett to drag themselves into the house around ten, both having been up and working for almost eighteen hours. They were both exhausted.

Jamie just pointed to the fridge and said, "Adam, if you're hungry, help yourself." She went off to her bathroom, took a shower, and fell into her bed, thankful for the long night's sleep that lay ahead. Unfortunately, no sooner did her head hit the pillow than thoughts of Ann came to her mind, and she slept restlessly.

Then, knowing something else had been bothering her, she woke up with a start. Where was Tippy, she wondered. With all of the things going on, she'd forgotten that the little stinker wasn't around when they'd arrived home. She tiptoed out onto the front porch looking for him in the corner where he usually lay. Then she walked barefooted out into the yard. Her feet picked up moisture from the grass and she began to feel chilled, wearing only her summer pajamas—not enough for an October evening in Iowa. She called out to the dog quietly and then felt stupid, as she always did, knowing the dog couldn't hear her anyway.

She got a flashlight out of the pickup, looked in the barn, around the chicken house, and in a few of the spots she'd known him to nap, but the little mutt wasn't anywhere to be found. Discouraged and cold, she decided to renew the search in the morning. She rinsed off her feet in the sink in the mudroom and dried them with a towel, then headed back to bed, even more troubled than before, trying to fight the negative thoughts out of her mind, but too tired to win the battle.

CHAPTER
11

Still unsettled by his visit with the farm manager, Benjamin, while driving down Highway 34, pulled out his cell phone and dialed Jan. No, she had no new news on the murdered farmer, and yes, she and Cindy had arranged to have someone available to dispatch for the remainder of the weekend. So that was good. Thank you, Jan, he thought, as he asked her for directions to Josh Flora's residence.

"Being nosy here I know, Sheriff, but what have you got going with Josh?"

"Oh, I just got done talking to the farm manager who takes care of renting out the farm that Carl was found on. The guy writes up leases, collects the cash rent, you know what I mean?" Without pausing for an answer from her he continued, "Anyway, this farm manager, guy named Hal Dallis, tells me there was some disagreement over who got to rent this particular farm. Apparently our dead farmer outbid Josh who'd been farming it, and there were some real bad feelings over that."

"Ah, well that's the first hint of any kind of motive we've had. But I sure hope it's not Josh. He's a nice person—anyway that's my take on him. Got a couple of kids I think." That was all she seemed to be able to offer.

"Well I'm off to see this Josh. Keep me informed. Okay?"

Half an hour later, Benjamin, having gotten lost only once, found the Josh Flora farmstead. Not fancy, no new large green machines parked all over the place, but it was well kept with a swing set out in the yard. He knocked on the door and got no response. Walking slowly out across the farmyard he could hear a pounding sound coming from one of the buildings and tracked that sound down to a surprised Josh Flora, lying under a combine, pounding on some sort of shaft.

"Hello, I'm Benjamin Willoughby, sheriff of Taylor County. Might you be Josh Flora?"

Sliding out from under the combine with a startled look on his face, a mixture of surprise and concern, "Yeah, I'm Josh Flora. What's up?" Josh pulled himself up to a standing position, dusted off his pants, took Benjamin's offered hand, and shook it.

"Well, Josh, you probably know that Carl Smith was found dead late last night?"

"Yeah, I heard that. What's that got to do with me?"

Benjamin noticed his defensive tone right off and how he seemed nervous, although that was hard to judge, not having met the guy before. He looked to be in his early twenties, and similar to a lot of the farmers around the area, he had calloused hands, was deeply tanned, wore blue jeans showing a lot of wear, and had grease stains on his clothes from working on machinery.

"Oh probably absolutely nothing, Josh. It's just that when something like this happens, we have to go around and question everybody. A formality, you know?" Benjamin tried to disarm Josh's attitude right away by opting for a friendly conversation where more information could be gleaned. "Anyway, Josh, your name came up only because Carl was found buried on the Dickenson farm, and I believe in the past you've been farming that place."

"Yeah, sure, *been* farmin' it, but not this past year. Carl rented it out from under me." And there was no doubt from the frown on Josh's face that he wasn't happy about that.

"Just to help me out here, Josh, my understanding is that the farm management firm that takes care of that farm, I believe they're called Iowa LandCo, they were asking you to pay two hundred dollars

56

per acre to rent the farm and you refused, so they rented the farm to Carl?"

"You got your numbers wrong. I woulda paid the two hundred. When I told that son-of-a-bitchin' farm manager I'd pay that astronomical amount, he drove right down the road to tell Carl, who already farms half the damn county, and Carl said sure, he'd pay two twenty-five. So, mister hot shit farm manager comes back, hands me a paper terminating my lease and that's that!" Josh was getting more worked up by the minute, his face showing a redder tone even through the tanned skin.

"And . . ." Benjamin started to ask another question but was interrupted.

"Now what do I do, lose almost half of my tillable acres? I've got this machinery here, debt against that, but not enough acres to farm. Does the farm manager care about that? Does Carl Smith care about that? Hell no, they don't! Does my banker care about that? Hell yes he does!" Josh's voice kept getting louder until he was almost yelling. "So guess what it does to me? I have to get a job at the factory working nights to make things work! How the hell would you like that? Work all day, then work all night! Hardly any time to see my wife or play with my kids, just because that son-of-a-bitch, Carl Smith, who doesn't even have any kids who want to farm, just wants to farm one more farm, add to his frickin' dynasty." Josh, having made the speech Benjamin guessed he had made a lot, took a deep breath, turned and walked out into the afternoon sunshine, his hands on his hips, holding a grease rag, looking out across his farm.

"I do understand your anger, Josh. Sorry things turned out like this for you."

There was no reply. Josh was still staring at something off in the horizon.

"Josh, did you have an exchange of words with Carl over this?"

Still no reply.

"Josh?"

"Get out of here! Now!" Josh yelled at him with more anger than he'd expected, catching Benjamin off guard. "And don't come back unless you've got a real reason or a warrant! Got that?" Having said that, Josh walked back over to his combine, stooped down and crawled back under the machine. In just a few moments he was pounding on the shaft again.

Benjamin, angered, but not quite knowing what to do about it, simply left the shop, walked to his patrol car and drove away, knowing he would have to deal with this Josh Flora again. But next time their confrontation would be on Benjamin's terms.

Walking into the Pigmy courthouse building, Benjamin looked at his watch and was surprised to see how late in the day it was. Shaking his head and thinking of all that needed to be done yet, he walked into the office and found their young informant, Henny, drinking a can of Mountain Dew and chatting with Jan.

"Well, how are we today, young Mr. Henderson? Where's your mom? I was hoping she'd come in so we could visit with her too," Benjamin was looking at Jan as he said this.

"Henny's mother is still ill, Sheriff. Henny just rode over on his bike to visit with us."

"Henny, is Henny your real name? I don't believe we established that last night, did we? Lots of things going on around here after you tipped us off to the whereabouts of Carl Smith." As he asked this question he noted that the youngster was still wearing the same clothes he'd had on the previous night, and they didn't appear to be any cleaner.

Henny smiled, turned, and looked at Jan and then back at Benjamin. "No, Sheriff, my real name is Chuck. My mom named me after Chuck Norris, you know the guy on TV—Texas Rangers. I'm probably going to join the Texas Rangers when I grow up, because I don't think we have any Iowa Rangers, do we?"

"Henny!" Jan interrupted, "I've told you twice now, don't let your imagination get the better of you, okay? Answer every question correctly and honestly or you could get yourself into a lot of trouble."

Somewhat chastened by her stern admonishment, Henny, not smiling now, nodded his head in agreement and replied, "Yeah, Henny, well actually Henderson. My mom named me Henderson James Henderson. I don't know why she did that, but if you met my mom . . . anyway, everybody just calls me Henny for short."

Benjamin was somewhat taken aback by the initial exchange between Jan and the boy. "Well, Henny, tell us again why you happened to be out on the Dickenson Farm in the middle of the night to witness what you saw?"

"Well Sheriff, I was . . . uh . . . actually, I was raccoon hunting.

Everybody knows those trees along the river are the best spot to find good raccoons and I had my flashlight shining up in the trees, tryin' to spot 'em." Henny shrugged his shoulders, end of answer.

"What? You have a gun you shoot them with? Where's this gun at? Are you even old enough to carry a gun on your own?"

"Uh, no Sheriff. I . . . uh . . . always use spears. Yeah, I throw spears up in the trees . . . try to poke 'em right between the eyes. And if I run out of spears, I always throw rocks. I'm pretty good at it. I killed a deer once with a rock out . . . "

"Henny, I've warned you for the last time. If you tell one more fib, I'm going to take you into the bathroom and wash your mouth out with soap. You got that mister?" Jan got right after him and was actually kind of surprising Benjamin, but still, she was making things better even if they were probably violating the kid's rights on several levels, not the least worrisome—interviewing him without a guardian present.

Caught in his lie and unable to disguise that, Henny, with a slight frown on his face, took on a sullen attitude and said nothing, then became preoccupied with something on his tennis shoe and started fiddling with it.

"Henny, let's go hop in the patrol car and drive over and visit with your mother." He was getting a look from Jan that seemed to be saying, good luck with that. But it did seem to bolster Henny's attitude, and he hopped right up and went out the door with Benjamin. As they loaded Henny's bicycle into the trunk of the patrol car, Benjamin noticed the worn tires and seat. The bicycle had seen a lot of use.

Henny did not care much for having to fasten his seatbelt in the patrol car, but he was absolutely fascinated with the inside of the vehicle and could hardly take his eyes off the shotgun setting upright against the middle of the dash. He rolled down the window and immediately spotted a group of children on the sidewalk as they pulled up to a stop sign. As the car stopped, Henny yelled out the window, "Hey, you dumb bastards, the sheriff says to get the hell home now! Beat it okay?"

"Hey, hey, quit that! Roll that window up now, you hear me?" Benjamin, extremely angered by the boy's crude outburst, continued, "You sit back in that seat and keep your yapper closed, understand?"

Henny, once again chastened, sat back in the seat with a wry look on his face and not another word was spoken on their short trip across town to his home. Pulling in the driveway, Benjamin remembered this place as probably the most run down property in Pigmy. The front yard was littered with trash, multiple broken down lawn mowers, a transmission from some vehicle lay right on the sidewalk—just a mess. An older style conversion van was parked in the driveway with not one, but three, flat tires. Getting out of the car and spotting a small tree growing right up through the cement, blocking the front door, Benjamin turned to Henny, "How do you get into the house? Is there another door around back?"

"Follow me," Henny said as he walked around to the front of the van and ducked under a broken garage door, leading them to a side entry where a door should have been but was missing from its hinges. Into the house, the filthiest one Benjamin had ever seen in his life, they went. Almost feeling his way through the dark rooms, following Henny, smelling stale grease and smoke, alcohol, and other smells he didn't even want to think about.

"Henny, we don't want to surprise your mom. You want to go ahead and get her, then come get me?"

Henny stopped and turned, giving Benjamin a questioning look. "Mom's asleep, she's always asleep. She says she likes to be asleep. She's right there," He was pointing at the couch as he said it.

On the couch, buried in multiple ragged looking blankets, was an overweight woman—very overweight—sleeping soundly, her hair tangled in the covers. A mess, thought Benjamin, living in a mess.

"Can you wake her?" Benjamin asked.

"I ain't wakin' her."

"Why not?"

"I just ain't wakin' her. You want to wake her, go ahead, but I'm going back outside while you do it." Then Henny, seeming to change his mind, shrugging his shoulders, turned and kicked his sleeping mother in the leg.

She groaned and sat upright, clutching the blanket in front of her and stared at them, trying to focus in on what was going on. Then, seeing the sheriff standing there near Henny, she sneered, "I'm not baling him out this time. He's all yours." Having said that, she turned and threw the covers over herself as she flopped back down on the couch with her back toward them.

Benjamin was caught off guard. This is not what he'd expected. He looked at Henny, who was in turn looking at him, giving him one of those "I told you so" shrugs.

"Well, Mrs. Henderson, we're uh . . . interviewing your son about a murder that's taken place."

"Screw you and get out of here!" came a muffled reply from a face buried somewhere in a grungy-looking pillow.

Shaking his head in disgust, Benjamin turned to Henny, "Come on, Henny," and the two ambled back through the house to leave. Benjamin could hear what he believed must be the furnace. There's no door on the house, it's a cold fall day, and the furnace is running. Oh brother, he thought. As they stepped through the empty doorway into the garage, Benjamin heard a grunting sound and a commotion coming from behind the garage. He turned toward Henny. "What the heck was that?"

Henny, with that look on his face that was now telegraphing to Benjamin that another lie was on the way, replied. "I don't know."

"Oh yeah? Well let's go take a look," Benjamin was thinking as he said this that he hoped there wasn't a mean dog out back waiting to take a chunk out of his leg. Around the corner of the garage, working their way through the weeds, Benjamin stopped—shocked at what he saw. Three muddy pigs were cavorting their way around a menagerie of junk, held in by a pen made out of junk. Broken gates, wheels, and several abandoned signs were wired and duct taped together to form a pen that kept the pigs from escaping. Though the pigs were muddy, they did look happy, and they were well fed and watered. They marched right up to the fence, and Henny immediately pulled a large milkweed out of the ground behind him and dangled it over the fence, giving the little squealers much joy as they nibbled at it playfully.

"Whose pigs are these? Your mom's?"

"Uh . . . no, they're mine."

"Where'd you get them?"

Henny, with a look of guilt on his face, struggled to come up with an answer. Benjamin was thinking, "Oh boy, here we go again."

"Uh . . . I found them when I was out raccoon hunting. They uh . . . kinda followed me home, and they were hungry, so I get all the scraps from the guy who runs the restaurant uptown, and they eat those."

"You feed them scraps? You mean leftovers that people don't eat at the restaurant?"

"Yeah . . . there . . . and I get some from the school lunch program too. You'd be surprised how much food people throw away. These little guys just love it."

Just as he said that, one of the pigs flopped down in a mud puddle, splashing some slop up and over the fence, hitting both Benjamin and Henny.

61

"Damn! Watch it!" Benjamin said, backing away and looking again at the pigs, wondering what the real story was on where they'd come from. "Henny, you got some mud on the front of your shirt. Go in and change your clothes. We're going back to my office."

"Can't."

"What? Why can't you go back to the office?"

"No . . . can't change my clothes. These are the only clean clothes I have right now that fit. Mom hasn't done laundry for a while," shrugging as he said it, clearly embarrassed.

"Well," Benjamin said, shaking his head, not quite sure what to make of that. "Well, let's go. Get in the car." Thinking as he said it—damn, a brand-new car no less, smelling like pigs.

CHAPTER 12

"Hey, Jan, I had to bring Henny back here for some more inter-rogation." Then turning his attention back to Henny who was following him, "Henny, go to the back room by the jail cells. There's nobody back there now. Why don't you take a shower and find some clean clothes. I know they all say sheriff's department on them but that's okay, huh, just 'til we get your other stuff cleaned up a little bit okay?"

"Sure, Sheriff, you got clean towels and everything back there?"

"Yes we do, Henny. If you need anything, there's a phone back there, just push the red button and it'll dial up here, okay?"

That was okay with Henny, and he headed back into the jail area. When he was out of hearing distance Benjamin turned to Jan and said, "That was worse than I thought it'd be. That kid is living in a hell-hole over there. Any idea where his father is?"

"I don't know if his mom is even sure who Henny's father is. I know that's a terrible thing to say, but it is what it is."

"You think we ought to call Human Services, do some sort of

63

intervention?"

"Well, I guess I don't want to be the one to make that call, you know. Kid that age, maybe things work out well, maybe not."

Benjamin didn't know quite what Jan meant by that, but he knew he had to do something. "Listen, I need you to do something for me." He reached for his billfold, pulled out some cash, and handed the money to Jan. "Would you please go somewhere and buy that kid a full set of clean clothes, all of them you know, and a good pair of tennis shoes? Make sure he gets a good meal and then drive him back to his house when he's ready. Watch him go in, okay?"

"Sure, Sheriff, anything else?"

"Yes, we still don't know what the little shit was doing out there when he came upon somebody burying Carl Smith. Keep working on him, okay? And yeah, there are some half grown pigs out in the yard behind his house, probably stolen. Try and get that straightened out too, okay?"

"Pigs? Man this whole murder thing is getting more complex all the time," Jan replied, shaking her head back and forth.

Benjamin walked across the street and enjoyed the evening special, featuring roast beef and gravy, at June's Restaurant. He drank two cups of black coffee with his meal and contemplated the growing list of problems he had to deal with. A murdered victim in his county would be plenty to deal with, but now he had a young lad that probably should have some sort of intervention. Oh yeah, remembering his phone conversation with Brightwall of the DCI, he also had some sort of a drug dealer right in his backyard. He shook his head as he thought man, could I use some help. Somebody from the DCI would be coming by Monday, but still that was a day away and these bases needed to be covered while the trail was still hot.

Well, Benjamin thought to himself, you can only do what you can do. He finished the excellent meal, paid June, and headed for his patrol car. Upon entering it, he picked up just the faintest scent of swine and thought about going somewhere to get an air freshener, but he had other things more pressing to take care of. On the radio, he called in and reported to the office that he was going out, one more time, to walk around the crime scene and check things over. He had no idea what he was looking for.

Ten minutes later he rolled into the driveway of the site that was now a mass of crushed cornstalks due to everything that had transpired the last few days. There were tracks everywhere, a hole dug out of the black Iowa soil, and a backhoe, setting down the road, still surrounded by police tape. He pulled his flashlight out of its holder and climbed out of the car. It was a beautiful fall night with leaves blowing around gently, coyotes yelping and howling off in the distance, and a harvest moon bathing the area with its nightglow. Benjamin was startled by a set of eyes near the hole, reflecting the beam of his flashlight, and then, just that suddenly, he chuckled, realizing the eyes belonged to a small raccoon dragging an ear of corn backwards as it tried to escape his light. So maybe Henny was telling the truth, there were at least some raccoons out here.

Then, as if someone turned off the light switch, a bank of clouds rolled in and shut off the moonlight and it became very dark. The darkness didn't bother Benjamin. He'd been in a lot of dark alleys in his career, but he was somewhat alarmed when the howling coyotes stopped almost as one, and then the rest of the woodland near the cornfield went strangely silent. He wondered why. Is it my presence here, the flashlight?

Those thoughts were interrupted by the sound of a vehicle starting somewhere on down the road from the driveway Benjamin had entered. No headlights came on for a little bit and then he could just pick them up going over the hill. Benjamin hopped into his patrol car, gunned it out the driveway, and hit his lights as he flew up the road, calling Jan as he did. It was probably just a couple of teenagers, but still, protocol was protocol. He raced over the hill and could tell that the vehicle ahead had begun to accelerate, then it slowed down and came to a stop at the side of the road. Benjamin slowed his car and stopped a short distance behind it. He aimed his spotlight through the back window of the car ahead and saw a single male adult. He reported the plate number to Jan and got out of his car. He exited his patrol car and had proceeded nearly halfway to the stopped vehicle when his emergency beeper went off. He stopped in his tracks with surprise and murmured to himself, "What now?" He went back to the car and reached for the radio microphone. "What's up?"

"I ran that plate, Sheriff. You've got Roydel Nuxton's car stopped. Be careful, okay?"

"Whoa! Roydel huh? Our resident drug runner. Okay, I'll keep an eye on him. Thanks for the heads up."

"You want backup? Cindy's still here. She can handle the radio and keep an eye on Henny. I can be out there in a few minutes."

"No I think I can handle him, but thanks. Just stay close to the radio, okay?" Having said that, he clipped his holstered gun onto his belt and headed back towards the car, still setting ahead, visible in his lights, with cigarette smoke drifting out of the driver's window. Shining his flashlight at the car and walking in an arc toward the driver's door, Benjamin called out, "Driver, please put both of your hands out the window!"

"Shit," Roydel mumbled and threw his cigarette out the window. He made a halfhearted attempt to lay both of his arms out the car window.

"According to the license plate, this car is registered to Roydel Nuxton. That be you?" Benjamin knowing the answer to that question, seeing the tattooed arms and the attitude of an ex-con in full presence.

Roydel felt his temper raging but reminded himself to hold on and remember how to play the game. "Yes sir, I'm Roydel Nuxton and this is my car. I have a license, registration, and insurance card available for your inspection."

Benjamin was taken aback, expecting to take some lip off of this guy. Well, don't let your guard down, he said to himself peering into the front of the car with his flashlight. "All alone I see. I'm not interested in your driver's license right now, Roydel, but I would like to know what you're doing sitting out here in the dark, right down the road from where a man was murdered not two days ago. Got a good answer for that?"

Roydel didn't reply right away. He started to reach for a cigarette to give himself time to think up a plausible story. "You care if I have another smoke?"

"You keep your hands on that door. You can smoke later. Answer my question. What are you doing out here?" Benjamin's voice took on a firmer tone. He did not want to fool around with this guy.

"Hey, I live just down the road a couple of miles. I was headed home and I had to take a whiz. Couldn't hold it you know? So I stopped to take a leak, no harm, nobody's around. Hey, go back there and check the weeds, you'll be able to tell where I . . ."

"I'm not going anywhere, Roydel. I'll take your word for it. You care if I search your car, check for weapons, drugs, that kind of thing? Won't take long."

Roydel's plan of holding himself together was quickly slipping away, and his anger was rapidly taking the upper hand. He could feel

66

it but could do nothing about it. "Why? A guy stops to take a leak on a country road and you got to run him down with your lights ablazin', pull him over, and now we're talking about a search? Man, a little tense tonight aren't we? I mean shit, I ain't done nothin'."

"You didn't answer my question Roydel. I said, do you mind if I search your car?"

"Hell yes I mind. I just cleaned the thing up. Don't want no lawman slobberin' all over everything!" Then pulling himself together a little bit, "Hey, you want to search this car? Fine, go ahead. But I want to see the warrant first, okay? Two can play this game, Sheriff."

And he was right, thought Benjamin. It was a game. According to the rules, if he wanted to search that car without Roydel's permission, he'd have to stay here and watch it while someone else, probably Jan, tried to find a judge and convince the judge to sign a search warrant. That would probably take most of the night if they managed to pull it off, and maybe nothing would be gained. Benjamin made up his mind.

"Listen, Roydel. I'm new to this county, but I'm not new to law enforcement. I've spent most of my life dealing with crime and quite a bit of that crime revolved around drug problems. You hear what I'm saying?"

"Yeah, shit, I hear you. Look like you haven't got my attention? You want a round of applause or . . . "

"Shut up and listen. I'm getting word that you're running drugs to Des Moines, and I'm getting that information from people who probably know what they're talking about. And when I have time, I'm going to make it my business to find out what you're up to and haul your sorry ass in and send you off to the pen so you'll be out of my hair. You understand that, dumbass?"

Feeling his anger start to storm out of control, listening to the smart-mouthed cop, hearing those threats, Roydel could almost feel himself reaching down for his gun. Oh man . . . shit . . . pull it out and put three quick ones in that loudmouth's chest. See what a big man he is then.

"Get your ass out of here and remember what I said. Enjoy your vacation now, 'cause you'll be back in the big house with all your boyfriends in short order."

Having said that, Benjamin turned and walked back to his car. He was tired of dealing with things he'd assumed he would never have to deal with in the quiet countryside of southern Iowa, apparently not as quiet as he'd thought.

CHAPTER
13

Jamie awoke with a start. She slowly sat up, feeling a really nasty headache, and discovered she'd overslept. "Damn," she berated herself. "How'd I do that?" Then she remembered the long day yesterday. The cattle were out when they had arrived home and she had had a troubled night sleeping, thinking of all the things that were wrong with her relationship with Adam Hawkett. She lay back down feeling sorry for herself and began working into a really good funk. Realizing that wasn't going to help, she forced herself up and out of bed. She downed a couple of ibuprofen tablets, then started making a pot of coffee while noting that Hawkett and Andrea were still asleep in their respective bedrooms. So they'd all overslept. Looking at the clock she realized that church would begin in a little over an hour so she hustled out to get the chores done that couldn't be postponed. Adam could finish when he got up. He might as well she thought. Not once in our relationship has he offered to go to church with Andrea and me . . . hadn't even offered.

She ignored the complaining milk cow. Hawkett would soon milk her . . . hopefully. She watered the pigs and checked the chickens.

The sheep could stay in the same paddock they were in, so they would be okay until tomorrow. A quick glance at the cattle and she could head back into the house and get ready for church. On her way to the pasture Jamie glanced out into the alfalfa field that the cattle had gotten into while they were gone. She spotted a black object, climbed the fence and walked towards it. A sense of dread grew with each step until she was sure of what she saw. A black cow lay on her side, legs extended and stomach puffed up like a hot air balloon. Her eyes were bulging and her tongue was hanging out, dead from ruminant bloat. "Oh no, oh no . . . " Jamie kept repeating to herself as she walked closer to the dead cow, knowing, as she walked, that the cow had eaten too much alfalfa during the herd's escape, much more than her complicated rumen could handle. Too much gas had been produced in her stomach, and the pressure had caused the animal's collapse, suffocation, and death. With no hope of salvaging any of the cow for meat, the animal was just a total, senseless loss.

Jamie stood silently looking at the animal, a bred heifer that would have delivered her first calf next spring, an animal Jamie had selected because of the reliable performance of all her ancestors in the herd. She was now just a dead object, worthless to everything in the world except flies, maggots, and other scavengers. Jamie wiped away some tears and took a deep breath. These things happened, but still, that didn't make it any easier. She turned around and peered across the hayfield and adjoining pasture making sure that no other animals were lost. She wondered if they'd missed this heifer when they'd chased them during the night or if it had already succumbed to bloat before they had arrived home. With a heavy heart and in a real state of depression she walked across the hayfield, climbed the fence, and headed for the house.

She met Hawkett as he stepped out onto the porch with a cup of coffee in hand. "Morning," he said to her. She didn't reply but kept walking towards him with a look in her eyes that told him something was wrong. "What's wrong?" he asked.

She stopped, put her hands on her hips, looked at the ground, then sighed, not wanting to get too emotional over this and start crying irrationally. "When the cows got out in the alfalfa yesterday, or last night, or whenever the hell they got out, one of them must have gotten too much alfalfa in her and she's laying out there bloated and dead. I don't know if we missed her last night or if she was already dead and we just didn't notice her in the dark. I just don't know."

70

Hawkett, looked out across the field, "Where, I don't see her."

"You can't see her from here, but trust me, I know a dead cow when I see one." Jamie didn't even attempt to keep the irritation out of her voice. "Listen. I have to get Andrea up and get to church. When you have time, would you take the tractor out, hook a log chain to the dead heifer, and pull her out by the compost pile? We're going to have to bury her deep in organic matter and let Mother Nature take over before she starts decaying and smelling. Okay?"

"Yeah, I guess. You want me to do that, huh?"

"Well, I guess you're not going to church with us, right? I mean you've never even offered to go in the weeks you've stayed here, so I'm guessing you're not going today. Right?" The irritation still in her voice caught Hawkett off guard. He didn't like her tone, but he held his tongue, turned, and just walked away from her. He heard the screen door slam.

Things didn't get any better at church. A groggy, grumpy daughter had been difficult to wake. Jamie, preoccupied with thoughts of the loss of her cow and the meeting with Hawkett's wife the day before, was in a mood and she just couldn't get out of it. Trying to pray, trying to listen to the sermon, trying to be thankful for all of her blessings just wasn't working today, and that made her mood that much worse. On the way out of church she ran into Thelma Oldham, her neighbor, and they chatted briefly. She liked Thelma and her sister-in-law Pearl. They were both good neighbors, but Thelma had always been nervous about the unmarried man living with Jamie and wouldn't leave the subject alone. As they parted, Thelma told her to be sure to say hi to her boyfriend.

71

CHAPTER

14

      Benjamin was at June's for breakfast early Sunday morning, enjoying a cup of coffee and chatting with some of the locals, all of whom were aching to discuss the murdered farmer. As usual, he had to avoid direct questions, but in the conversation he picked up on another lead. One of the farmers present made mention of the fact that he knew that the murdered farmer had borrowed all of his money from the area Farm Credit Bank. This fact had come up during their discussion of what might happen to the farms Carl owned, speculation about his debt, and other general farm gossip, most of it irrelevant to Benjamin's investigation. But the idea of talking to Carl's banker appealed to him, and when he got back to his office, he made a point of searching for leads on someone at the bank he could visit with. He realized it was Sunday morning and his odds weren't very good, but one call led to another, and finally he had Carl's banker on the phone.

      The banker's name was Robert Olde—just call me Bob—and he seemed to be very willing to visit with Benjamin over the phone about the murder investigation, although he did remind Benjamin that there were probably questions he couldn't answer—protecting the privacy of Carl and his wife Emily.

"Well, let's take it one question at a time and see if you can enlighten me any, Bob. Of course you know that Carl Smith died from foul play?"

"Yes, I was saddened to hear that. Carl had been a good client of this bank and a valuable resource in his community. I'm sure he'll be missed by many."

"Yes, that's probably true. Listen, Bob, can you confirm to me that Carl and his wife borrowed money from your institution?"

"Yes, I can tell you that they borrowed money from us for operating loans, machinery purchases, and land investment as well."

"That was my understanding from scuttlebutt but just wanted to confirm it. Are you aware of any financial stress or . . . uh . . . circumstances that might be problematic for the Smiths?"

"Well, Sheriff, I can't, of course, give you any specific details. I can say that the Smiths borrowed a large sum of money and were considered good customers."

"Can you tell me how much a considerable loan would be?"

"Well, again I won't make any specific reference to the Smiths, but some of our larger grain customers have operating loans and real estate debt that amounts to several million dollars. Again, not giving you specifics, but that's a hint as to what farmers like Carl and Emily might have borrowed."

Benjamin was sitting there shocked at the astronomical amount of money that the banker had casually mentioned, trying to remember his next question, "Man-oh-man, Bob, that's a lot of risk. I mean how do these farmers handle that load?"

"Well, you have to remember, a lot of them have quite a bit of equity built up in the farms they own. Let's face it, real estate has been a darling of the financial portfolios for some time now. Secondly, most of our large grain farmers use some form of government revenue insurance to protect them against bad weather or falling markets. Again, not mentioning the Smiths specifically, but a lot of farmers like them do just that."

"Oh, I see. That's how a guy like Carl can afford to spend two hundred dollars an acre to rent a farm, say, like the Dickenson farm he was found on?"

"Well, I was thinking Carl was giving more like two hundred

twenty-five an acre to rent that farm, maybe it was another farm, but yes, that's a large part of their gamble, knowing there's a bit of a safety net to fall onto."

"But of course that doesn't cover the loss of human life, you know what I mean? I mean how will Carl's wife, Emily, carry on now? The poor woman has lost her husband who probably ran most of the machinery and managed the business I suppose? How does that figure into everything?"

"Well, I hate to sound like a broken record, Sheriff, but there are things about the Smith's personal business I just can't comment on without legal permission. I can tell you it's not uncommon for us to re-quire our higher risk clients to carry large enough sums of life insurance to cover such a situation."

"You mean it's possible that there's a life insurance policy for Carl out there worth a million dollars or more?"

"I would say that is very likely, Sheriff, and his wife Emily is probably the first beneficiary."

The call ended a few minutes later with Benjamin learning little more and thanking Banker Bob for his cooperation. Sitting there daydreaming, he thought about the possibility of a huge life insurance policy existing, with the man's wife as a beneficiary. He wondered if she could run a backhoe and thought, hell, she drove everything else on the farm, why not a backhoe? He was also thinking it was the first hint of a motive for Farmer Smith's death, and he'd have to follow up on it.

CHAPTER
15

Back on Jamie's farm, things were beginning to calm down a bit. Jamie was still in a down mood, but felt she was working through it, and the beautiful fall weather certainly did help to brighten her spirits. They'd gotten the dead cow thoroughly buried in a large pile of compost, well away from the buildings. Now nature would have to take its course, turning a once valuable breeding animal into recyclable fertilizer to be spread out across one of her fields the following spring. Having the dead animal out of sight seemed to help everyone's mood a little, and Jamie, Hawkett, and Andrea enjoyed a quiet lunch of hamburgers and potato salad.

Afterwards, Hawkett retired to a lounger in the living room to read one of his favorite magazines while Andrea curled up on her mother's bed for a much-needed nap. Jamie went out to take a walk around her farm, trying to catch up on some spiritual reflection that'd been blocked out while in church that morning. And indeed, it was a beautiful fall day for a walk around the farm. She walked out across the cow pasture, climbed over the fence, and proceeded up the tree-covered hillside.

She ambled through the trees and brush until she reached a favorite clearing that allowed her to turn and view her farmstead below. Stepping away from her work and looking back at it always brought a sense of pride and accomplishment to her. From this vantage point she could see the different animals grazing, her gardens, and the farm buildings, and if she sat here long enough, she would probably see Hawkett or Andrea come out and take on some activity. This was good. She leaned against a tree and took deep breaths of the fragrant fall air, marveling at the beautiful array of colors the fall foliage provided. Things had not gone well yesterday and this morning, but they were turning around now, and she could handle her problems once again. One more deep breath and off she went, back down to her farmyard.

Jamie found Hawkett busy changing oil in the pickup and Andrea half asleep on the front porch swing, holding her favorite doll and struggling to wake up from a very good nap. Before Jamie had a chance to draw near the little girl, she heard an approaching car and stopped to look. There was so little traffic on their road, and her place was the final inhabited house before the dead end, so an approaching car was something worth noting. Unless someone was lost or just sightseeing, and that did happen once in awhile, it was likely that they had an unexpected visitor.

Jamie was thinking that the vehicle, traveling at a fairly fast rate, was going to zip on past, but the driver hit the brakes, and, after the vehicle skidded slightly out of control, it whipped into her driveway going too fast. Several laying hens that ran loose around the farmyard were pecking at the gravel in the driveway and picking up a little grit for their gizzards. The approaching vehicle—a newish-looking high-dollar SUV—dodged two chickens and ran over another one as it skidded to a halt. Jamie could feel her temper rising, wondering what was so important that this speeding idiot had just killed one of her hens. She was watching the chicken do its final death throes when things went from bad to worse.

Out of the car appeared Ann Mora, dressed in another one of her provocative outfits, with her hair and makeup making her look like a movie star. Ann was glancing around nervously. "I hope I didn't hit any of those chicken things. Don't you people put up any warning signs? I mean, they were just walking across the driveway and . . ." Spotting the dying chicken behind her on the driveway she gasped, "Oh, oh, oh, please tell me I didn't. I did, didn't I. Oh, my, I'm sorry, so sorry. Can we? Is it? Do you want me to take it to a veterinarian? I . . . "

This chatter was doing nothing to relieve Jamie's temper as she walked over and picked up the chicken. It didn't appear to have endured much physical damage, making it a good candidate for a meal in the near future, seeing as it would never lay another egg. With just a tad more aggressiveness than was necessary, she grasped the dead chicken by its legs, put her boot down on its head and pulled upward, decapitating the creature right in front of Ann.

Leaning against her SUV, Ann let out a sound, somewhere between shock and disbelief. She tried to cover her eyes, but it was too late. Assessing her role in the death of this creature, and Jamie's calloused reaction, Ann responded, "I'm so sorry, so sorry. I'll pay you for the chicken, or I'll buy you a new one." She looked on as Jamie held the beheaded chicken over the edge of the driveway and let the blood drip out of its carcass.

Jamie, her temper subsiding a little bit and, quite frankly, enjoying every bit of Ann's suffering, replied, "Don't worry about it. We have over a hundred of them walking around and will probably replace most of them before next spring. You just hurried up this one's trip to the freezer a little bit."

Now Andrea had joined the group and was studying the situation. She was surprised at what she believed was foolish behavior on Ann's part and couldn't understand why an adult would carry on like that, as she studied the chicken's head lying there. She hadn't enjoyed the meeting with Ann the day before and wished the woman hadn't shown up at their farm. These events painted a deep frown on her face.

Hawkett walked over from where he'd been working on the pickup and took in the view. He fought back a smile as he found the situation quite comical, but then he noticed the faces of the three females and decided that this was a dramatic situation, not a funny one, and he'd darned sure better act that way.

He was quite taken by surprise at Ann's appearance on Jamie's farm and wondered how she had figured out the way there. But of course, Ann had her sources and she could track things down. But still, he wondered why she had come, and, all the while, he wasn't missing the fact that Ann was not at all hard to look at, dressed as she was.

"Oh Hawkett!" she cried out, running up to him and wrapping

her arms around him. "Thank goodness you're here. I . . . I seem to have killed one of your girlfriend's chickens. I'm so sorry, but the silly thing practically threw itself in front of my tires. I braked and swerved, but it was just too late. And then, this woman, your girlfriend I guess, walks up and murders the thing right before my very eyes . . . me wanting to load the poor creature into my car and drive for help."

Hawkett, feeling her body close to him and knowing it felt good, but seeing the brown eyes boring down on him from both the mother and daughter nearby, knew that he was in trouble. He tried to push Ann away gently, desperately trying to think of the right thing to say, but knowing there was absolutely no way out of this mess.

Jamie saved him—again . . . "What are you doing here, Ann? What do you want? Surely you're not here to purchase any fresh food from us, although I'd be willing to give you a pretty good deal on this chicken. It's not quite as good as a younger bird, but, cooked properly, it'd make a good meal for you."

Hawkett watched as Ann regained her composure and took control of the situation—like only Ann could do.

"No, I'm not here to buy anything. I came here to see Adam." She turned to look at Hawkett with a smile on her face. "There were some memories stirred at our reunion yesterday, and I couldn't sleep a wink last night wishing I'd spoken some different words and expressed my feelings of closure somehow—tried to deal with buried emotional issues that sprang to life yesterday." Turning to Hawkett again, moving towards him, "Uh, Adam, is there somewhere we could talk? I mean more privately? I don't want to upset these farm people." She glanced casually back over her shoulder towards Jamie and Andrea.

Hawkett, seeing no way out of this situation and knowing it would do little good to ask Ann to just leave, thought he'd better let her have her say and then work on damage control with Jamie later. "Sure. Let's . . . uh . . . let's just go over here and sit on the bench by our . . . well . . . er . . . Jamie's garden."

"Oh thank you, Adam." She smiled at him like he'd just given her a second chance on life or at least had come up with a solution for world peace. The two walked across the farmyard to the garden and sat down on the bench. Once there, Ann broke into some sort of animated conversation with Hawkett. Jamie could not hear what was being said and was glad she couldn't, or at least that's what she told herself. She got down to the business of processing the chicken, bringing scalding hot water, a large bowl and a butcher knife from the kitchen. She noticed Andrea had disappeared and wondered what the little tyke was up to.

As Jamie slipped the processed chicken into a plastic bag for freezing, she noticed the other two adults walking towards Ann's SUV. She sighed deeply—glad that this fiasco would soon be over. Wouldn't it? Then feelings of insecurity and yes, damn it, jealousy, overtook her as Ann wrapped her arms tightly around Hawkett, then reached up and kissed him passionately.

Finally, longer than Jamie thought it should have taken him to, Hawkett pushed his ex-wife away and gently worked her into her SUV. Jamie watched as Ann backed the vehicle around carefully in the yard. After tapping the brakes repeatedly, looking for other chickens, she finally drove out of the driveway. Jamie started toward the house to put the chicken in the freezer, when all of a sudden she heard a scream, and the SUV braked to a halt right out on the road in front of her house.

"What the hell now?" Jamie murmured to herself.

Out of the vehicle jumped Ann, yelling hysterically and running around to the other side of her SUV. She seemed to have a tissue in her hand and Jamie watched, mystified, as Ann picked some object off of the passenger seat and pitched it across the road toward their house.

Looking more closely, Jamie realized it was the head of the dead chicken. "Andrea," she yelled, "you come here right now, young lady!"

CHAPTER
16

Roydel was restless. He paced up and down the length of his trailer house, glancing out the window, looking for something but not quite sure what. The encounter with the sheriff the night before had really set him off—got him to rememberin' the time he spent in prison. Shit, I'm not going back there—no way man. He lit up another Gold-Tip, drew hard on it, and blew smoke out in front of him, watching it settle on his sofa. Working at trying to calm himself for over an hour now, he told himself, "Roydel, chill down boy. You just had a bad run-in with the law. Just let it pass, things will be cool. Go huntin', drink a beer—shit go for a ride in your car, man, just chill down." But the "chillin' down" part just wasn't working.

He kept thinking about what his poor deceased mother would always say when something really bad happened. "These bad things, they always happen in threes." Thinking about the time his dad blew an engine in their pickup, then the electricity got turned off for failure to pay their bill, and then what? Sure enough, number three comes along and his poor old daddy gets caught robbing a drug store down in Purity,

Missouri. He got less than a hundred dollars, three cartons of cigarettes, and a bag of prescription drugs that turned out to be sold to some old gal to treat hemorrhoids. His haul sure wasn't worth finding out that somebody caught the numbers on his license plate and remembered it long enough to hand it to the local law. So yep, there came bad thing number three. Daddy was back in the pen, and they still didn't have any electricity. Roydel took stock of his current situation.

Number one—I get stiffed on my drug money by that pissant tellin' me there was a problem. Yeah, I should have pulled on him and then he'd know a real problem when he saw one.

Number two—I'm out researchin' the murder site, see the backhoe setting there and get to wonderin' what could be stolen off of it. Take a little look-see, then get caught sneakin' away by Mr. Big Prick Marshall!

Now, number three—what's it gonna be? Hey, he thought, that rhymes. Number three—what's it gonna be. He repeated it in his mind. "Oh shit, that's gotta be a really bad sign."

He couldn't help it anymore. He needed to see a good sign and get some relief, so he pulled his cell phone out of his pants pocket and punched in the number he wasn't supposed to use except on meeting nights.

"Hey, what are you callin' me for on this phone? Better be pretty damned important, and make it quick."

Roydel, not liking that tone at all, replied, "Yeah, well it is important, asshole. You stiffed me five hundred dollars the other night. When am I gettin' the rest of my money?"

"I told you, there's a problem. That's all you need to know. Now don't call me on this number again until I give you permission."

Roydel started to yell something into the phone but could tell he'd been cut off and knew the son of a bitch had hung up on him. Furious, he hit the redial and became angrier still when a series of unanswered rings turned him over to voicemail. He tried to leave a threatening message, but his anger caused him to sound like a fool so he threw the phone to the floor of his trailer. Now his Nuxton temper was out of control, and he was gonna have to find some relief. He slammed open the door of his trailer and started to run across his homemade deck. He caught the heel of his boot on a board, tripped, and rolled down the wooden steps, smacking his head hard. Lying there in the grass and staring up at the sky, he growled to himself, "Somebody's gonna pay!"

CHAPTER
17

Well, thought Benjamin, he had learned some things. Maybe not much, but still the bit about the huge life insurance policy was really interesting. That unpleasant lead would have to be tracked down. He tried imagining himself asking Emily Smith about the life insurance policy and thinking of the look that would come over her face when it dawned on her why he was asking such a question. That put a damper on his mood. Thankfully, everything else in his world seemed pretty quiet, and there would be help from the Iowa DCI tomorrow, so things couldn't get any worse. Could they? Jan, the magnificent Jan, had control of the office, and it was getting late in the afternoon, so he decided to drive out to the Jamie Chamber's farm for a much anticipated dinner. It was yet another beautiful October day. He drove slowly out of Pigmy and turned onto the dead end road that led to her farm.

The first farm he drove by was where Pearl and Thelma lived. He grimaced remembering the run-in he'd had with Pearl only two days prior. Maybe he should stop, try to reason with her a little bit, tear up the ticket. But no, dammit, there was already a nice dent in the front left quarter of his car and a cleaning bill on his pants, assuming the stains could be removed. No, she could come into town and pay her bill or take it to the magistrate court and see how far she got there.

He turned into Jamie's farmyard, drove up the lane and parked. He was really delighted to see little Andrea running across the farmyard to greet him. As he stepped out of the car, she ran up to Benjamin and gave him a hug. He was truly touched by the little girl's affection. Benjamin had no family of his own. Jamie, Andrea and Hawkett were his family, his "make-believe family" of sorts. Anyway, he cared deeply for all of them, probably actually loved them, but that word wasn't part of his vocabulary. So maybe it had been a really bad past few days, but for the next couple of hours he could sit back and really enjoy the people he was with, and he couldn't have been happier.

As Hawkett came walking up from a distant pasture, Benjamin watched him and gently shook his head. It was still amazing to think that only a few months ago he and Hawkett had been partners in the murder investigation division of the State of Iowa Department of Criminal Investigation, and the one case here in Southern Iowa, where a banker had been found murdered not a quarter mile from where he stood, had transformed their lives.

"Farmer Hawkett, how're things out in your fields? Corn growing, pigs getting fat, that sort of thing?" Willoughby asked with a glint of amusement in his eyes.

"Hey, how are you, big guy? There are lots of things goin' on out here where people actually work for a living. Not like you civil servants who ride around in air conditioned cars and pester the poor people of Taylor County. How's the murder investigation coming? Got that little problem all sewn up?"

"Aw, don't bring up that kind of unpleasantness. I come out here to relax and enjoy the farm hospitality you folks are so good at, and then you start bringing up this murder business. Hell, you might as well go into town and sit in June's restaurant so you can bug me with the rest of the townspeople. But I will say that not much progress made yet on that front."

The two men bantered back and forth good-naturedly for a couple of minutes, then walked up the sidewalk, across the front porch, and into the house where they could smell the delicious aroma of Jamie's cooking. Ben's first hint that not all was well was when she greeted him. Although she certainly was polite and pleasant, it just didn't sound like the usual Jamie, and a small flag of worry sprang up in his thoughts.

Gathered around the large oak table garnished with fried chicken, mashed potatoes, homemade bread, and fresh applesauce, the three adults and Andrea held hands and prayed. Benjamin was trying to concentrate on the words of the blessing, but he was salivating so much and anticipating the food that his mind just wasn't in it. However, when eating at Jamie's house, a prayer was said before every meal, and he willingly participated.

Although he was already stuffed beyond belief from the wonderful meal, Benjamin gladly accepted the homemade peach pie smothered in fresh homemade ice cream—made possible by Flossie the cow, whoever milked her, and whoever cranked the handle on the ice cream maker. He scooted his chair back from the table and, wanting to think of something to talk about related to farming, mentioned the three pigs he'd discovered yesterday in the backyard at Henny's.

He immediately had Jamie's attention. "Three pigs, how big?"

"I don't know, maybe a foot tall and a couple feet long. Is that what you mean?"

She chuckled, "Well no, we usually describe pigs by weight, but I get a general idea from what you've said. What color are they?"

"Well, they're probably black and white, some spots I think. The little devils had been rolling around in the mud and it was kinda hard to tell what color they were really. Why do you ask?"

"Sometime in the past three weeks, three pigs have gone missing from my weaning pen. We didn't see them running outside the pen and we haven't found them dead. It's been a real mystery, and I just bet that little crook stole them from us." Jamie wasn't smiling anymore and everybody in the room could feel her getting angrier as she spoke. "What was this Henny going to do with them—sell them?"

"He said he was trying to start a little pig farm of his own. I know it sounds bizarre, and I also know the kid lies easily, but it did look like that's what he was trying to do. Believe me, the place he lives in is already a pigsty to begin with. His mother is a complete waste and it looks like the kid takes care of himself. It's no secret he was the one who saw Farmer Smith being shoved into that hole last Thursday night—claims he was out raccoon hunting." Benjamin shrugged his shoulders. "Well, when I get back into town, I'll find out where the pigs came from for sure. Anyway . . . can you positively identify your pigs?" He smiled as he said it, but saw from the look on Jamie's face that she didn't find it at all amusing.

"Yes, I believe I can. I mean they probably look just like their littermates that we still have, assuming they've been fed and cared for."

"Oh yeah, they looked plump and healthy to me. If he doesn't fess up, I'll have you come in and take a look at them." Benjamin paused momentarily, contemplating the issue. "Well, this is the first good news I've had in a while! I've probably solved a mystery. Wonder if any more pigs or other animals have been stolen by this kid?"

"Not stolen pigs, but we have a pup that's been taking off at night, and I'll bet Tippy has met Henny somewhere along the line. I suppose they're friends?" She snorted, thinking of their trusted farm dog gleefully helping somebody steal from them. That darned pup. Something would have to be done.

"I'm just amazed," said Hawkett. "This kid is actually trying to start a little pig farm in his backyard at Pigmy. I mean where did he even get the idea to do something like that? Were his parents farmers? Has he worked on a farm? I mean most kids, when they go bad, get into drugs, vandalism, theft, that sort of thing. This kid apparently found theft, but not like anything I've ever heard of."

"I don't know if he was ever around a farm," replied Benjamin. "Story I get is that nobody is sure who his dad is, and he's not around—and the mother is a complete waste." He stopped his line of conversation, remembering there was a five-year-old with big brown eyes listening to his every word. Wishing he'd said less, Benjamin shrugged.

"Yep, that's where the problems begin," Hawkett said. "Kid has no parents, or a bad parent, dad leaves, or all of these, and they just get off to a bad start. I feel sorry for a kid who has no . . ." Now Hawkett, catching the silence of the room, realized he'd stuck his foot in his mouth. A little girl who'd lost her father to suicide and his widow were both staring at him.

Jamie started to say something, then stopped as if to reconsider her words. Then thought, what the hell, "You think a child needs a father huh, Adam? Think that's a very important part of bringing them up, fulfilling their needs?"

"Well yeah," nervous now, after hearing the tone of her voice, knowing something was troubling Jamie and pretty sure he knew what it was. Well dammit, he was getting kind of tired of dancing around with this issue. "Is this about us getting married so you can call me your husband and Andrea can call me her dad? That's it isn't it? Follow your rules on how life has to be. I've been married once and ended it with a divorce. Ben's been married twice and divorced twice. You've been married once and look how that ended up." He wished with everything in his soul that he hadn't said that, but he had, and the hurt it inflicted on both mother and daughter was obvious.

Tears started flowing from Jamie's eyes, and Andrea slid from her chair and ran from the house. Benjamin, who had been caught off guard by this turn of events and was wanting to fix things, fumbled with his thoughts. Before he could think of anything to say, Hawkett, feeling remorse and desperately wanting to say the right thing, blurted out, "You want to get married . . . call up your preacher and we'll get married . . . solve everything. Okay?"

Jamie stood up from the table and quietly said, "Excuse me," and left the house alone, presumably following her daughter.

The two men sat silently for a few moments, stunned by this turn of events and speechless. Benjamin felt both anger and disappointment toward Hawkett's outburst. Still, he was no shining example, being a twice-failed attempt as a husband. He felt bad, really bad, about the hurt he was seeing here.

"That probably wasn't the right thing to say, was it?" Hawkett asked, needing to say something to break the painful silence.

"No, I don't believe it was."

"Well, dammit. Haven't I been good to her? Don't I carry my weight around here? You think she's being abused? Hell, I can tell you that's not the case. I mean, I've been living in this house for almost three months, day and night, and I can tell you there's been absolutely no hanky-panky. Can you believe that?"

"Well . . . " Benjamin wanted to say something to indicate that their sex relationship, or lack of, was something he had no interest in hearing about, but he was cut off.

"Then I say, okay let's get married. You heard me. And out the door she goes. Doesn't even bother to reply."

"Could be how you posed the question . . . "

More silence. "Well, this is just no good. We can't go on like this and dammit, I hate this idea of getting married just so you can say you're married. The woman and her beliefs. Man, is she stubborn." Hawkett was still ranting away, but the tone of his voice had changed from indignation to self-doubt. "Well, what do I do now?"

"You're asking me?" Benjamin replied with surprise. "I don't know. Go after her—tell her you're sorry?"

"That's not going to do it. We need some space. Living like this, together all the time. Hell, you can't see the forest for the trees in this relationship. And it's as much my fault as it is hers. She didn't ask me to move in here. I just took advantage of her kindness when I was at a . . . what . . . down point in my life?"

"You were a drunk dealing with depression."

Hawkett winced, "Wow, thanks for the honesty. Don't remind me okay?" Hawkett slid back from the table and looked out the window. He couldn't see Jamie or Andrea anywhere. He was feeling . . . sad . . . depressed. He sure knew what people meant when they said they had a heavy heart, because he had one right then. "I need to step away for a while . . . get hold of my thoughts . . . you know."

Benjamin frowned, wondering where this line of thought was going. He suddenly found himself trying to come up with a reason to get out of there "pretty darn quick" and let these two sort things out.

"Benjamin, s'pose I could bunk up with you in town for a couple of days? Maybe do some kind of start over thing with Jamie? Call her up for a date? I don't know. I promise it'll be just for a couple of days. Man, I just don't want to finish tonight and start tomorrow with this crap hanging over my head."

No, no, no. Benjamin did not want him to move into town with him, but this guy had been his partner and closest friend for over fifteen years. And maybe Hawkett was right. These were two intelligent, mature humans. Maybe a little separation would help them clear their heads. Although he was shaking his head no, he responded, "Sure."

CHAPTER
18

Both men rode back to town in the patrol car in a very somber mood. The break up had been a whole lot more than either one had anticipated. A couple of guys trying to "fix things" and man it had turned really painful. Jamie had cried softly, saying she was sorry . . .repeatedly saying, you don't have to do this. Hawkett, stoic, thought that he was doing the right thing and then not knowing how to not do the right thing. He was almost in tears when little Andrea ran to him, wrapped her arms around his legs, and wept.

Benjamin wanted to turn the car around and haul Hawkett right back to the farm to talk things out. He was angry and hurt, not knowing why these things always turned out this way. Who was he to intervene anyway, having failed two marriages. But still . . . seeing that little girl cry . . . .

"Sorry, Ben. Didn't . . . uh . . . know things, I mean, I didn't know there'd be that kind of reaction. I . . . uh . . ."

"Oh shut up." And that was the extent of their conversation. The two men rode the short trip back into Pigmy, unloaded Hawkett's few possessions, and set him up with a place to stay. A place to stay—for the weekend only? Benjamin wondered.

Benjamin called into his office. Nothing new was going on. Finally things had calmed down a little bit. Henny was sound asleep in new clothes, lying on a bed in one of the unlocked jail cells, happy as could be. On hearing that, both men decided to call it a night, maybe get some good sleep time and try to start over fresh on Monday morning—go back to trying to "fix things."

Roydel was feeling better by the minute. He'd been smoking weed since early afternoon and had started drinking cold homemade raspberry wine shortly after. The wine tasted so good, and by the time Hawkett and Benjamin were calling it a day, he was on a sweet, sweet high, his troubles behind him, and hungry for action. Well, hungry for something, and a sausage pizza from the Quick Mart in the nearby town of Clarinda would hit the spot. Just thinking about that sausage, cheese, and thick crust made his mouth water. He made the call on his cell phone to place his order, and the woman on the other end said it'd be ready to go in about twenty minutes.

Damn good, Roydel thought, as he headed toward his car, a little wobbly in his step. He told himself he could control himself—avoid doing anything stupid and give the law a chance to pull him over to take a blood alcohol test. No, he'd be careful he thought, forgetting that he was still carrying a joint with him—taking hits on it as he drove towards Clarinda. He saw very few cars on the drive to Clarinda and pulled into the Quick Mart right on schedule. His stomach was really, really anticipating thick slices of cheese-laden pizza, and as he entered the brightly illuminated store, he could smell the pizza immediately. As he took it from the same lady he'd visited with over the phone, he could feel the heat from the pizza through the cardboard box. Up to the cash register to pay, Roydel strutted. He pulled a wad of cash out of his pocket, then seeing two people ahead of him, he thought—come on people—I'm starving here.

The young woman ahead of him carried only a Mountain Dew. That wouldn't take long. But the guy, a fat longhaired guy with baggy clothes on, had several items, and Roydel could feel his temper begin to flare. Dumb ass, he thought. Nothing better to do but take up everybody's time.

"Will there be anything else, sir?" the cashier patiently addressed the fat guy in the front of the line.

"Oh yeah, I need . . . I need a pack of Pall Mall Lights."

Turning to the cigarette display the cashier replied, "I don't believe we have any Pall Mall Lights. We have the regulars and we have the super menthols, but I don't believe we have any lights." She turned to the customer for his decision. He stood there as if lost in thought, trying to make a very important decision. Roydel felt another tinge of anger and was trying to hold it together, but was needing a good draw on his weed to hold himself steady.

"Well okay . . . I guess I'll take the Pall Mall Regulars."

She grabbed a pack of cigarettes, scanned them and said, "Your total will be . . . "

"Oh and yeah . . . I need three Powerball tickets," he turned and smiled at the two people standing behind him in line. Smiling . . . but why? Roydel was wondering why that face seemed so familiar.

So, as the seconds turned into minutes, the cashier pulled three tickets and ran them through the process. She announced that he had won two dollars and she'd take that off of his bill now and . . .

"Oh and yeah, I need three *Firecracker 500* lottery tickets. Man I'm on a roll now. Might as well pay my bill with more winnings." He turned around again to glance back, this time right at the scowling Roydel. He seemed to enjoy holding everybody up, and Roydel was tired of holding back.

"Hurry up, dumb ass. Pay and get the hell out of the way!" Roydel had succeeded in getting the cashier's attention. She glanced at him nervously as she tried to accommodate the customer in front of her—all the while knowing that a storm was brewing.

The fat guy turned around and glared at Roydel with a real "tough guy" look on his face that Roydel bet he developed by staring in the mirror. "You talking to me?"

Roydel held it in for about three beats then yelled, "Yeah, I'm talking to you, dumb ass. Hurry up!" He still felt that he knew this guy and was trying to place him from somewhere.

The fat guy suddenly smiled, "Hey, Numbnuts, is that you? Haven't seen you since you dropped out of high school. Heard you was in prison. Must be out now, huh?" Not waiting for a response, he turned back toward the cashier and, finding out he'd won no more money, started to dole out the amount of cash he owed. But then he paused as if remembering, "Oh and yeah, I need some cigarettes for my wife. Damn. What is it she smokes? Better not get it wrong." Again he began studying the rows of cigarettes stacked behind the counter.

Roydel gently pushed the woman ahead of him out of his way and stepped ahead, placing his hand on the fat guy's shoulder. He'd finally recalled that this guy was someone he'd known in high school. He couldn't remember his name, but the guy had called him Numbnuts, the nickname from his schooldays that he hated with a passion. "Pay and get out of here now. Hear me, jackass?"

"Hey, chill out, Numbnuts!" He turned as he said it and accidentally knocked Roydel's pizza box to the floor. Everybody watched the fresh steaming pizza roll out of the box and onto the dirty floor.

"Hey, I'm not payin' for that, Numbnuts. It was your fault, you dumbshit. Just have a little patience okay? You ain't gotten much smarter than you was in high school, have ya."

Anger was replaced by rage, and Roydel walked quickly out of the convenience store and over to his car. He reached into the front seat, retrieved his Glock, and then strode right back into the store. After banging the door open and holding the gun up in the air he had everyone's attention, including the cashier, who screamed and scrambled for cover.

"What is my name?" He spoke loudly and glared directly at the fat guy, who in turn stared at the gun and the angry man holding it. The overweight man was at a loss for words and real fear was evident in his eyes.

More loudly, Roydel repeated himself, "What is my name, my real name, dumb ass?"

With his voice quavering he answered, "I don't know. Alls I remember is Numbnuts."

"Wrong answer, dumb ass!" Having said that Roydel put three shots right into the fat guy's chest. The gunshots made a deafening noise in the otherwise quiet store. He walked over to a nearby display and grabbed three bags of potato chips. As he walked out of the store, he looked at the fat guy lying there, with blood gushing out of him and spilling onto the white tile floor, and he remembered his pizza, crushed underneath the dying man.

CHAPTER
19

Benjamin was in bed trying to sleep, but was restless and unsettled by the events that had taken place between Hawkett and Jamie. He was lying there, staring at the ceiling and thinking about little Andrea, when the phone on the nightstand beside his bed began to ring. While struggling to locate the phone in the dark, his cell phone began ringing. He knew something big was up.

"Yeah, what it is?"

"Sheriff!" It was Cindy and he could tell she was excited.

"What's up?"

"Sheriff, somebody got shot over in the convenience store in Clarinda. Don't know if the guy is going to live or not. Anyways, the sheriff in that county, Page, you know . . . "

"Yes, Cindy, I know Clarinda is in Page County." He tried to keep the irritation out of his voice but was not getting the job done. It did however help to calm her down a little.

"The sheriff over there says that Roydel Nuxton shot the guy—just gunned him down in front of a bunch of witnesses! He wants you to call him right away. They're out now looking for Roydel's vehicle, but he wants you to talk to him right now!"

"Oh great, just great. Okay, I've got a number here for them on my cell phone. I'll call them right away. Any other catastrophes in the works?"

"No, Sheriff. Not a word all night. Jan went home two hours ago. You want me to call her up?"

"Not yet. Let me find out what the hell is going on . . . and Cindy?"

"Yes, Sheriff?"

"Thanks for getting right to me. Good work."

"Sure, Sheriff. Just doing my job."

Benjamin laid the cell phone down and turned on a lamp, trying to collect his thoughts. For some reason, he hated to call another law officer while sitting in his underwear, so he dressed, plugged in the coffee-maker to heat up some old coffee, and dialed the Page County Sheriff.

Ten minutes of phone conversation pretty well summarized the entire situation and the steps that he would need to take. Roydel had apparently shot some other patron in line at the convenience store over some sort of prior row. The gunshot victim was probably going to die, or maybe was already dead as they spoke. Were they certain that Roydel had done the shooting? Hell, they had his name and phone number on a pizza box smashed on the floor. They had his picture shooting the guy on the security cameras. What else did they need?

By this time Hawkett was awake and listening to Benjamin's half of the exchange and was getting a pretty good idea of what was going on. He began to wonder how his old partner was going to handle the situation.

"My mistake," grunted Benjamin as he pulled on his second shoe. "I was thinking I'd taken a quiet boring job as a county sheriff. Thinking I'd had enough of this kind of shit when I worked with the DCI. Thinking I wanted to ride into retirement dealing with little or no violent crime, and now I seem to be up to my ears in trouble. Murder, drug running, now more murder. Damn!" Shaking his head as he spoke, "And I just don't have the manpower to deal with this." He stopped tying his shoelace as if he had a sudden idea and sat up looking straight at Hawkett. "Hey, just like the old days, huh? Me and you off on a chase?"

"Yeah, except I'm not in law enforcement anymore. I'm just a peace loving pedestrian now."

"Not tonight you aren't. Get dressed. I'm going to deputize you when we get to the office and get a gun for you. I'm in trouble here and I need help. Okay?"

Well, thought Hawkett, what could he say? His old friend was in trouble. Could he say, hell no, don't want any part of this? And then, thinking to himself . . . hell yes, I want part of this. He felt the adrenaline run like it hadn't for a long time.

"Sure Benjamin, I'm in. What's up?"

In fifteen minutes, maybe less, Benjamin, Hawkett, Jan, and Cindy were gathered in the sheriff's office. They were listening to radio chatter and trading phone calls and information with other law personnel out hunting for Roydel. Benjamin was surprised that Jan had gotten there so quickly, but, as she explained it, she'd been having trouble sleeping and had picked up the story on her police scanner.

Benjamin immediately deputized Hawkett. He found a badge for him in one of the desk drawers and asked Jan to witness the few words he said. With that done, she pulled their spare handheld radio off the charger rack and gave it to Hawkett.

"You got a weapon for me?" That question caught Benjamin off guard, and he turned to Jan who was shaking her head no.

"Here, take my Beretta. It's loaded, eight shots. You aren't going to need them, but still, there you are. I'll use the shotgun in my car if we do any kind of approach."

"All right, here's what we're going to do. We've been asked to go to Roydel's residence out south of town—trailer house he has there. It's pretty unlikely that he's there, but we'll drive out and secure the area. They've got three of the Page County Department's cars out looking for him and two state patrol units assisting, so there's not much more we can do. Just keep our eyes open. Cindy, are you good to go here? Keep a cool head and keep us informed. If they catch him somewhere, we don't want to be sitting out there all night waiting around for nothing."

"I'll handle things here, Sheriff."

"Okay, Hawkett, you ride with me. Jan, you bring your car and stay out on the road when we drive in if we don't spot his vehicle. If we do spot the vehicle, we'll wait out on the road and study the situation a little, make a plan, okay?"

Everybody nodded in agreement.

"Okay, let's go. And remember, we don't want to be killed or kill anybody. So be careful, very careful, but if you have to shoot, shoot to kill."

Jamie sat straight up in bed. Damn, she finally had passed out and now the thoughts and regrets were nagging at her and she felt the emotional pain setting in. She should have backed off, not pushed him like that. She should have . . . oh, what the hell.

She checked her daughter lying beside her, thankfully asleep on a tear stained pillow. She'd not expected Andrea to react the way that she had. The little girl was truly, deeply hurt that Hawkett was leaving. Well, why not? She had never known her real father, was too young when he'd hung himself out in the barn. Remembering that incident took Jamie to a whole new low, and she crawled out of bed, wanting to be somewhere else, trying to shake the pain.

She tiptoed out onto the front porch, carrying a heavy comforter with her, and sat on the porch swing in the cool autumn air. She wrapped the comforter around every part of her body. Looking up into a full harvest moon, she tried to find the Jamie who could tackle this kind of misery and bring herself up and out of this emotional pain, but she wasn't able to do it. All right, she would cry for a while, let the tears run, let her feelings run their course.

She jumped in fright when Tippy, coming from out of nowhere, jumped up on the swing and curled up next to her. Well, at least the little stinker wasn't off running around somewhere tonight. That was good. She pulled the pup close to her and stroked its head. "Oh, if you could only hear little dog, what a sad story I could tell you." Tippy's eyes were locked on Jamie, and the little dog abruptly stretched his head toward hers, and licked a tear off her face.

CHAPTER
20

In and out—that had been Roydel's plan. He'd screwed up big time, and the weed and wine-induced high that'd made him act so stupidly, was quickly falling, as the reality of the situation sank in. Damn, damn, damn, don't lose my temper. How many damn times had he told himself that, but now he'd done it. Boy, had he done it! It was time to run, find somewhere to hide down in the hills of Missouri maybe, he didn't know. He'd taken back roads all the way home from the scene of the shooting. At least he'd had the sense to do that. It had really taken time, but he knew he wouldn't stand a chance out on the highway. After backing his car around behind a corncrib, where it couldn't be seen from the road, Roydel ran around inside his trailer house gathering the things he had to have—clothes, cash, extra ammo. He was out the door and headed for his car when he saw headlights from one, no shit, two cars coming down the road. He knew who that was.

Ambush them here? How many would there be in two cars? These questions went running through his mind as he tossed his possessions into the car, grabbed his handgun, and then peeked around the corner of the corncrib. He spotted the two patrol cars coming to a stop on the road. Two Taylor County patrol cars, well that was good. He would not have to be dealin' with any SWAT teams yet. Then remembering his last encounter with a Taylor County patrol car, he hoped that "Mr. Sheriff Bigmouth" was in one of them. Yeah. That'd be nice to see him lying on the ground, like that sumbitch in the convenience store.

Over the radio, Benjamin asked Jan to keep her car back a couple hundred yards, to get out on the opposite side with her firearm, and to keep her eyes open. Hawkett and he had already exited and moved to the opposite side of his patrol car. There didn't appear to be a car parked near the trailer and there were no lights on, but still, he thought, be cautious. Benjamin took a spotlight and worked it over the trailer and everything in the yard. No sign . . . good. He quietly reported this to Jan and then reminded her again to keep her eyes open.

"What do you think, Hawkett? Nobody around here? You hear anything?"

"Don't see anything, don't hear anything."

"I suppose we could walk up to the trailer, take a closer look before we report this to the other units."

"Yeah, I think that would probably be wise. How do you want to do it?"

"Well, I'll take the shotgun and you take my Beretta. We'll spread out about twenty yards apart and walk in unison, slowly and quietly, okay?"

Benjamin reached into the patrol car and pulled out his shotgun, catching the stock on the car frame and wincing at how loud that had sounded.

"Uh Benjamin, do you have any vests we can put on? I don't think we're gonna get shot at, but still . . . "

"Damn, no. They're back in the office. Brand new ones I just ordered. Shit, how did I forget those?"

"Want to go back and get them?"

"Oh hell." he swept the light back and forth across the yard. "Nobody's here. I'll betcha' old Roydel is miles and miles away by now. You want me to send Jan back to get them?"

Hawkett paused, "Let's just go check things out, get it done."

Roydel stood behind a walnut tree growing on a little rise about two hundred yards behind his trailer house. Hoping, man he was really hoping, the cops would see no lights on in the house and not see his car, and just leave. But no, dammit all to hell, thanks to the bright moonlight, he could clearly see that two men were outside their car and starting to work towards the trailer—probably that damn sheriff and some deputy. He'd take that sheriff first—try to get close enough so he could look him in the face and say, "Remember me?" Then put two or three rounds right into his belly.

Or, he could run through the timber and fields, cross-country, find another farm, find a car to steal if he had to. Roydel was weighing his options while waiting to see what the police were going to do, how far they'd push him. He was thinking he could run on foot, but it'd take a lot of time—time for the police to get more police, form roadblocks. No, he'd best stand and fight, kill these two, then deal with that other patrol car setting down the road, wondering how many people were in it. He had his Glock and three spare loaded clips in his pockets. Enough to shoot his way out of this mess—confident of that.

Benjamin spoke softly, "All right, let's take a little look-see at the trailer house. Keep wide apart and try to have a place to go if shots are fired. I still don't think he's around here anywhere, but you just never know."

Hawkett nodded, thinking to himself—not four hours ago I was living the life of a farmer, sitting in a farmhouse with people who probably love me, and now I'm carrying a loaded gun into a potentially dangerous situation. He shook his head as he thought it, catching Benjamin's attention.

"What?"

"Oh, nothing, I'm ready to go when you are."

Benjamin whispered into his radio, "Jan, you see us okay?"

"Yes, Sheriff."

"Good," thought Benjamin, but if she could see them from her position, on this moonlit night, so could anybody else, making him wonder if they shouldn't call for more backup. But still, this wasn't their first time walking into a situation like this, and both men had always walked away before.

"Let's go."

Not twenty paces into the driveway, a cat jumped out from behind a bush and scurried in front of them. Both men caught their breath and aimed their guns. Hawkett almost fired at the darned thing and said to himself—man, pull yourself together. They moved forward and Benjamin motioned for Hawkett to stop while he went on up the steps and quietly walked across Roydel's makeshift deck, feeling it sway slightly under his weight. Stopping, he tried to calm his breathing and listened for any sounds. Hearing nothing, he worked his way around the patio furniture to the door of the trailer house and again listened. He pulled out his flashlight and quickly glanced into the nearest window. Still nothing—good.

Well, it's time to step things up a little bit, he said to himself, and get this over with. Leaning against the side of the trailer, he yelled out, "Taylor County Police. You in there, Roydel? We need to talk to you!" His voice sounded extremely loud in the cold, still country air. Both men waited for a reply, a light to come on in the trailer, anything. Nothing happened. Benjamin yelled out the same command again, and again they waited. Nothing.

"I don't think he's here. Walk around to the back of the trailer and I'm going to go in."

Hawkett nodded and did just that, carefully picking his steps, and using a flashlight to work his way around to the back of the trailer house. There was no back door, so if Roydel came out, he'd have to come through a window, and they looked too small for anyone to get through very quickly, so he relaxed just a little. The situation was looking better all the time. He heard Benjamin yell, "I'm in!" Then he could hear his partner working through the trailer, three times yelling out, "Sheriff, Taylor County." Then another yell, "Nobody in here."

Hawkett took a deep breath and felt his shoulders relax. He realized how keyed up he was and how tight his muscles were. Walking quickly around the other side of the trailer house to meet up with Benjamin, his flashlight picked up a reflector on the front of Roydel's car, setting behind the corncrib. He instantly went to the ground, reaching for his portable radio. He keyed the mike and whispered hoarsely into it, "Ben, we've got a car setting out here behind one of the farm buildings."

That brought Benjamin right back out of the trailer and kneeling down behind the deck—wondering what car? Where? Did it mean anything? Could be some abandoned piece of junk setting in the weeds. He spun around, hearing movement behind him, then relaxed a bit seeing Hawkett moving quickly up to his side.

"Where's the car?"

"Behind that farm building—right over there," he pointed with his gun.

"What kind of car? Do you know?"

"No, a newer car though," almost reading Benjamin's mind. "Could be the one he's driving. Kinda' tan colored I think. Hard to tell in the dark."

"Ah, that's not good. He was driving a tan Chevy when I had a run-in with him the other night. And, I'm pretty sure that's the car they were looking for on the all points bulletin they were issuing from Page County."

Both men were quiet for a few moments, running their flashlights back and forth across the side of the corncrib but seeing nothing. "Well, if he's here, he knows we're here. And, he's had a chance to do something stupid. At least that's not happened," said Hawkett, staring out into the darkening view. Clouds were working their way under the moon, and the night began to darken even more.

"Well, let's move to that corncrib and get a look at the car—but that's all. If it *is* the car they're out looking for, we're backing out of here and calling for backup—lots of it. No use being a hero and getting gunned down in the dark. I don't want to end anybody's life out here because we were stupid. You go around the far side of the crib, and I'll take this end nearest us. Check the crib out real well when we get there. Make sure he's not in it, on top of it, or even in the car. Okay?"

"I'm ready," Hawkett was holding the Beretta up in front of him.

"Okay, let's go!"

Roydel watched the two policemen heading for the corncrib, and peeking in and around it with the flashlights. He knew that they had his car and that more cops would be on their way. He was cornered and guessed there was only one way out, and the sooner the better.

He had to get that car and get the hell out of there. That was his only chance. He had to draw them away from it somehow, and he was pretty sure of what he needed to do.

He started working quickly and quietly down the hill toward the other police vehicle parked on the road. There was at least one person behind that car, and as he got closer, he thought—just one—good. It looked to be a female officer. She was standing behind her car looking down the road towards the trailer house, holding a radio in one hand and a gun in the other. Roydel figured he was fifty yards, maybe less than that, from her car, and she had no idea he was there—standing behind some cedar trees along the road. The moonlight was quickly being replaced by darkness as clouds continued to roll in.

Better get the party started now, he was thinking. He smiled, extended his Glock, and fired four quick rounds, taking out both tires on the driver's side of her patrol car and a fifth shot took out the back window. He heard her cry out in surprise and then heard her gun firing back toward the trees. Roydel was already on the move, running as fast as he could, back towards his car, hoping the other two cops would fall for his plan.

They did. Benjamin yelled out, "Damn. He's headed down the road—trying to get away—shooting at Jan!" The two men turned and started running out the driveway towards the road, trying to help the ambushed Jan, hoping she was still on her feet and still breathing.

Hawkett, much faster than his partner, raced across the road and into the opposite ditch, calling to Jan on his handheld. Benjamin moved as quickly as he could. Hearing a noise that sounded like someone stumbling and cussing, he turned to look behind him.

He felt his knee buckle under him and cried out in pain as he collapsed and rolled along the gravel driveway. Holding onto his gun and feeling around on the ground for his radio, he tried to get control of the situation. He knew they'd screwed up big time. There was panic in his heart—not wanting to find that Jan had been hurt.

"Jan's okay. I'm with her. Where are you at?" Hawkett's announcement over the radio brought some relief to Benjamin's mind.

"I tripped—fell down. I think I hurt my knee, but I'm okay. Where the hell is Roydel? Did she get a shot at him?"

"She says he fired from some brushy looking trees behind her. Got both of her tires shot out. We don't know where he's at. She said she fired back at him, into the trees."

"Stay right where you're at, keep your eyes open, and call for help!"

"She already has. Are you okay?"

"I'm fine just . . . oh shit!" Benjamin heard Roydel's car start behind the corncrib and knew that things were going to turn bad really fast.

Knowing he'd botched this whole affair but not having time for regret right now, Benjamin got to his feet using the shotgun as a crutch. He reached to retrieve his radio, but there was no time. Roydel's car lights came on and around the crib his car roared, sliding out of control on the grassy farmyard, but then taking off again, coming right down the driveway towards Benjamin. Roydel thought out loud, "Oh yeah, got you now, fat boy," as he pushed down on the accelerator and headed right at the sheriff.

There was only one possible thing to do—no time to get out of the way and dive for cover. Roydel had him. Benjamin lifted the shotgun and fired, pumped, and fired again into the windshield, then rolled to the ground. The car's tire just missing him as the Chevy veered sideways off the driveway, and piled into a fencepost by the road.

CHAPTER 21

Jamie got up early, skipped her morning coffee, and got right to work. She was determined to shrug off the depression that the previous night's events had brought upon her and fall back on the old Jamie Chamber's belief that hard work and a positive attitude were the foundation stones to a happy life. Thankful that it looked like another beautiful fall day, and knowing that that would help, she started with the chores: feeding the pigs, moving the ewes to a new paddock of grass, and gathering the eggs deposited by her free range hens in their portable henhouse.

The constant bellowing from behind the barn reminded her that there was a cow to be milked. It also reminded her that she would have to do Hawkett's chores as well, and just that quickly, she was depressed again—lonely and lost. Feeling tears coming, which made her angry with herself, she hustled to the barn and ran the cow in, "cussing her good" in the process, and then feeling guilty and foolish in the same instant. This was going to have to stop. Soon, her daughter would be out there, and she didn't want Andrea to see her acting like this.

It'd been a while since Jamie had milked the cow, and she was surprised at how quickly her hands and forearms ached. Flossie danced around a bit, almost tipping the milk pail, then turned her large bovine head around to look back towards her milker. That did bring a little lift to Jamie's spirits—realizing that the old cow knew someone else was milking her. "What? Hawkett do a better of job of milking you than I do old girl?"

"Mom, are you talking to our cow?"

Jamie laughed out loud, looking towards the barn door at a half-awake Andrea, still in her pajamas, carrying her special blanket and wearing a pair of her mother's muck boots that went up well above her knees.

"Yeah. I was just asking Flossie if maybe she'd give us some chocolate milk today instead of that regular white stuff. What do you think? Would that be a good idea?"

"Mom, Hawkett always tries to pull that one on me and I know that Flossie can't give chocolate milk, okay?"

Well, so much for that humorous comment, Jamie was thinking to herself. "You'd better head back to the house and put on your work clothes. And make your bed and pick up your room, too. I'll be coming in with the milk in about ten minutes. Okay?"

"Okay, Mom." Andrea turned and left the barn.

Having rested her arms and hands a bit, Jamie got back to filling the stainless steel bucket and, after two more stops to rest, she managed to strip the cow dry. She turned Flossie back out to pasture and headed for the house.

Halfway to the house she heard someone yell, "Hey, Jamie." She turned to see her neighbor, Pearl, walking quickly up the road towards her house. Jamie wanted to get the milk into the house for processing and check up on Andrea, but that could wait just a bit. Pearl acted as though she had something important to say, but Pearl always acted that way.

Jamie watched her neighbor as she walked down her driveway. "Where's your bicycle, Pearl?" She regretted that question the minute it'd left her lips, remembering the wreck Pearl had caused the previous Friday.

"Sheriff wrecked it!" Pearl was trying to talk, but was slightly winded, and Jamie was thinking, why not? A woman her age walking this far and that fast—it was really pretty impressive.

"Oh yeah, I forgot. Are you going to get a new bike or can your old one be fixed?"

"Well that depends on how the lawsuit comes out. If I win, and I'm pretty damn sure I will, then the sheriff's office will be furnishing me with a brand new bike and probably about ten-thousand dollars in damages!" Pearl was getting herself worked up as she spoke.

"But didn't you run into . . ." Jamie stopped herself, no need to go any further with this conversation. It would be pointless.

"Did you hear about the shooting?"

"What shooting?" Jamie realized as soon as she asked, that that was why Pearl had walked all the way to her place—what Pearl perceived to be exciting new gossip.

"Sheriff Benjamin Willoughby, himself, shot Roydel Nuxton! Big gun battle out at Roydel's place last night I hear."

This was no longer exciting new gossip but bad news that involved someone Jamie felt very close to. She needed to know right away what happened to Benjamin. Was he okay? She was wanting to ask if Hawkett had been involved. And if so, was he okay? But Pearl cut her off.

"Thelma went to town this morning and came home with the news. She says Roydel isn't dead, but he's hurt pretty bad. Somebody said there were over a hundred shots fired! Said Roydel tried to mow down the sheriff with his car! Wow, sure wish I could have been there and seen that fight." Pearl was shaking her head back and forth in wonderment.

"Is the sheriff hurt? Anyone else involved?"

"I think maybe something happened to the sheriff, but I ain't sure. Thelma doesn't always hear the best, I can tell you. Half the time I have to yell."

"When did you say this happened? Last night?"

"That's what Thelma says. Some time later today we're going to go into town. If I hear anything else, I'll let you know." And with that Pearl spun around and headed right back up the driveway and out onto the road, having accomplished her important task.

Jamie watched as she walked away, wondering what could have happened. She remembered that Adam and Benjamin hadn't left her place until after nine o'clock. Well, it didn't matter, she was going to have to get to the bottom of this and find out what had happened, who had been hurt, and how bad the situation was. The anger and hurt she had felt was replaced with purpose, and she made a quick inventory in her mind of what had to be done to take care of her farm before she could head into town.

A little over an hour later, Jamie and Andrea left the farm in their pickup truck. It started a little hard, but at least the darn thing started. Jamie dropped Andrea off at Pearl and Thelma's for one of her weekly visits—an occasion that her daughter and the Oldhams loved. Though she warned the ladies not to, she knew that Andrea would be pampered and spoiled for the next hour. Jamie drove on into town. She parked on the square, shut the truck off, got out, and started walking apprehensively toward the courthouse. She was headed for Benjamin's office, wondering if she'd run into Hawkett in doing so, and how that would go. It didn't matter; she still had to find out how they were.

When she walked into the office, Jan was the only one visible and was talking on the phone. Jan waved at her and pointed at the coffee pot. Holding up her hand, she gestured that she'd be with her in a minute. Jan knew about the relationship between Jamie and Hawkett and knew that Sheriff Willoughby joked about Jamie being his adopted daughter, so it was no surprise to see her sitting there with a concerned look on her face.

When she got off the phone, Jan got right to the heart of the matter. "Okay, this is what I can tell you. There was an incident last night in which Roydel Nuxton was severely injured in a gunfight with the sheriff and others. Benjamin strained his knee somehow, maybe when Roydel tried to run him down with his car, maybe earlier, I'm not quite sure on that point. Anyway, Hawkett, Deputy Hawkett now, took Benjamin to Clarinda to get his knee checked out and to meet with the Page County police while they're there."

"Deputy Hawkett? When did that happen?"

"Last night when it was evident we didn't have enough manpower, and Sheriff asked him if he'd help. Pretty damn glad we had him as it turned out."

"And Hawkett wasn't hurt, neither one of them were seriously injured ?"

"No, and for the record I'm okay too, even though I was actually the only one that Roydel shot at."

"Oh, I'm sorry. I didn't mean to take it for granted . . . "

"Hey, that's okay. While you're here, you want to meet the noto-

106

rious bandit who I understand has probably been stealing pigs from you?"

"What? The kid Henny something?"

"Yeah, we still have him sitting back in an empty jail cell, watching TV, ordering pizza delivered, living the good life. Kid doesn't want to go home."

"He's back in one of the jail cells? Sure. I'll go visit with him. I'm not violating any of his rights or anything am I?"

"He's not going to be charged with anything. We're just holding him, waiting to find out how to handle the situation. His home life is just not adequate."

Jamie walked back into the jail cell holding area beyond the main office. In a cell with the door open lay Henny. He was comfortably positioned on a cot, with a number of pillows behind his head, reading a Playboy magazine.

Jamie cleared her voice and startled the young boy. He immediately dropped the magazine over the other side of the cot, but the look on his face said he knew he was busted.

"Who gave you that magazine?"

"Nobody gave it to me, I found it up there," pointing, as he spoke, to a shelf on the hallway wall that had piles of police procedural manuals on it.

"Does the sheriff know you're sitting back here reading that kind of magazine?" Jamie was taking the role of a mother here and wondering to herself as she did—what business was it of hers what this little delinquent did?

"No," he replied so softly that she could hardly hear him.

Jamie grabbed a wooden chair and carried it into the jail cell. "Mind if I sit and visit a little?"

Again, in a solemn tone, "No."

"The sheriff tells me you're in the pig business. Got three gilt pigs out behind your house here in town. You going to sell them, make a little money when they get bigger?"

"No, I was gonna raise 'em up and then breed 'em and raise a bunch of little pigs," shrugging as he said this, probably knowing that the hammer would be coming down soon.

"Oh, I see. Start a little hog operation of your own." She paused for a little bit, taking in the boy's appearance, the new clothes he was wearing, and thinking that he was awfully thin.

"Mind telling me where you got your three gilts? And before

you tell me, Henny, remember that I raise a few pigs on my farm and when they're born I ear-notch them for identification purposes. I can go anywhere and identify my pigs by their color, sex, and ear notches." Telling him this, she watched the look of guilt on the boy's face intensify.

Trapped for a reply, knowing that any lie could be quickly debunked and things might get even worse, he searched for another plausible answer.

"I found them wandering around in a field outside of town. I thought they might starve to death if I didn't feed them so I brought them back into town and . . . "

"Quit your lying!" Jamie felt anger rising up inside of her, disgusted at what lengths this kid was going to, to deny his guilt. "Those pigs disappeared from my farm. They disappeared one at a time over a three-week period. Somebody stole them, and you and I both know who that was. Right?"

He didn't answer but just sat there looking at her.

"My question is, do I press charges, get you arrested, and sent to jail?" Knowing as she said this, the boy would never go to any type of jail for his crime, probably wouldn't even get his hand slapped. "If you man-up and tell me the truth right now, I might not have to press charges."

"Yeah, okay."

"Okay what?"

"I stole the pigs from your farm."

"That's better." Jamie got up and walked around the jail cell thinking to herself. "Okay, here's what's going to happen. First, the pigs come back to my farm. Got that?"

Henny nodded his head up and down.

"Secondly, and I'm assuming there's nothing wrong with the little porkers, secondly, as penalty for this theft, you're going to have to pay the piper."

"Pay what piper? I ain't even got any money."

"No, paying the piper is just an expression for saying that . . . well that you feel bad about what you did and you're willing to do some work on my farm as restitution for your crime." She didn't think he knew what the word restitution meant, but believed he was absorbing the essence of her message.

"Work, what kinda work?"

"I don't know, taking care of animals, cleaning up around the buildings, whatever needs to be done."

"When do I have to do this work?"

"You can come out after school . . . maybe on weekends? Figure out something with your mom. Don't let it interfere with your school-work. Get that all done first, okay?"

Henny nodded his head. "How long do I have to work for you to . . . you know . . . to even things up?"

"That'll be up to you, Henny. You did a stupid, dishonest thing. Here's your chance to right your wrong. See if you're man enough to do it, okay?"

Jamie stood up, "Well, we'll see you . . . what . . . today after school? You'd better talk to the sheriff and tell him the deal. And, buddy, you'd better get the heck out of here and get back to school. Maybe Jan will write some sort of excuse for you if you ask her politely."

After a short talk with Jan, Jamie left the courthouse feeling a little better. She wondered if she'd done the right thing with the young boy. She felt greatly relieved that neither Benjamin nor Hawkett been injured. Lost in her thoughts, she walked around the corner of her pick-up and suddenly caught sight of them pulling up in Benjamin's patrol car, with Hawkett driving. Now what, she wondered, locking eyes with Hawkett as he parked the patrol car near her pickup and got out.

"Hey," he said, looking over the top of the car, not quite sure what to say.

"You both okay?"

"Yeah, we're okay . . . well Benjamin's got a knee injury of some sort," nodding toward the sheriff who was slowly getting out of the passenger side of the patrol car.

Benjamin stood up slowly and shut the door of the car. He turned and faced Jamie with a serious look on his face. "I . . ." He began to speak to her, but then he shrugged, looked back at Hawkett, and slowly hobbled down the sidewalk towards the courthouse.

"So, you're back in law enforcement, huh?" Jamie said.

"Well, Benjamin was in a tight spot last night. I was here, I . . ."

She interrupted him, "How long will this last? Is this a whole new career thing? You getting a place of your own? What?"

Hawkett didn't like this. He'd done nothing wrong and now he felt like she was berating him, making him feel guilty and hell, guilty of what? He turned and looked away, feeling angry and not wanting to say something stupid and make things worse. He finally turned back to say something, but when he did, he discovered she was already inside her pickup and turning the key. She backed out without looking at him again.

CHAPTER

22

Benjamin limped over to the coffee pot. He was feeling a little better—the pain pills were kicking in—and he poured himself a cup. He sat down at his desk and took a couple tentative sips of the hot coffee. Hawkett came walking into the office and Benjamin surmised, that given the short time lapse since leaving their patrol car, not much of a conversation had taken place between Jamie and him, and that was disappointing. "I shouldn't sit down, might fall asleep. Man, am I tired." Benjamin said, trying to remember when he'd last slept.

"We're all exhausted, Sheriff. We need to take turns getting some sleep," Jan, as always, gave good practical advice.

"Boy, you got that right. Well, any loose ends here? Roydel's being guarded by a deputy in the Clarinda Hospital. At least the Page County Department's got that covered. Glad he's over there. What else?"

As if on cue, Henny came walking out of the jail cell area and over to Jan's desk. "Jamie said if I asked you politely, you might write a pass for me so I can get back into school."

111

Jan looked at Benjamin and he nodded his head. "Okay, I can do that. What's your teacher's name?"

Jan completed the note, folded it, and stuck it in the pocket of Henny's new shirt. "You brushed your teeth yet today?"

"Yes ma'am."

"Okay, get on over to the school and if there are any problems, have them call me, okay?"

"Yes ma'am."

"And Henny," Benjamin interjected, "stay out of trouble, okay?"

"Yes sir. Got a new job now so I'll be keeping pretty busy."

"What new job?"

"Mrs. Chambers hired me to help take care of her animals. Says she's going to pay me ten dollars an hour, and I can work as many hours as I want."

"Jamie told me you were going to help her on the farm, but I don't recall her saying anything about it being a paid position." Jan questioned him, " Are you sure about that? If I catch you lying, you're going right back into that jail cell."

"Oh." He was caught again in a fib. "Well maybe, uh . . . well I better being goin'. See ya."

"That kid! Is there any hope for him?" Benjamin asked.

"There's always hope, Benjamin." This coming from Hawkett, surprised Benjamin. "I'm going to go back into the jail cell and replace Henny—get a nap. Call me if you need me."

"Yeah thanks. What else we got going, Jan? You need to go home and get some rest? I can watch things here for a while, and Cindy should be back in later this afternoon."

"You know, I think I'll take you up on that offer. Things should be quiet around here for a while, shouldn't they?"

"Well, we had a murder, we had a problem with a drug runner, and we had this kid stealing pigs and living in an inadequate home-life. Somehow, Roydel is going to be tied into the murder of Carl Smith, I just know it. And Jamie seems to have come to terms with Henny, found a way to make him pay for his theft, and maybe working for her will be good for him in other ways. So, I say yes, things are kinda under control. You take the rest of the day off. I'll see you tomorrow."

"Thank you, Sheriff." Jan started to walk towards the door. "Oh, there is one more thing."

"What?"

"The County Magistrate called to remind you that the court will be in session tomorrow, and she hoped that you would be in attendance to help with security and to answer questions that might come up. You know, people disputing their traffic tickets? Oh, and she did say Pearl Oldham was coming in to fight that ticket you gave her for riding her bicycle on the sidewalk. Says Pearl got pretty vocal over the phone, talking about lawsuits, etc. Anyway, I think maybe that's why the Magistrate wanted to make sure you were going to be there—to help deal with Pearl."

"Oh criminy. Just what I needed." Benjamin shook his head back and forth.

"Yeah, if she calls again today, tell her I'll be there." He immediately realized what a stupid thing he had said considering that Jan would be gone for the rest of the day, but shrugged, passing it off to being overtired.

After gathering up some personal items, Jan turned and left.

Benjamin promptly lifted his feet up on his desk and within minutes was snoring loudly.

Leaving the courthouse in a bit of a huff, Jamie was outside of town before she remembered her pigs. She had a rack on the back of the pickup that would hold them, so she turned around—determined to load the little porkers up and get them back home. Jan had told her where Henny lived with his mother, and in a small town like Pigmy, the place wasn't hard to find. Jamie had driven by it before and wondered who lived in that run-down dump. Pulling into the driveway she surmised that things hadn't got much better. She exited her pickup and knocked on the door, tried the doorbell, which she didn't think worked, and finally gave up trying to get any response. Again, based on the information Jan had given her, this was no great surprise. She worked her way through the junk around to the back of the house and quickly located the stolen pigs.

She was surprised to see the good condition they were in. Somehow, little Henny must have found feed for them, because they were just about the same size as their littermates at home. She was also impressed with the fence Henny had made out of junk, and the little pig hut that appeared to be bedded with straw. She dragged some extra panels around and made a small catch pen.

Having cornered the pigs, she hauled them, one at a time, over the fence and around the building and hoisted them up into the back of her pickup. This was no small task since the pigs weighed nearly forty pounds each and fought her handhold on their back legs every inch of the way.

Finally—sweating, winded, and smelling of pig—she climbed into her pickup and headed home to return the stolen pigs to their rightful pens.

CHAPTER 23

Benjamin woke with a start, his legs involuntarily jerking and knocking a coffee cup off the corner of his desk. Before he got his balance and bearings, he almost rolled out of his chair. He stood up and stretched. His injured knee was still stiff and sore, but he'd work through it. He retrieved the empty coffee cup, unbroken, off the floor. His immediate instinct was that he was hungry, and no wonder he thought, as he checked the time. It was almost two o'clock.

How was it possible to sleep in that position for over three hours? No wonder he had such a cramp in his neck. He hoped no one had entered his office during the nap, wondering if a considerable amount of snoring hadn't accompanied his deep sleep. There were no phone messages. Good. Things were still pretty quiet. He walked back into the jail cell and observed Hawkett sleeping soundly.

Back in his office, he phoned June's Restaurant and asked if she'd fix them a couple of burgers and some fries, and deliver that to the Sheriff's Office. He made a new pot of coffee and poured himself a cup, then took three ibuprofen tablets and sipped the coffee carefully to wash the pills down. He was amazed at how well he was getting along with his sprained knee. When he'd gone down, the previous night at Roydel's, he'd thought he'd broken something. That was not the case now.

One of the waitresses who worked at June's came walking in with a big bag of fried food. It smelled heavenly to Benjamin who'd not yet eaten that day. He thanked her and gave her a generous tip. Then he went back into the cell area and woke Hawkett.

"Hey, you hungry? I've got some food out here. It's up to you."

Hawkett sat up and made a gesture with his hand signifying "sure", trying to wake himself up. Soon he joined Benjamin, and the two men ate silently, drinking cans of Diet Coke that Benjamin had retrieved from the department refrigerator.

"Man that hit the spot. Not as good as Jamie's but . . ." Hawkett let it go at that, thinking about her and not wanting to go there.

"Yeah. Now if we just had a couple pieces of her homemade apple pie with hand cranked ice cream you guys make out there. Of course you aren't out there." Benjamin was thinking he probably shouldn't have said that, but he had, so there it was.

Both men deposited their wrappers and napkins in the trash and sat down. "Well, I think it's time we reviewed this case—I mean, if you're still a deputy. I guess we should talk about benefits, hours, that sort of thing. The job's here if you want it. I know there's nobody with anywhere near your talent that could apply. Unless I'm screwing up things between you and Jamie? I don't really know where you are on that."

"Been no new developments on that front I guess. I'm not sure what the next move should be, or if there should be a next move. I just don't know. But yes, I'm interested in being a deputy for now. I've got nowhere else to go, nothing else to do," Hawkett answered, shrugging his shoulders.

Just then, Jan walked in, looking fresh and rested—a smile on her face. "Hi boys, been in any more gun battles today?"

"Hey, I thought you were taking the rest of the day off. What are you doing here?"

"Sheriff, I slept hard for a while but then woke up and just couldn't find anything I wanted to do around home. I don't know, maybe I'm a slave to this place. Probably isn't healthy that I enjoy my job here like this."

116

"Well, since we're all here, we might as well review where things are with these current problems and decide where our priorities lie." Having said that, Benjamin pulled a marker out of the drawer of his desk and approached the whiteboard. "Let's list the problems we don't have answers for. Then we'll brainstorm some solutions. Let me start, and you jump in whenever relevant."

"First off, I suspect that Roydel had something to do with the death of our buried farmer. We need to go out and check his trailer house, look for . . . hey. Weren't we supposed to be getting some help from the DCI? Weren't they supposed to get somebody down here today? Jan, have you heard anything?"

"I'm just pulling something up on my computer, an email from one of the DCI administrative assistants who works for Brightwall. Okay, it basically says that there were four different murders in Iowa over the weekend, and the DCI can't get anybody down here right away. They feel, possibly because you worked for them, that you can handle things by yourself. Huh, wonder what they'd think if they knew you had Hawkett working for us as well—two former DCI employees. Anyway, it says to forward all forensic evidence you have to them and they'll help analyze that. Blah, blah, blah . . . and then call if you want to talk to Brightwall himself," she shrugged. "Guess that answers your question. Email came in early this morning. I just missed it. Sorry."

"Great, just great," Benjamin said with a look of disgust on his face. "Alright, first things first. Farmer Carl Smith . . . am I correct that he's already in Des Moines awaiting an autopsy?"

"Correct, Sheriff. I got the paperwork on that by fax this morning as well. Nothing done yet, but they have the body anyway." Jan replied.

"Good. We need to see if they can pull a slug out of him to see if we can match it up to any of Roydel's guns."

"What's Roydel's motive for murdering Smith?" Hawkett brought up a point that worried Benjamin a little.

"Honestly, I don't know, but I caught him lurking out near the murder scene last Saturday night, sitting out there doing—I don't know what—claiming he'd just stopped to take a leak. But up to something, just too much of a coincidence to have a known felon in the same vicinity as an unexplained murder."

Benjamin stared at the board a bit, seemingly lost in thought. "Okay, we need to visit with Carl's wife, Emily, about any possible connections with Roydel, good or bad. And I need to visit with her about the life insurance payment she's going to receive. Probably nothing to that, but it's a subject that has to be looked into, in any murder investigation."

While he wrote two notations about Emily Smith on the board, he informed Hawkett about his interview with the Smith's banker that'd led to information about the life insurance policy. He turned to his two partners, "What else?"

"How's Roydel doing? Any chance we could question him about the murder or about his relationship with Carl Smith?" Jan asked.

"I've heard nothing beyond what we learned this morning, to answer your first question. Apparently his injuries aren't life threatening, but the buckshot tore his face up pretty good. He's probably going to need some plastic surgery, but yes, I think he can talk to us if he wants to. Hawkett, you want to go try? I know he sure as hell won't have anything to do with me given the circumstances."

"Yeah, sure, I'd be glad to give it a try."

"Okay, what else?"

"The backhoe, Sheriff. We were going to try and find out who owned it. We thought that it belonged to Carl, but some of his neighbors said they'd never seen it on his farm. Did anybody get a serial number off of it?" Jan was asking this question, and feeling a little guilty because she knew no one had gotten the serial number, and was more or less just implying that somebody should get it done.

"Right you are," Benjamin said, as he noted "identification of the backhoe ownership" on the board. "You want to take care of that, Jan? Run out, get the serial number, make and model, and run it through the computer. Clear up that matter?"

"Will do, Sheriff."

"Let me interject here," said Hawkett. "What's the deal on this backhoe? Did you guys use it to dig up Carl's body?"

"No, actually we got a backhoe from a construction company here in Pigmy. The owner/operator volunteered to come out and dig up the hole the night we found Carl. The backhoe we're talking about, the one Jan's going to try to identify ownership of, was parked just down the road from the entrance into the cornfield. We assume it was used to bury Carl."

"I see. So you were approached by Henny, telling you that he'd seen a body buried out in a cornfield on the Dickenson farm? You followed up on his information and found a freshly dug hole out in the cornfield. Then you got volunteers to help dig up the hole, using a back-hoe from town, while the other one was parked down the road. Have I got that right?"

"Yes you do," Benjamin was wincing, remembering what a poor job they'd done of preserving any evidence at the crime scene.

Hawkett nodded his head, acknowledging that he now understood.

"Okay, I'll try and interview Emily Smith. Hawkett, you take our patrol pickup over to Clarinda and try to interview Roydel. Jan, when Cindy gets in here, will you run out and see to the backhoe, take care of that?" Both Hawkett and Jan nodded in affirmation. "Anything else?"

"You remember the magistrate's request for tomorrow?"

"Yeah, I'll take care of that. Is that all?"

"Well, don't forget this is rodeo week. We have a parade and festival to deal with Wednesday, and then the rodeo parking problem, Friday and Saturday nights."

"Oh heck, I forgot all about that. Man, well we'll have to get some volunteer help from the county reserves to handle that. Let's talk about it again tomorrow afternoon, okay?" And with that the three Taylor County officers got busy with their assigned tasks.

Jamie was actually rather surprised to see Henny come pedaling his trusty bike into her yard right after school as promised. The first thing he did was get off his bike and hug Tippy, who seemed just as glad to see Henny. The mystery of where Tippy was going at nights was becoming clearer. Jamie realized that she'd have to deal with that problem as well.

"Did you get your pigs back? I stopped at my house to check before I came out here and I seen they was gone."

"Saw they were gone, not seen," Jamie corrected him.

He seemed just a little puzzled, thinking that Jamie might be kidding him, but he couldn't quite figure out the humor in it. "Yeah, well, did you get them or not?"

"Yes, Henny, I got them and they're back where they belong," She gave him a stern look as she said it, trying to make a point, but it obviously buzzed right over the little boy's head. Jamie again noted that his new clothes looked just a little large for him, but that may have had something to do with the fact that the kid was pretty thin—almost to the point that he looked just a little unhealthy. She made a mental note to herself to sit the boy down at her kitchen table before he returned home and make sure he had a healthy meal.

"So, we gonna go out and do something with the pigs? I really like taking care of them. I was starting to train your pigs in town to do a few tricks."

Jamie couldn't keep from smiling, wondering what tricks he was teaching these pigs and at the same time noting that he was admitting that he'd stolen the pigs and didn't seem to have much remorse about it. "Oh really, what tricks were you teaching my pigs while you had them in town?"

"I almost had Spot trained to roll over when I touched her on the head with a little stick."

Jamie chuckled, "Spot! The pigs are all spotted! How in the world could you tell one spotted pig from another?"

"Oh, I just knew that the one had a big black spot right in the middle of its back and the name seemed to kinda fit. And I had one I was training to fetch a . . ."

Jamie interrupted him, "Hey, we've got work to do, remember? You've got a debt to pay back for your crime. Let's get over there to the garden. We have several rows of potatoes that haven't been dug up yet—should have done it a long time ago. Anyway, we've got to get it done before this beautiful fall weather stops, and Old Man Winter sends us a cold front and puts some frost in the ground."

"Dig potatoes! I thought we was going to take care of pigs!"

CHAPTER
24

Hawkett didn't much care for the patrol pickup he was driving. Darn thing was noisy, didn't even have a radio, and it constantly pulled to the left. Well, he was doing something anyway. He was involved in an investigation and was getting back into the work he'd known before landing on Jamie's farm in that bizarre set of circumstances last August.

He looked at his calloused hands guiding the steering wheel, hands that had been soft last August when he first walked onto her farm. The farm had changed him physically. He'd gained a lot of muscle tone and lost some belly fat. He felt better about himself physically than he had in years. And mentally—wow! Big change there, too. He hadn't had a drink for what—a couple of months? And better yet, the need for a drink wasn't there. So, he asked himself, if I'm physically and mentally stronger than I've been for years, why do I feel so bad right now? He knew the answer to that. He missed her, missed working with her, missed being with her. Missed seeing little Andrea, teasing her, watching her play, watching the relationship between her and her mother. Missed working on the farm, taking care of the animals, being part of something important. Then what the hell had gone wrong? Was it really all his fault?

He thought about these things as he cruised along Highway 2, heading west toward Clarinda. He was depressed, but wasn't failing to appreciate just how beautiful the scenery passing by him was. It was another October day, warm enough to drive with the window open. Better enjoy it while it lasted, he thought. This was Iowa, and the weather could be much different tomorrow.

Hawkett sighed as he recalled another uncomfortable thought—remembering Ann showing up at the Farmers' Market in Des Moines and then again at Jamie's farm. What the hell was the woman thinking? After all, it'd been Ann who had dumped him, walked out on their marriage, hired an attorney and that was that. Then all of a sudden popping up in his life again, like she had?

Well he could say one thing, she sure did look good. He began comparing her to Jamie, but that wasn't really fair. Jamie wasn't at all hard to look at—she just never fixed herself up like Ann. Wondering to himself how the two women would compare if they both had on farm clothes and then seeing them dressed to the hilt with makeup and sexy dresses.

Then, wondering to himself—what was wrong with him? Why was he thinking these things? Yeah, Ann looked hot, and she acted like she wanted to hook up again. That could be exciting, but it wasn't her that he missed. He missed being with Jamie, missed her more than he'd ever missed anyone.

Hawkett pulled into the Clarinda Hospital parking lot, locked the pickup, and found his way to where Roydel was being taken care of. He was glad to see there was a deputy parked in a chair outside of Roydel's room, although the guy looked to be in his seventies. He was a pretty obese fellow who, Hawkett noted, was asleep.

No hospital staff seemed to be alarmed that he was walking towards Roydel's room and the deputy was off in la-la land snoring softly, so Hawkett entered the room. He was not surprised to see a mass of wires and tubes strung about the bed, coming from an IV bags and monitors, and attached to the sedated and sleeping patient. He *was* surprised to see that Roydel's face was completely wrapped in bandages, making him the slight appearance of a mummy. Hawkett wondered if he dared wake Roydel—nudge him a little maybe, when a woman entered the room behind him. She was not a nurse, like he'd surmised, but a woman, possibly in her late thirties. She was dressed in clothes a teenage girl might wear—too small for the body that was in them. Short-shorts on a woman who, quite frankly, would have looked a lot better wearing blue jeans, or better yet a skirt, thought Hawkett as he surveyed her red hair (obviously dyed), heavy blue eye shadow, and thick mascara.

"Who the hell are you?" she asked. "You another copper?"

Copper? Her use of that term made him smile, and, from the look on her face, that didn't improve her opinion of him. "I'm a deputy with the Taylor County Sheriff's Office." He felt surprised that he had said that so easily, given the short time he'd been deputized. "Who may I ask are you?"

"Erlene Bass. I'm engaged to be married to this man you guys about blew the face off of. Think that was really necessary to scar the poor man up for life? You guys get a big thrill out of nearly blinding this poor soul?" As she spoke her voice got louder, and her yelling woke up the deputy outside who entered with a nurse right behind him. The deputy was both embarrassed and put out that people were coming and going without his permission, and the nurse was angry at the disturbance and pretty quickly had run them all out.

Hawkett did take note of the fact that Roydel didn't move a muscle during the encounter. Apparently he was under too much sedation, and it appeared that an interview wouldn't be possible at the moment.

He'd stop in at the Page County Sheriff's Office as a personal courtesy and casually mention the ineffective deputy; maybe some good would come out of this trip. He'd get this trailer park beauty off his back. She had followed him down the hall and continued to berate him with "colorful" language. He'd also visit with the sheriff to find out who the hell Erlene was and how she fit into any of this.

Benjamin was having much better luck with his interview, sitting across the kitchen table from Emily Smith in her Ranch-style house, drinking a cup of strong black coffee and eating food that neighbors had prepared. He knew there were many stages of grief when a loved one is lost, and she was currently dealing with some anger issues. Letting him know someone needed to "fry" for murdering her husband or at least spend the rest of their lives locked in a little jail cell somewhere far away, hopefully being assaulted by the other prisoners. She was angry that a funeral had to be arranged, and all the headaches that went with that—in-laws that weren't offering to help and a deceased husband who'd refused to buy a gravesite years ago when she'd brought the subject up. She was angry that their one daughter, who lived out on the coast, was taking her sweet time getting home, thinking her problems were so much greater than her mother's. And finally, she was mad because her husband's body was still waiting in Des Moines for an autopsy, clouding the issue of when the damn funeral would be anyway. Benjamin watched her grab tissues and cry silently, letting her calm down a little more before he proceeded with questions, still dreading bringing up the life insurance policy.

He had learned that there was definitely a connection between Roydel and her deceased husband. She'd told him Roydel did work for the Smiths once in a while. Actually, he had his CDL and could drive their grain trucks. He had not been dependable at all. He came and went when he needed money, and he sometimes took much longer than he should have running grain to Kansas City or St. Joseph. The Smiths wondered where he'd been and what he'd been doing with their trucks in the unaccounted time. Still, he never damaged a truck and there were no other problems. She said she had personally never cared for the man, but Carl kept using him. Twice Emily asked Benjamin why he was asking about Roydel, and both times Benjamin dodged the question. Emily said that Roydel had worked for them as recently as two weeks ago, so the connection seemed to be getting stronger. But what was the connection, Benjamin kept wondering.

She seemed to be getting control of herself again, so Benjamin decided to press on. "Uh, what about your personal welfare now? Will you be able to carry on with this farming operation? Did Carl arrange for any kind of life insurance to make life easier for you?" He was thinking as he asked it, he'd done a pretty good job of sneaking in the question about the huge life insurance policy.

"Life insurance, let's see . . . I think we do have a policy on Carl, now that you say that. To tell you the truth, I'd not thought of that. I think it's a pretty big one, too." She stopped and blew her nose in a fresh tissue and brushed her hair out of her eyes, before continuing. "Yeah, we have a really big policy, maybe a million dollars. The outfit that finances us made us carry that policy, and man, I'm glad they did. I mean, Sheriff, you can't imagine how much debt we have. Carl, he just couldn't quit, couldn't wind down and retire, he just had to be adding one more farm, one more tractor. I said to him once, 'Carl, you're going to be dead one day and you haven't even got a child that wants to take this farm over. How come we keep doing this, keep taking on more and more?' You know what he said? He said, 'because it's all I've ever done and all I know how to do'." She shook her head. "The man was smart but also a fool. We never enjoyed anything. We just worked. Get one crop out and haul grain all winter getting ready to put another crop in the next spring." Still shaking her head, she took a drink of her coffee. "You need more coffee, Sheriff? Need that warmed up?"

"No, thanks, I'm fine. So, any plans for the farm now, Emily?"

She shrugged, "Guess I'll go talk to the banker and our attorney. Find out what we're worth, or I guess what I'm worth now, financially. Let them sort things out. If I could come out of this with a place to live I'd be happy. I've no interest to keep working like this. I've done enough work in my lifetime. And believe me, I have no understanding how the financial side of this place works. Carl always took care of that. Heck, there's over one hundred thousand dollars in the safe in the other room, and I have no idea where that came from! No, it'll probably cost me a small fortune, but I'm going to let our attorney handle everything. Have a farm sale, sell our land, and get out from under this mess!"

Benjamin was still thinking about the large amount of cash stashed away in their safe in the other room. Why in the world would they have that amount of cash? Surely all grain sales were paid through checks. "Did you say you had over a hundred thousand in cash in your safe, in this house?" Benjamin asked, just wanting to make sure he'd heard her correctly.

"Oh yeah, he'd get the money out once in a while. Count it here on the kitchen table and make some notations on a notebook he kept with the cash. I never had any idea what he was doing, always kinda figured he was just showing off. Get me to quit griping, show me what a big money guy he was."

"My first thought is that you should get that cash into a bank. If you want me, or one of my deputies, to accompany you while you're doing it, we'd be glad to do that. Emily, it's not a good idea to keep that much cash around your house."

She snorted, "Yeah, Carl must have thought of that. He's got some sort of fancy gun he keeps in the safe, right on top of his pile of cash."

"That's no good. I suggest you get the money into a bank and get rid of the gun. Did you say he had some sort of a notebook he kept? You said he was what, keeping track of his cash in it?"

"Yeah, I guess. He didn't seem to act like it was any of my business, which was business as usual around here," she said with some anger in her voice. "I'll get it if you want to take a look. I'm sure I couldn't make heads or tails of his figures."

"Sure, Emily," thinking this investigation was about to take on a whole new direction, but what? Benjamin was also thinking that there was no need to worry about a search warrant. She had volunteered to let him see it. With some effort, she slid away from their kitchen table and walked out of the kitchen into an adjoining room. Benjamin could hear her grunting as she bent down, and then the clicking noise of her working the combination. Moments later he heard the door to the safe bang shut.

She returned with a grave look on her face. "Well, this can't be good. There's no money, no notebook, and no gun in the safe. It's completely bare!"

CHAPTER
25

"Somewhere around a hundred-thousand in cash!" Hawkett was astounded at hearing Benjamin's report, as they sat in the sheriff's office drinking coffee and comparing notes. "Are you sure she just wasn't making that up? I mean why would anybody have that kind of cash at home, even in a safe, unless they were up to no-good?"

Benjamin nodded, "Well that's probably the answer—our deceased farmer was up to no-good. But doing what? In cahoots with Roydel over drugs somehow? That's the most likely scenario given what's happened and what little we know. If Roydel knew he had the money in his safe, that'd be motive enough. He worked for the Smiths part-time, hauling grain. Somehow he must have figured out Smith had that kind of money around and knew how to open up that safe. Unless of course he forced Smith to open it up at gun-point."

"Or Emily Smith is right in the middle of this deal, maybe working in tandem with Roydel," interjected Jan.

"Could be, could be," repeated Benjamin, "but if she is, she should get an Oscar for her acting job. I mean, she's the one who pointed out the money was gone. If not for that, we'd not even know about it. Anyway, it'd be a good question to run by Roydel, see if we can shake anything out of him. You have any luck with him this afternoon, Hawkett?"

Hawkett reported that his trip to the hospital had been a waste of time. He also reported that the deputy on guard was incompetent, and that the Page County Sheriff's Office had been informed and was going to deal with that problem. He also gave them a colorful description of his run-in with the angry woman, Erlene Bass.

"Who's this Erlene?" Benjamin wondered aloud.

"She's Roydel's on-again, off-again girlfriend," answered Jan. "They've been running around together for years. They broke up when Roydel was in jail for a stint. Haven't seen her for a while, but what I remember of her a few years ago, she was a real floozy. I believe she worked as a stripper, part time. Grew up in a good family, but she sure as heck didn't turn out that well."

"Well that's the first I've heard of her. Was she living out in his trailer house with him?"

"Honestly, Sheriff, I don't think so. I think I heard tell that she'd run off with some trucker. How she shows up at Roydel's bedside this quickly is a mystery in itself."

The three adults sat in silence for a few moments, contemplating the case at hand. Then Benjamin slid his chair back, stood up and walked over by his marker board, preparing to make a notation about the money and Erlene, when he spotted the post about the identification of the backhoe.

"Oh . . . hey, Jan? Did you find out who actually owns that backhoe out there that probably buried Carl?"

"Yes I did, Sheriff. Got the serial and model numbers and ran it through the system. Guess who the owner is?"

"I don't know, apparently not our dead farmer, Carl, so please tell me it belonged to Roydel Nuxton."

"Can't do that, Sheriff. The backhoe belongs to Iowa LandCo, the farm management firm that's in charge of renting out the farm that we found Carl Smith buried on."

"Iowa LandCo. Yeah, that's the farm manager guy I met with over in Red Oak. Hey, he was a real peach I can tell you." Benjamin shook his head back and forth. "That guy made me glad I'm not farming for a living. So what do they have a backhoe parked out here for? My guess is they don't figure on going to these extremes to get rid of farmer clients. I better talk to that guy again. What was his name?"

Jan was looking at her notes, "Dallis, Hal Dallis. I've got his cell phone number here." She gave Benjamin the number.

Benjamin dialed the number and had a short visit with Dallis. He found out that the backhoe belonged to his company, and that they loaned it out to tenants to do repair work on terraces and tile lines on farms they managed. He seemed to be pretty proud of that fact, said he knew of no other farm management firms that offered this service to their clients.

Hal also mentioned in the conversation that he might be coming to Pigmy that Wednesday afternoon. He was thinking about driving his pickup in the Rodeo Days parade—throw a little candy out to the kids. Having learned that, Benjamin asked him if he'd stop by the office to visit, and Dallis tentatively agreed.

Benjamin hung up and reported what he'd learned from Hal, then looked at the clock. Seeing that it was getting later in the evening, he wondered how the time kept disappearing. "Jan, would you order some pizza? Would that be okay with everybody? I'm buying."

An hour later, the three adults were sitting around the office eating pizza and drinking Diet Cokes when Henny walked in. He said "Hi" as he headed for the jail cells in back.

Benjamin stopped him. "Hey, where are you going?"

"I'm going to bed. Thought I'd just sleep back in the jail cells again. That okay with you guys?"

"Why don't you stay at your house? Your mom probably doesn't want you staying here all the time."

"Mom's gone, Sheriff. I stopped by there after working for Jamie. No sign of her, and I think her suitcase is gone. I don't know, but I think she may have moved out."

"Moved out? Well hell, she would have said something to you. She can't have moved out."

"Well, she's not there and my pigs aren't there anymore. Jamie came and got them, so it's kinda lonely there. Thought maybe I'd just sleep here. I promise I won't make a mess, and I'll make my bed in the morning."

Benjamin was thinking, how could he say no to this boy, and wishing things were different for Henny—that he had a responsible

129

mother. "Yeah, sure, you can sleep back there. You got any clean clothes, got your toothbrush?"

Henny shrugged, "No, but I got these brand new clothes you guys gave me. Jamie wanted to wash them for me before I came back, but she didn't have anything else I could wear and I didn't want to wait around so . . . " he shrugged again.

"Well, find a towel and some soap, and take a shower before you go to bed, okay?" Benjamin was wondering what the heck they were going to do with this poor kid.

CHAPTER
26

Walking from his patrol car towards the courthouse, Benjamin heard a loud boom of thunder, and that, along with the darkening skies, made him think their Indian summer might be coming to an end. He felt a few cool drops of rain on the back of his neck just before entering the building.

The darkening skies and cold rain appeared to be a precursor of more bad things to come Benjamin realized after arriving at his office. A fax lay on his desk—a report from the Iowa DCI Crime Lab. The good news was that the report concluded that Carl Smith did die as a result of a gunshot. The bad news was that the slug retrieved from his skull did not match the ballistics of any of the guns they'd confiscated from Roydel. Benjamin shook his head as he re-read the report and wondered why it couldn't be easier, and then he thought about the gun missing from Smith's safe.

"Morning, Sheriff." Jan walked in carrying files for their monthly budget reports. "That's not the news we hoped for, huh?"

"No. No, it's not, darn it. I should have pressed Emily Smith for information about that gun she says is missing from her safe. I didn't think to ask her if she knew what the make or model was. According to this report, Carl Smith was shot with a .38. Maybe I'd better run out there and visit with her."

"Uh, Sheriff? Magistrate's Court starts in just over a half an hour, you know? I reminded you."

"Oh yeah, dammit. Yes, I'll take care of that first."

From out of the back room walked Henny wearing the same clothes, but his hair was combed, and he was carrying a paper bag.

"Hey partner, you off to school?"

"Yeah, Sheriff. Got me a lunch here that Jan made for me. Says I got to eat it all or she'll refuse to let me go out and help Jamie at the farm after school."

"Hey, good for you and good for Jan. Thanks, Jan."

Jan didn't look up from her work but raised a hand in acknowledgement.

Suddenly Benjamin had an inspiration. There wasn't going to be any real punishment for this kid for his theft of pigs, but still maybe it would be a good idea to take Henny into Magistrate's Court and allow him to watch other people pay for their violations—minor violations, mostly speeding tickets, but broken laws just the same. Might be good for Henny to see that there were some real consequences for breaking the law. Sure couldn't hurt, he thought.

"Hey, Henny, wait up. I think you need to appear in court this morning."

Henny stopped in his tracks and turned towards Benjamin with a look of worry on his face. Benjamin also had Jan's attention now as she had ceased working on the accounts and was looking his way.

"No, I don't mean we're going to make you stand trial or anything, I just think you should get a chance to see how the legal process works—what actually happens to lawbreakers. Jan, would you call the school and see if I can keep Henny out for a couple of hours this morning?"

"Henny, put your lunch in the refrigerator. If you haven't had breakfast yet, you can eat with me over at June's."

Half an hour later, Benjamin led Henny into the Taylor County Courtroom. The room was full of wooden chairs and benches, many old enough to be classified as antique, but polished and ready for use.

132

Several people milled around: some getting ready to contest their traffic violations or dispute debt obligations, a few high school kids awaiting trial for shoplifting, and two or three lawyers. They were all asked to stand as the magistrate walked in at exactly eight o'clock followed by her assistant. The magistrate read a short statement, one that she always read. It contained statements about her purpose, rights of the accused, and the expected behavior in her courtroom. Having said that she sat down and began addressing the first contested case of the day.

Arguing coming from the hall outside the courtroom interrupted her proceedings, and then the door opened with a bang. In walked Pearl, carrying a briefcase in one hand and rolls of paper under her opposite arm. Thelma, lugging some sort of a portable easel, followed her closely. Thelma seemed tentative, acting like she didn't want to be entering this place. She looked around timidly, searching for a place to sit.

"Ladies, please take a seat and be quiet. Court is already in session."

That stopped Pearl, and she glared at the magistrate. "Well excuuuuse me! I didn't know tax-paying American citizens were not welcome in this courtroom!"

The magistrate started to reply to that, but then, seeing the ladies sit down, thought better of it and got back to the case at hand. Benjamin had checked the docket and could tell that Pearl's appearance wouldn't be coming up for a while. He led Henny to the front row of seats and whispered to him to sit there and be quiet. Thinking he could slip out and get some work done in the meantime, he headed for the door, noting that Pearl Oldham was glaring at him as he walked by.

An hour later, the magistrate's assistant knocked on the sheriff's door. "Sheriff, Pearl Oldham's case is about to come before the magistrate."

"Okay, thank you, I'll be right there."

When Benjamin entered the room, he was irritated to see Henny goofing around with the high school kids, whispering something that got them all laughing, but he didn't have time to deal with that at the moment. Pearl, with the assistance of Thelma, was positioning a number of posters in the front of the courtroom. She had a picture of her damaged bicycle, among other things, and a diagram with a heading on it that said, *The Scene of the Accident*. Benjamin sighed. This was going to be fun . . .

"Mrs. Oldham . . . " the magistrate began to address Pearl.

"Call me Pearl, honey. We're all friends here, right?" winking at the magistrate as she did. Benjamin wondered what that meant.

"Pearl, I don't know what you're doing, but your appearance here is merely to establish the validity of a ticket you received for riding your bicycle on a city street. A violation of ordinance . . . " She turned to her assistant for verification. "Yes, a violation of Ordinance #442. Just exactly what are you doing?"

"Well, Judge, let me tell you. I intend to show the jury that on the tenth day of October, the year of . . . oh, whatever year this is, I was unlawfully assaulted by our local 'county mounty' and . . . "

"Wait, wait, just a moment here. You don't seem to understand what the responsibilities and parameters of this magistrate's court are. We're not going to deal with any of these accusations, whatever they might be. I suggest you hire an attorney and take the proper channels to do whatever it is you want to accomplish. Furthermore . . . "

Once again, Pearl interrupted the magistrate, "Your Honor, I understand the sheriff here is your buddy, probably writes your paychecks for all I know, but . . . "

The magistrate finally found her gavel and rapped it, with great force, on her bench, quickly gaining the attention of all in the room, including the high schoolers and Henny, and making her assistant jump. The room took on a new atmosphere, and that seemed to calm the magistrate. She took off her glasses, lowered her voice and said, "Mrs. Oldham, I'll allow you one minute to summarize whatever statements you want to make, then I'll ask you to sit down and remain quiet. And when you sit down, please take all this *trash* with you," pointing her gavel at Pearl's posters.

From the look on Pearl's face and stiffening body language it was clear that she was growing very angry and was ready to make some crude outburst. Benjamin sat and silently prayed that he wouldn't have to handcuff the old woman and lead her from the courtroom.

Pearl slowly turned and faced the people who were sitting in chairs, patiently waiting for their turn with the magistrate. She cleared her voice, then said, "Ladies and gentlemen of the jury, I intend to show today that . . . "

Again, the magistrate interrupted her, "Mrs. Oldham, there is no jury in this room."

Pearl appeared astonished. She turned away from the magistrate and pointed at the small group sitting in front of her. "Well then, who the hell are these clowns?" That declaration brought a hearty round of laughter from everyone in the room, except the magistrate, who was clearly getting angrier by the minute.

"Mrs. Oldham, I am done with you! Clean up your mess and leave this courtroom before I ask the sheriff to escort you out!"

Pearl started to say something, clearly upset and angry, but Thelma grabbed her by the shoulders and whispered something in her ear. For a few moments, Pearl stood there glaring at the floor, thinking things through, then apparently deciding to calm down, she shook her head back in forth, as if in disbelief. She began helping Thelma gather her "evidence". When Pearl bent down to pick up her briefcase lying on the floor, Henny, timing it perfectly, ripped the piece of paper he was holding. That action produced a sound creating the impression that Pearl had split her pants as she bent over. The room filled with laughter. Even the magistrate began to chuckle, but then she quickly restored her composure and wrapped her gavel on the bench three times, with great force.

"Order in the court!" she bellowed. When things quieted down again, the magistrate stood up and looked at Benjamin. "Sheriff, would you escort this young man from the courtroom? I don't want to see him in here again!"

Benjamin started berating the young boy as soon as they left the courtroom. "What in the heck did you think you were doing in there? That's a court of law, kid. The magistrate could have asked me to hold you in contempt. Do you know what that means?"

Henny, appearing to be chastened, made no reply.

They walked together in silence back into the office, and Jan could quickly surmise by their body language that something had gone wrong—Benjamin was angered and Henny was in trouble. But what had happened, she wondered?

"Alright, here's the deal, Mister. We're going to find a broom and you're going to sweep all the steps of this courthouse and the entire sidewalk running around the block. You understand?"

Henny nodded his head up and down meekly. "But, Sheriff, I've got to be out at Jamie's farm later to help out there, so . . . "

"No going out to the farm today, buddy." Changing his mind he said, "Tell you what, you get a note from Jan, get your lunch, and head for school. Within ten minutes of school closing I want you back here

135

sweeping. Understand?"

Henny nodded his head up and down—clearly not happy with the situation.

"And, if you don't do a good enough job sweeping tonight, I'll get a toothbrush and you can start cleaning all the toilets in this building. Got that, Mister?"

"Yes, Sheriff."

"Okay, get to school and learn something today, okay?"

CHAPTER
27

"Great, just great," Jamie uttered to herself, feeling the cold rain drops falling on her back as she worked in her garden. She was wishing the beautiful warm October weather could have held at least one more week, giving her time to complete the harvesting of her fall garden. She stopped digging potatoes and counted the pumpkins resting on the south side of her garden—wow, nearly a hundred of them. Those, along with the gourds, the Indian corn, and other ornamentals, needed to be put away.

It seemed like an insurmountable job, and here she was by herself. Andrea was trying to be helpful, but there was only so much a five-year-old could or would do. Jamie found herself wishing that Hawkett was there, and not just for the help, although she had grown used to his strong arms tackling the heavy lifting and more physically challenging jobs around the farm. She also missed the way she could complain to him about how impossible all this work was, and then feel relieved and calmed as she listened to him tell her to not worry—the work would either get done or it wouldn't. They'd do the best they could, and they had.

Ever since the day he walked into her life, a short three months ago, things had improved in a number of ways. She'd discovered he was the missing piece of the puzzle—not just for her but for her daughter as well. It was as if God had sent him to save her. Her thoughts drifted to all the things that had gone wrong in her life after her husband's death and the really dark period that followed. She'd only just been able to hold on, thanks to good neighbors like Thelma and Pearl and others—always there to do whatever they could and to offer a kind word. She knew the steady flow of help wouldn't last forever, and then Hawkett walked into her barn one day in the first steps of the murder investigation.

She shook her head. She had been so thankful to have met him and to have him living at the farm, but at the same time, so hurt that he wasn't there now and that she hadn't found a way to bend her "rules" just a little.

"Mom, we're getting wet!" Andrea interrupted Jamie's thoughts. She was playing on the other side of the garden, throwing a stick that Tippy continually retrieved for her. Well at least the dog was good for that—entertaining her child.

The rain was falling faster suddenly, with bigger drops, and they were cold. The wind was picking up as well, making Jamie shiver. "Hey, kiddo, head for the house and don't track in. Take your dirty clothes off and put on your grey sweatpants and sweatshirt, okay? Hear me?"

"Gotcha, Mom. Can Tippy come in the house? He doesn't like the rain either."

"No. Put Tippy in his pen in the barn. He'll be fine, and hurry up."

Jamie heard a ruckus on the other side of the barn and left the garden to go investigate. To her dismay, one of the old Hampshire sows was shoving straw and sticks into a nest in the corner of the pigpen, and Jamie knew what that meant. The old girl was getting ready to give birth. Jamie knew that if the sow farrowed outside in the cold rain, it was likely that the pigs would get chilled and die. She couldn't let that happen, so she grabbed a short panel and forced the reluctant sow into a small pen adjacent to the barn that housed a portable steel farrowing hut.

The hut measured nearly six feet wide and eight feet long, standing tall enough that a sow could walk into it, but too short for a human. Jamie threw half a bale of straw into the hut and watched the sow aggressively spread it around the pen, making her new nest. Good, thought Jamie, let it rain. This sow is in a warm hut that will shed water and her new pigs should be okay.

The rain was coming even harder now, so Jamie picked up four boxes of vegetables that she'd harvested earlier that morning and lugged them into the barn. She'd deal with them later. She took another look at the sow, still busy messing around, making her nest. Jamie longed to be warm and dry.

Warm and dry, but very uncomfortable, Roydel tried to get his one good eye to focus correctly. He wondered why it was watering like it was, wishing he could rip the "damn bandages" off his face.

"Honey, set still, your gonna' make a mess of all that work the doctors did on you. You want me to get ya somethin', Pumpkin?"

Roydel was thinking, man oh man, he was glad that Erlene had shown up. She was the only good thing that had developed from this mess, but if she called him "pumpkin" one more time he might have to hit her with something—knock some sense into the woman's head. He mumbled, "Hey, Erlene, how bad am I? Am I gonna live or what here? I mean, the way I'm feelin'—I need to die to get better."

"Baby, you're gonna live. That's the good news."

Roydel didn't like the tone of her voice when she said "good news", making it sound like the bad news was going to be really bad. "Dammit, woman, what's the bad news? Spit it out."

"Hey, no need to get snippy with me. I ain't the one who fired a shotgun into your face."

Roydel sighed, "Yeah. Sorry, baby. That damn sheriff. I'm gonna take care of him another day. . .get him in my sights and . . ."

"Well you see, Pumpkin, that might be a problem—gettin' him in your sights. You done lost one eye in this deal and the other one's got a little damage and your nose got about half blown off. I don't know. I got a peek this morning when they were changing the bandages and it didn't look good." She shook her head back and forth, showing her concern. "But the doctor says you'll still be able to smell with the part of your nose that's left. That's good, isn't it, baby?"

"Part? What the hell!" He tried to raise his hands up to touch his face but one was bandaged to the point he couldn't flex it and the other

139

had a set of handcuffs securing it to the bed railing.

"And you're gonna have some scarring. I don't know how bad, but there was some glass from the windshield blown into your face and it really cut deep," Erlene said these things quickly, wanting to get the bad news over with as soon as possible.

Strangely, Roydel didn't respond with any sort of a threat or insult, and that touched Erlene deeply, seeing a side of her man she'd not seen before.

"You mean . . . " Roydel's voice was soft now, "you mean I'm gonna' look like some sort of Frankenstein monster, scare little kids, have people starin' at me when I go out?"

"Baby, I don't care what you look like," taking his hand in hers, pushing the handcuff out of the way so she could hold it firmly. "I'm here and I ain't leavin' you. I'm pretty sure we can get a plastic surgeon to fix you up and . . ."

"Fix me up! Hell, woman. Do you know what that'd cost? Thousands and thousands of dollars. Where do you think that money's gonna' come from?"

"Don't get all worked up, Roydel. We'll find a way to get the money. Ain't you got any stashed away? After all, she thought, if he didn't have anything, it might change her feelings about not leaving him. She wanted to be loyal and loving, but not dirt poor.

"I got maybe twenty thousand put away."

Erlene was thinking to herself, twenty thousand dollars was a lot of money, but not enough to live on for very long. "Baby, I know I been gone, but I'm back now. While I was gone, what have you been doing? You got a job or what? Maybe there's some insurance benefits or unemployment—something like that."

"Erlene, did you think I'd gotten a job at the sewer plant while you were gone? Think I was working eight to five, building up my pension plan, hoping to become a foreman someday? Huh, Erlene, does that sound like your boy?"

"Then what? How'd you get the twenty big ones? What have you been up to, Roydel?"

He sighed again, wondering what to tell her, but the drug running scheme looked to be dead for now. What could it hurt?

"I was running meth from a supplier down in Missouri to an up-line guy, just playin' the role of middle man—distribution not sales—that kinda thing. It was a sweet deal, yes sir. But then there was a problem

140

with that deal and now a problem with this new sheriff of Taylor County and now . . . Shit, I can't see or take a pee without a nurse helping me."

Roydel was feeling the weight of his situation coming to full realization. He felt like he might start crying and was wondering how that would work with one eyeball missing from the socket—wondering where the tears would come from and where they'd go. Then getting hold of himself, he gathered his anger and began thinking about what to do now. Today.

"Erlene, they got me handcuffed to this bed for a reason. Soon as they can, they're gonna wheel me out of here into some damn jail cell, read me my rights, and start filing charges. That can't happen, Erlene. You gotta get me outta here as soon as you can. You hear me woman? Get me outta this hospital. We gotta run."

"Hey, keep your voice down, Pumpkin. There's a deputy sitting right outside this room packin' a gun, not to mention you bein' hand-cuffed to this bed. How we gonna get you outta here? I mean we can't exactly *hotwire* a hospital bed."

Roydel was silent for a moment. "I'll think of a way outta here. You make sure you get us a van or somethin' that I can lay in the back of, if I can't sit up. You hear me, Erlene? Get a van, get it fueled up, and be ready to go when I say."

CHAPTER
28

Benjamin sat with Hawkett and Jan, drinking hot black coffee and recounting how things had gone in court earlier that morning. His emotions transitioned from anger to humor, as he observed his co-workers smile at the mention of Pearl trying to address the "jury", yet both of them could read the disappointment in his face when he spoke of Henny's behavior.

"When are we going to make the call to Child Services and get the ball rolling on Henny's future?" Jan asked the question, realizing nobody wanted to talk about it, but knowing that things couldn't go on the way they had—the small boy living in limbo—sleeping in their jail cells.

Benjamin took a deep breath and shook his head back and forth, not wanting to answer her question or do what he knew he had to do. "Have you been back out to his house? Mom come back yet?"

"I've been there three times. Not a soul around. The neighbors say she's gone, somebody picked her up in a Ford pickup with a topper. That's all anybody seems to know."

"How in the hell could a mother, even a pathetic mother like her, just take off and abandon her child?"

"Not the world we grew up in is it, Sheriff? Sad situation. Breakdown of families, multiple fathers who just leave, kids with no supervision, no direction. May be the greatest challenge this country faces. Wish somebody could fix it."

The two men shook their heads in agreement. In somber moods, all three were drinking more coffee for something to do while their minds were lost in thought.

"Well okay." Benjamin slapped the top of his desk with his hand, startling both Hawkett and Jan, who spilled some of her coffee in the process. "Life goes on, always has. Time to get to work. Let's prioritize."

He stood up and took his marker over to his whiteboard. "Nothing here from last time we need to keep." He sprayed the board with cleanser and wiped it clean.

"Alright. Number one—the death of Carl Smith. What do we know?"

Jan reviewed the notes from her case file. "He died of a gunshot wound to the head from a .38 caliber handgun which we don't know the ownership or location of. He was buried late at night in the middle of a cornfield. The backhoe used to bury him was owned by the farm management firm, Iowa LandCo. The backhoe was supposed to be somewhere on that farm. It was no surprise the company furnished a backhoe for its clients to use, repairing tile lines, that sort of thing. Carl Smith rented a lot of farmland, most of which was managed by Iowa LandCo. He outbid other farmers to get it and this did cause some anger. We know that for a fact. Case in point—Josh Flora. Carl was paying two hundred dollars an acre rent for a lot of it or two twenty-five, depending on who you talk to. His wife, Emily, was his partner. She seems to be the quiet, mousy type, wanting more from life than work, work, work, but she was married to the guy and what else was there? Maybe not happy living with him but fear of living without him?" Jan paused.

"Go on please," said Benjamin, finding a comfortable position to sit on the corner of his desk.

"We know that he was in good standing with his banker. We know that he carried a large life insurance policy and both his wife and the bank will benefit from that, depending on their total financial situation. We've heard no rumors that Emily was running around with anybody else or that there was any kind of horseplay. The most damning thing seems to be that they occasionally hired Roydel Nuxton to haul grain, and he was "highly unreliable" according to Emily. We know that she says a gun and money are missing from their home safe. I do find it interesting that she's not in here, angry, and demanding we find the money or do something about that." Jan shrugged her shoulders. "What else?"

Hawkett, who'd sat quietly taking in the discussion, spoke up. "There are three solutions to this murder, and we all know what they are. Roydel, Roydel, and Roydel. We all know that trouble attracts trouble and the coincidence of him living in that same general neighborhood, working with the Smiths, and being a professional criminal, are just too great to discount in any measure. We need to get Roydel in a room and question him, get him worked up, and see what he spits out."

"Yeah, but he's lying in a hospital one county over and those guys have control of him. Can't blame them for wanting to take care of their own murder case, but hell, at least they know what happened and who did it," lamented Benjamin.

"What about the DCI? Anybody headed toward Southwest Iowa? Are we gonna be getting any help from those guys?" asked Hawkett.

"Email message I got yesterday said no. There was a lengthy message about budget cuts—too many murders. They did again offer to do whatever they could," Jan shrugged. "Oh, and Carl Smith's body is to be returned today. They're supposed to deliver it to the funeral home here in town so at least Emily can have a funeral for him. I guess that's good—get some closure on that front for her and the neighbors."

"So what do we need to do here? Suggestions?"

"Go see Emily again," said Hawkett. "Press her. I think there are things she's not telling us. The money and gun gone from the safe that she just *happened* to discover while you were there? That's sounding a little suspicious to me. I don't think there's any downside to pushing her, even if you don't learn anything more. And then there's Roydel. Like I said earlier, he's in the middle of this. We need to find out if we can question him yet—the sooner the better."

"I couldn't agree with you more. I'll go out and visit with Emily before the day's out. Hawkett, call the sheriff in Page County. Find out when and where we're going to get to question Roydel. What else, Jan? Are we ready for this rodeo parade coming up tomorrow night?"

"Well, I've notified all the reserve deputies. They'll be needed

144

for parking, helping to oversee the parade route, that sort of thing—and all four of them are ready and willing to help, so that's a good thing—one bright spot this week."

"Good, good. Yes, thanks Jan. I hope we're all around to help with the parade—help this town enjoy their annual event. Kinda looking forward to watching the rodeo one night myself. Just love watching the horses and the big bulls. Love those bull-riding events."

"I'm hoping you get that chance, Sheriff. I must say that this job seems to have gotten much more stressful since you came on board. Just coincidence I know, but we've gone years and years without much violent crime and look what we're dealing with now." Jan shook her head back and forth.

A ringing phone interrupted the discussion. Jan picked it up and said, "Taylor County Sheriff's Office, what can I do for you?" She waited for the response, then said, "Yes . . . yes, he's right here." Jan looked at Hawkett while she cupped her hand over the receiver. "It's your girlfriend . . . what's her name . . . from Des Moines. You want to talk to her here or take it in the back office?"

"Ann? Ann Mora? Hell. She's not my girlfriend. She's my former wife. Why in the hell is she calling me? How in the heck did she even know to reach me here?"

"Do I look like Sherlock Holmes? You want to talk to her or not?" Jan replied with just a touch of irritation in her voice.

"Yeah, sure. I'll take it on the back phone," he said as he got up and walked out of the room, knowing Benjamin's eyes were boring a hole right through the middle of his back.

Out on the farm, things hadn't improved much. It was cooler, yet the rain had stopped. A brisk northwest wind was blowing around and through Jamie's farmstead, forcing her to dress more warmly. She knew the temperature would continue to drop during the next twenty-four hours to probably well-below freezing, and there was still some garden produce she needed to harvest.

The good news was that the sow had settled down and some new pigs were busily working at her side, jostling for a position to suckle milk. They appeared comfortable in their new straw-bedded home, out of the harsh weather. She decided to tackle the work in the garden

145

and do what she could before chores and darkness determined the end of her day.

"Hey neighbor," Jamie looked up with surprise as Pearl and Thelma came walking up her driveway. Both were dressed in bib overalls and heavy sweatshirts, with mud boots on as well.

"What's up, ladies?" Jamie responded, not wanting to chit-chat—needing to get busy and work.

Thelma shrugged her shoulders and said, "We're here to help you finish up with your garden. We heard you were having quite a time getting it done and saw what this weather was doing. So we came."

"Well that's very kind of you, but how did you know I was having trouble? Where did you get that information?" Jamie was hoping they would say from Adam Hawkett—that he was worried about her.

"Oh, a little bird called us on the phone," Thelma said with a smile as she started loading pumpkins into a wheelbarrow. "We got nothin' to do, old retired ladies. Glad to get the chance to be helpful to somebody."

Jamie was thinking—a little bird—who would that be? Then suddenly realizing who, she turned towards the house and caught a little face quickly duck away from the window. That little stinker. She would have to have a talk with Andrea. The little girl knew she wasn't supposed to use the phone without permission. But, there they were, two people willing to help and Lord knows she could use it. As if on cue the sun peeked out from behind the clouds bringing warmth and brightness and Jamie's sense of hopelessness suddenly turned into one of guarded optimism.

Andrea came out, surprisingly dressed appropriately, with boots and a coat—work clothes. At last, with the help of three more, things were starting to happen. They kept at it and produce started moving from the garden to the root cellar, bringing Jamie tremendous relief.

Right after school, Henny came racing into the yard on his bicycle, and Jamie was glad to see him as well. She wasn't aware that he'd been forbidden to come out to the farm after school, and that he was supposed to be sweeping sidewalks as punishment for his behavior in the courthouse that morning.

He was wearing the same clothes that he had worn the previous day and that upset her. The little guy had no coat on and was shivering when he got off his bike. Jamie took him into the house and found a hooded sweatshirt—one that was far too big for him, but with the sleeves rolled up she thought it would work. In addition, she located a pair of Andrea's boots that were still too big for the little girl. They were a tight fit for Henny but much better in the weather than his tennis shoes — already muddy and soaked through with splatter from his bike.

To add to her afternoon of pleasant surprises, Henny dug in and got to work without complaining. Jamie was secretly waiting for the moment she could announce the new litter of pigs, knowing how excited that would make the little wannabe pig farmer.

Pearl had been working steadily since arriving and seemed to be uncharacteristically quiet, especially for Pearl. At one point she looked over at Henny and asked him if they'd met somewhere before, trying to remember where she'd seen the kid. Thelma, working nearby, hoped Pearl didn't remember that Henny was the little wise-guy who'd pulled the prank on her in the courtroom earlier that morning. Thelma was sincerely hoping that entire ugly incident was behind them, but still, chuckled to herself, as the paper ripping sound had really been quite humorous.

After about an hour of working steadily, Thelma offered to go into the house and get some coffee and bring it out. Maybe they could sit in the barn for a spell and relax, she thought. Jamie agreed that it was an excellent idea to keep the mud out of the house. She thanked Thelma and added that there were some cinnamon rolls on the kitchen counter that she could bring out too.

The group convened to the barn and sat down on square bales of hay. They enjoyed coffee, cinnamon rolls and milk from a thermos that Thelma had filled for the little ones. Everyone felt good about their progress and felt a strong sense of accomplishment. It reminded Pearl and Thelma of days gone by when farm families had worked together for threshing and other huge tasks.

"Oh, Henny." Jamie thought the time was right to give him a chance to see the new baby pigs. "Why don't you go around to the other side of the barn and check out our new litter of pigs? Andrea, show him where okay? You two guys just look? Don't get close to the pen and rile the sow up, okay? Hear me?" she yelled as the two kids raced out of the barn.

Jamie and Thelma gathered up the cups and napkins, and got ready to get back to work while Pearl blew off steam about the morning's fiasco in court. She relayed how the judge and sheriff had conspired to "railroad" her case through the courts with no chance for an honest verdict. Jamie listened, pretending to be sympathetic to Pearl's story, but finding it quite humorous. She tried not to smile and secretly wished she could have been there.

The three adults headed back toward the garden. With the wind having calmed and the sun's warmth stronger, Jamie began thinking about the effect the weather had on a person's attitude. She thought about how depressed she'd been earlier in the morning and how charged up she felt now. Yeah, she was still missing Hawkett, but other than that, life here on the farm looked pretty darned good.

Then she heard Andrea scream.

CHAPTER
29

Ann wouldn't say how she knew to call him at the Sheriff's Office. She had her "sources" and he believed her. She was, after-all, an investigative reporter for a Des Moines television station, and Ann was good at what she did. She said it didn't matter how she knew to call the Sheriff's Office, she was just thankful that she could talk to him, hear his voice, and know that he was okay. She told Hawkett that she knew about the incident at Roydel's and had worried about him being injured. She had tracked his whereabouts using information she'd picked up from the TV station's crime division. They were always looking for exciting stories to boost their viewer ratings.

She told him she was in the neighborhood and felt the need to talk to him, but refused to tell him what had brought her there. Hawkett believed she'd probably driven to Pigmy from Des Moines just to see him. Knowing he didn't want to see her, but still touched by her concern, he began to remember times when their marriage hadn't been all that bad—times when they'd been close, really close.

He told her they could meet. He didn't know why. He should

have told her he didn't want to lay eyes on her again? That wouldn't have been quite truthful however, remembering how good she had looked and felt and the intoxicating smell of her perfume.

He began to feel guilty and wondered why. Hell, he knew why. It was Jamie. But, hadn't she the same as kicked him out—all because he'd refused to marry her—right then, on the spot. But no, that wasn't quite true. She'd been patient, and what'd she say as he was walking out? "We don't have to do this?"

Okay, so now he was feeling guilty about meeting up with his old wife. He wondered how he'd gotten caught up in this mess. He didn't consider himself a ladies' man, but he did feel that he might be caught at a critical juncture in his life. Hawkett told himself to not get carried away. Maybe all Ann wanted was an interview about the Roydel Nuxton thing. Hell, he thought, he was tired of worrying about all this. What would be—would be.

Bolting out of the barn, Jamie tripped and landed face-first in the mud. Awkwardly she scrambled back to her feet, stumbling as she tried to move quickly. Her heart pounded as again she heard Andrea's screams for help. The sow on the far side of the barn was growling angrily. Jamie could hear baby pigs squealing and the metal hog-hut being hammered against the barn wall.

Around the barn she ran and was horrified by what she saw when she got to the other side. Henny was on top of the slippery hog-hut, holding on for dear life, but just barely doing that. A piglet was trapped under the bottom edge of the portable structure and was squealing its lungs out. The old sow, thinking Henny was to blame for her pig's distress, was trying to get to him, sink her teeth into his hide, and protect her piglets.

Jamie could see blood on the little boy's leg. She realized the sow must have bitten him at least once already. She couldn't believe he'd been so foolish as to crawl into the pen, but there was no time for that now. Knowing that if the old sow got him down on the ground—got four hundred pounds of teeth and anger on top of the little boy—she'd kill him.

Looking around, Jamie saw a metal bushel basket. She grabbed it and leapt into the pen, fully conscious that the sow might get them

150

both. The little pig, still trapped under the building, kept up its shrill squealing. As the sow moved about, she stepped on her other piglets, getting them to join in the ruckus too, and this was driving their mother to even greater depths of anger. The sow turned her anger towards Jamie and charged at her with teeth barred. Jamie did the only thing she could think to do. She shoved the bushel basket over the sow's head and blocked its attack.

Feeling the force of the sow's momentum shove her back against the fence, and almost over it, she held the basket firmly over its head. She knew that it was all that stood between life and death. She yelled at Henny to get out of there, but he was clawing the wall of the barn and looking for something to grab hold of—all the while trying to keep his foothold while slipping and sliding on the curved steel roof. The sow backed away from the basket, but Jamie stayed right with her, shoving and pushing, trying to keep her feet under her, not knowing what else to do.

Shocked and wearing down, she saw the situation getting even worse, until miraculously Pearl made her way over the fence and moved toward Henny. She yelled at the boy to come to her—to jump. Thank God, thought Jamie. Henny jumped. He went leaping off the farrowing hut towards Pearl's waiting arms. Of course, the force of his impact was too much for the old woman—slamming her into the side of the pen but catapulting Henny over the fence and out of danger.

Still skirmishing with the sow, Jamie could see Thelma reaching over the side of the pen for Pearl, trying to help her get out of harm's way. Finally, with both Henny and Pearl out of the pen, Jamie let go of the basket, turned quickly, and dove over the fence, landing squarely on an empty feed bucket. Rising to her feet, she felt a sharp pain in her ribs where she'd landed on the bucket. She winced, but then set about determining the condition of the other two.

Thelma was helping Pearl sit down against the side of the barn. She had a spot of blood on her forehead and appeared injured. Jamie turned and went to Henny who was crying tears of fright and pain. She looked down at the blood seeping through a rip in his pants.

Andrea, still quite shaken, was crying and kept saying, "I told him not to go in there, Mom. I told him not to go in there." Tears were running down her cheeks and her body was trembling.

"Andrea, calm down. Let's worry about that later. I need your help now. Go to the house and get the first aid kit, okay? Run!" That seemed to soothe her daughter as she turned and sprinted for the house.

"Henny, sit down on the ground right here." Jamie pulled a pocketknife from her pocket and used it to carefully slit his jeans so she could examine the wound. It wasn't a long cut, but it was deep and bleeding freely.

Andrea had returned with the kit, so Jamie took some gauze and pressed it firmly against the gash. Then she looked up at Henny and asked, "Are you hurt anywhere else?"

"No, I don't think so. Why was that sow so mad, I didn't hurt her pig. I was just trying to help," he sniffled as he spoke.

"Just try and relax Henny. We'll have you fixed up here in a little bit." Jamie continued to put pressure on Henny's injury as she spoke over her shoulder, "Thelma, how bad is Pearl?"

"I think she's okay. She hit her head on the fence. It stunned her a little bit, but she says her vision's not blurred. I don't see any evidence of a cut or anything. This blood on her forehead is not hers. It must be off the boy's leg."

"Is she right, Pearl? Are you okay? Do I need to call an ambulance?"

"Hell no. I've been hurt worse than this hundreds of times. Just give me a minute, then I'm going to crawl back into that pen with a ball-bat and teach that old bitch a lesson."

Thelma interrupted her, "Pearl! Don't use that foul language around these kids, please!"

The ensuing banter between the two women gave Jamie the reassuring feeling that Pearl was okay—bless her heart. The old woman had taken quite a chance by going into the pen like that.

Jamie thought about what had just happened and what could have happened and then felt the tears coming. She choked them back. There wasn't time for tears; she had an injured boy to take care of.

Ann walked into the Sheriff's office and looked around. Seeing Benjamin, Hawkett's old partner in crime, she wondered how it was going, the two . . . what . . . partnering up again to fight crime? Just like the old days?

"Hey, how's it going?" Jan gave Ann a greeting. Maybe it was a little half-hearted, but still she was trying to be pleasant. She found it difficult to be congenial however, after smelling the expensive perfume and noting the pricey clothes that had just entered their office.

"Benjamin, aren't you going to at least say hi to an old friend?" Ann was addressing Benjamin's back.

He turned to face her. "Oh . . . hi, Ann. How's it going? You're looking for Hawkett, I suppose. He's in his . . . uh . . . back office. Right through there." Benjamin nodded his head toward the door leading back into the jail cells.

"Oh." Ann felt that everyone in the place was acting like somebody had died. She wondered what *that* was all about. She dropped her jacket on the edge of Jan's desk and tentatively walked into the cell area. She found Hawkett sitting in a chair, reviewing the Taylor County Employee's Handbook, trying to figure out the health benefits, but getting nowhere doing it as he thought about his ex-wife.

"Hey, Adam, love your office. It's the first time I've seen somebody use a jail cell theme for decoration?"

"Yeah, well this isn't actually my office, Ann. It's . . . you know. It's . . . well . . . the jail cell area."

"Hey, I'm impressed. First I find you living out at Old McDonald's Farm with your honey, now you're using a jail cell as your office. Do they give you a car to drive or do you have to ride a mule?"

"Did you drive all the way down here to insult me?" He remembered her sharp tongue and how mean she could get, but at the same time he was a little shocked. This was not the kind of conversation that he thought they would be having.

"No, I'm sorry. That was very rude of me, and I apologize. It's just . . . seeing you like this . . . it just wasn't the way I pictured you ending up."

"Well, my life's not exactly over." Hawkett was contemplating telling her how much he loved living on that farm, how wonderful his friends were, and how he had a woman he loved, but all that sounded so stupid with him sitting in the back of the jail. Instead he asked, "Ann, what are you doing here, what do you want?"

"Hey, I'm sorry. I don't know why I say these things sometimes. I'm sure you're doing fine here with your old buddy Benjamin. Still fighting crime, huh?"

"I'm helping him out through a rough spot here—local farmer got murdered," Hawkett shrugged his shoulders.

"So, you're not a farmer now? What's up with that?"

"We," Hawkett paused, trying to find the right words. "We've split up, Jamie and me. Don't know if it's permanent. You know how it goes. Things are said—people get hurt." He shrugged again.

"I understand. We've been down that road, right?"

"Yeah, I guess we have."

"Hey, stand up will you?"

Hawkett stood up—not knowing why. He quickly found out when Ann walked up to him and wrapped her arms around him. She laid her head on his chest with her blond hair tickling his chin. Man . . . feeling so good, smelling so good.

"Adam, I have a confession to make," She didn't move and neither did he. "When I saw you standing at that booth at the Farmers' Market last week, I fell in love all over again. I remember why I married you but for the life of me I can't remember why we broke-up. I mean . . .yes, things were said . . . hurtful things, and I know I was guilty and I'm so ashamed." The words were coming faster, and Hawkett could hear the pain in her voice. It surprised him to see a side of Ann he hadn't seen for a long time. Was that a tear working its way down her cheek?

She hugged him even more tightly. "Anyway, sometimes people can put things behind them—start over again—build on past mistakes, you know?"

Hawkett cleared his voice. He felt he should say something, but what? You walked out on me, I didn't walk out on you?

"Well say something, Adam. Don't leave me hanging here." Ann looked up at him with tears welling up in her eyes.

He remained silent. His confused mind was volleying thoughts of loyalty and lust.

Suddenly everything became clear to Hawkett. Finding his true feelings, wanting to quit playing games and get his life back on track, he took Ann's hands in his, looked into her eyes, and spoke.

CHAPTER
30

Bone-tired, Jamie drove her pickup up Main Street in Pigmy. It'd been quite an afternoon. Fortunately, the medical clinic was still open by the time Jamie had gotten Henny into town. The doctor thoroughly cleaned and treated the wound, putting in five stitches. After wrapping it with gauze and tape, the nurse gave him a tetanus booster.

Andrea was in the reliable care of the Oldhams. They were no doubt treating her like a princess and spoiling her rotten. Well that was okay. She'd had a rough day too . . . quite a bit of stress for a five year-old.

Jamie slowed down and steered the pickup into a parking space near the courthouse. She had made up her mind, she would take Henny back to the sheriff, find Hawkett, and invite him out for supper—for just the two of them. She would leave Andrea at the Oldham's for the night. They'd agreed to that. They weren't given a reason why, but they didn't need one. Thelma and Pearl were always happy to have an overnight guest to brighten up their boring lives.

She'd offer Adam the invitation, and then, if he accepted, and she prayed he would, she'd beat it home, finish a few chores, and get cleaned up. Then she would prepare his favorite meal, light some candles, and pour a little homemade wine. She planned to create some romance and start acting like a woman he could love—not just one he could live with.

"How you doin', kid?" Jamie asked Henny. He was strapped behind the seatbelt on the passenger's side, a little quieter than usual—one lollipop in his mouth and another in his pocket—gifts from the staff at the clinic for his brave performance.

"I'm okay, it doesn't really hurt that bad."

"Great. Well, let's get you back to the sheriff's office and tell them what happened." Jamie checked out her appearance in the pickup's rear view mirror. She coaxed hair away from her eyes and checked her teeth.

After she got out of the pickup, she went around to Henny's side, opened the door, and unfastened his seat belt. "You can walk okay, can't you?" she asked while helping him out of the truck.

"Yeah, sure, Jamie. I can walk by myself."

The two of them started walking slowly down the sidewalk toward the courthouse, and then Jamie froze. She felt her heart sink. Hawkett and his former wife had just emerged from the courthouse. They stopped, faced each other, and embraced, and then parted ways.

Jamie felt the tears coming, and she knew she wasn't going to be able to stop them this time. With her voice breaking she said, "Henny, get on into the Sheriff's Office, I'll see you later." She turned and quickly walked back to her pickup, jumped in, slammed the door, and left.

Henny entered the courthouse, and Benjamin, remembering the morning's problems with him, looked at the clock, and then barraged him with questions. "Hey, where have you been? You were supposed to be sweeping off the sidewalks after school. What's going on here? Why are you wearing that sweatsuit? You been playing with the other kids or what?"

"Jamie bought them for me after we went to the doctor. The sow ruined my pants, so she bought me this stuff."

"Whoa, whoa . . . let's back up here, mister. As I recall, you were supposed to come right over here after school. What's all this about Jamie, a sow, what?"

Surprisingly, Henny fessed up to disobeying Benjamin's orders and told of his run-in with the sow, the women saving him, and his trip to the doctor. He told the story slowly, pausing to answer questions from Benjamin and Jan. He was careful not to leave anything out, not to make anything up, to humbly offer his belief that his life had been saved, and that he had acted very stupidly. Benjamin, Jan, and then later, Hawkett, were all of the belief that they were seeing a different boy than the original Henny.

"Well, you've certainly had quite an experience," Benjamin said. He was still trying to imagine Jamie and Pearl in a small enclosure with a raging sow. He'd seen the teeth on those things—really wicked. "But, you've still not swept these sidewalks, you know."

Henny interrupted him. "I know, Sheriff. I'll go get the broom now and get started on it right away." This statement caught Benjamin off guard. He was expecting some wise-crack comeback from the kid or the claim that he was hurt too badly. But no . . . he was already heading out of the room.

"Hey, get back here." Benjamin said. Henny came back into the room. "You had supper yet? Jamie get you anything?"

"No, well I had a lollipop they gave to me at the doctor's office."

"That's not enough. Let's go over to June's and get a burger. What'd you say? Hawkett you want to go? I'm buyin'."

"Yeah sure." Hawkett was still pondering the incident out on Jamie's farm—what had happened and what could have happened. He was feeling badly that he hadn't been there when she needed him. Or, maybe she didn't need him. He hadn't heard from her since . . . when? A couple of days ago?

"Jan? You joining us or you want me to bring you something?"

"No, Sheriff. I'll watch things here. Cindy will be in shortly to handle calls. I'll take a break then—maybe go on home and do some cleaning, laundry, fun stuff . . ." She was smiling at him. "Thanks anyway."

After finishing another great meal of June's famous cheeseburgers, French fries, and malts, the three returned to the sheriff's office in the courthouse. "Well, now what? Any new messages, Jan?"

"No. It's quiet as can be. Cindy's here, and I'm out of here unless you need me."

"Nope, I think we can handle things. Hawkett, you want to hang around here while I go visit with Emily Smith again?"

"She's probably not out on her farm, Sheriff," Jan said. "Remember they returned Carl's body to the funeral home and tonight is visitation for friends and family there. Emily's probably already over there greeting people."

"Oh yeah. I don't suppose it would be very good publicity to be grilling her in front of a bunch of grieving people. Well heck, guess I could go over and pay my respects. See who's there—maybe learn something. Hey, Henny, ever been to a funeral home?"

"Nope, don't think so."

"Well, come with me. It'll be good for you to see how people turn out to show kindness during someone's time of need."

"What about the sidewalks?"

"Tomorrow, right after school, and don't forget this time. Understand?"

"Gotcha, Sheriff."

Benjamin had never been in this funeral home before. He hadn't met the proprietors and expected them to be older people who carried an aura of sympathy. He was surprised to find that the local funeral business was being managed by a younger, upbeat couple. He introduced himself and Henny, and they, in turn, told him where the family was, what arrangements had been made, and where the body was if they wanted to view it.

Benjamin turned and whispered to Henny, "You ever see a dead body before?"

"You forgot, Sheriff, I already seen this guy once, remember? Seen him get shoved into that hole?"

"Oh yeah," Benjamin, feeling like an idiot, was glad he had whispered the question to the boy. "Well, if you want, you can go take a quick peek at him again, lying over there in that casket. Don't touch anything, okay? I'm going to go over here and say something to his wife, Emily. You get done, you sit over there on those chairs. Hear me? You can ask questions later. Okay?"

Benjamin left Henny standing on his tiptoes, staring at the dead body of Carl Smith. He walked into the visitation room where a crowd of people was standing around talking quietly amongst themselves, taking turns giving Emily hugs and offering their condolences. He saw a guy who looked familiar and then he remembered who the man was. It was the farm manager for Iowa LandCo, Hal Dallis. Hal had just walked up to Emily and was giving her a big hug, holding on for some time, and talking softly in her ear. That raised Benjamin's attention. He was surprised that the farm manager was even there. Didn't he say they only met once or twice a year? Still . . . there were probably lots of people in the room who may not have seen the deceased on a regular basis. That hug didn't look normal though. It looked personal.

Finally his turn came and he took Emily's hand. He told her how very sorry he was, and assured her that everything possible was being done to locate her husband's killer. She thanked him for coming and turned to the next person. Benjamin thought she seemed a bit rude and quick with her dismissal of him. But then again, he wasn't actually a friend or relative.

He went back into the viewing room and was pleased to see that Henny, as he had been instructed to do, was sitting on a folding chair, behaving nicely. Benjamin once again felt that maybe the encounter with the sow had scared some sense into the boy.

He was also surprised to see the young farmer that he had questioned. Benjamin couldn't remember his name at first, but then it came to him. Josh . . . Josh Flora . . . was headed directly for Emily. Benjamin remembered Josh's bitterness over losing a rented farm to Carl Smith. He wondered if there would be some fireworks or some sort of outburst. But no, Josh went up to Emily and started talking quietly. He even gave her a hug. Benjamin was trying to equate Josh's current behavior with the behavior he'd witnessed while visiting with him on his farm. It just didn't add up. The only thing he could determine was that maybe the guy was the real forgiving type. He'd like to visit with him again to get some sense of whether or not this was the truth, just to settle his curiosity.

Before he left, Benjamin decided to take a quick peek at the corpse. When Benjamin looked down at the body he gasped. Surprise quickly turned to anger when he saw the stick of a lollipop protruding from the dead farmer's mouth—locked between his upper and lower teeth. Benjamin was forming a mental picture of the candy sphere inside the corpse's mouth. He turned to glare at Henny, but the little rascal was gone—probably predicting that he would be in trouble. It appeared that no one else had viewed the body since the lollipop had been inserted, so Benjamin figured he could quickly do damage control.

He glanced back and forth, and seeing no one close by, Benjamin discreetly reached into the casket and gave a slight tug on the lollipop stick. The damn thing wouldn't budge, so he pulled a little harder. He wiggled the stick around a little but the lollipop wasn't coming out. He wondered how in the heck that kid had gotten it in there in the first place. Frustrated, Benjamin turned once again and saw a young lady walking towards the casket with tears streaming down her face. He knew he had to do something. He quickly reached again for the stick. This time he got a really good grip on it, gave it a yank, and then watched in horror as the deceased's dentures came flying out of his mouth with the lollipop still inserted. Losing his grip on the stick, he saw the dentures soar across the room, strike the back of an older woman, and crash to the floor— shattering into pieces.

The room fell silent. The people assembled first looked at the shattered dentures and then at Benjamin. With looks of disgust and disbelief on their faces, they tried to process what had just happened. Benjamin felt himself turning bright red as he desperately tried to think of something to say—anything that would explain what had just happened. He quickly grabbed his cell phone out of his pocket, held it to his ear like he was hearing a message, and then spoke into the phone like it was a radio. "Ten-four, I'll be right there!" He couldn't get out of that building fast enough.

CHAPTER
31

Outside of the funeral home, Henny was nowhere to be seen. Benjamin checked both the front and back seats of his patrol car and the kid wasn't there either. He drove slowly, checking the sidewalks and alleys on his way back to the courthouse, thinking he'd spot him, but that didn't happen. Then, he was sure he'd probably find the boy sitting in one of the jail cells when he got back to the office, but neither Hawkett nor Cindy had seen him.

Benjamin looked at his watch. It was past 8:00 P.M. He wondered where Henny could have gone. He was angry at being humiliated at the funeral home like that. He wondered what people were saying and what he'd have to put up with at June's, or worse yet, at his first employee review with the Board of Supervisors. When he found the boy, and he was confident he would, he'd give him a real reprimand this time—one that Henny wouldn't forget. No more feeling sorry for the boy, giving him slack because of his lousy home life. Either the boy would come around or he wouldn't. Benjamin was sure of that. Still, nothing could be done until Henny was found, and that should probably be a priority.

"Hawkett, would you drive over to Henny's house, see if the boy is there? Check all through the house . . . out back . . .I don't know. A lot of places he could be hiding out there. There're some abandoned vehicles in the drive, check those out. Oh, look for his bike too—a little gray colored thing. I think they call them mountain bikes. Okay?"

"Yeah, sure. I'll go take a look. If I find him, what? Just haul his butt back in here?"

"Yeah, he's gonna get an ass-chewin' when I find him. I don't even want to tell you what happened over at the funeral home." The frown on Benjamin's face indicated to Hawkett that it must have been pretty serious.

"Before I go, I'm gonna' have to give you some more bad news."

"Oh no, now what? Something else Henny has done?"

"No, I just called over to Page County to try and line up an interview with Roydel. Seems that won't be possible since Roydel is gone—escaped."

"Oh hells bells. When? How?"

"Well, they're not sure. This is how it was told to me. It seems that sometime around three this afternoon a fire started on the backside of the hospital. I guess smoke was really billowing up the side of the building, and everybody got pretty excited I can imagine. Anyway, the deputy, who was supposed to be guarding Roydel, grabbed a fire extinguisher and ran outside and doused the fire. Turns out it was a bunch of trash burning away inside a dumpster. Then about that time, the fire department shows up and everybody is high-fiving the deputy and wondering what could have started the fire, etc. Then the deputy finally got around to remembering that he was supposed to be guarding a prisoner and hustled back up to Roydel's room. Says he peeked in and Roydel appeared to be sleeping soundly. It wasn't until about an hour or so later that a nurse went in to give Roydel his scheduled medication, only to discover that sheets were stuffed under the blankets in such a manner as to make it look like he was sleeping there. Says it looked like his head was lying on his pillow, partially covered with blankets, but turns out it was actually a bowling ball wrapped in tape." Hawkett laughed as he reported this, knowing it wasn't funny for a number of reasons, but still.

"What about the handcuffs?"

"I was told it looked like a pair of bolt cutters had taken care of those."

"He had help. Probably his girlfriend, what was her name?"

"Introduced herself as Erlene Bass, and I'd bet you're right—she helped her sweety escape."

"When were they gonna let us know? Put out an all points?"

"Whoever I talked to said they were issuing one as we spoke."

Benjamin, his mind full of questions and thoughts, walked over and poured himself a cup of coffee, trying to sort out things as he did. "Do you agree with me, Hawkett, that Roydel is still our number one suspect for Carl Smith's death?"

"Couldn't agree more."

"We both know who the person is that witnessed Carl being shoved into that hole."

"Henny."

"We'd better hurry up and find that kid."

Hawkett heard an uncharacteristic note of panic in Benjamin's voice.

After Hawkett had left, Benjamin grabbed his cell phone and dialed Jan's number.

"Hey, Sheriff, what's up?"

"Jan, Henny has taken off. Probably right around here somewhere, but keep your eyes and ears open okay?"

"Sure, Sheriff. How come he took off? You makin' him sweep too many sidewalks?" she said with a hint of humor in her voice.

"Listen, Jan, we've got another problem. Roydel's escaped from the Clarinda Hospital. Right now nobody knows where he's at."

"Oh damn. Suppose he'll head back to his farmhouse?"

"No. I'll have Hawkett drive out there, but Roydel's not that stupid. Plus, I'm not sure he can even drive. We're betting that his girlfriend's hauling him somewhere."

"Yes, I would agree." Jan paused, ". . . and this makes finding Henny a little bit more urgent, doesn't it. I mean he's probably not in danger, but just to be on the safe side . . . How come he took off? I thought you took him over to the funeral home."

"Well . . ." Benjamin paused. He didn't want to tell her what had happened at the funeral home, but knowing that she'd hear about it before the night was over anyway, he decided to fill her in. He told her about the incident that had led to the broken false teeth bouncing across the floor, about his humiliation and anger, and how Henny—knowing he

163

was in *big* trouble—took off.

"Well," she was trying to suppress her laughter and show him a little bit of sympathy, but it wasn't working out very well. "Well, Sheriff, I don't know what to say. Darn kid's just into one thing after another. I mean, I like the little guy and I feel sorry for him, but I don't know. He may be too screwed up to turn around. I really hope not, darn it anyway. I am sorry for what happened to you. That's not fair either. I mean you're trying to be good to the kid. I don't know what to tell you. I'll keep an eye out for him and make a few calls. If you want, I can come back in and help organize a search.

"No, I don't want you to do that. The weather isn't terrible out, and we have no real knowledge that he's in danger. Kid's so darn resourceful, he's probably got other hideouts he goes to. Who knows anyway? Thanks, Jan."

He started to say good-bye, then had a second thought. Lowering his head and speaking in a quieter tone, not wanting Cindy to overhear his inquiry on the other side of the room, he said, "Oh, by the way, tell me what you heard in the conversation earlier today between Hawkett and his ex."

"What do you mean, what I heard? I didn't hear anything that you didn't . . . "

Benjamin cut her off. "Come on now, Jan. You've never lied to me before. It's common knowledge that you can go into the women's restroom, stand on the toilet, and hear every word spoken back in the jail cells, through the vent. You were gone for a good fifteen minutes while they were back there, not that I was keeping track, but I think you may have a pretty good idea what was said. Don't worry, I'll keep it between the two of us."

She didn't respond for a little bit. Benjamin was picturing the look of indignation on her face, surprised that the old sheriff knew about the standard procedure of snooping on prisoners that way. Illegal, yes, but effective. No wire-taps or court orders needed. Worthless information in court, taken illegally, but useful in many other situations—like now.

"Okay, you got me, Benjamin, but give me your word, this is between you and me. Nobody else, okay? I mean Hawkett would really be pissed if he knew I was eavesdropping on their conversation. But in my defense, it's always beneficial to have knowledge of how the personal lives of our staff . . ."

"Please Jan," he interrupted her again. "What was the gist of the conversation? Is he getting back together with that bimbo again or what?" Benjamin was anxious to know.

"Well, Sheriff, you'll be proud of your boy. Clearly she wanted to get back together with him, I mean I almost had pity on her, listening to their conversation. But Hawkett didn't waste much time telling her that he had somebody else he was in love with and wanted to spend the rest of his life with. Almost like listening in on a damned soap opera, I tell you. But he did say the right things, and I do have more respect for him now than I did before. I like Jamie and her daughter a lot, and I'm pretty sure he's the guy for her. His comments back in the cell today sure helped reinforce my opinion of that. Any questions?"

"No, Jan, thanks. And don't worry. This will be between you and me." Benjamin was smiling as he said it and thinking at least one thing had gone right today.

Hawkett drove the department's pickup across town to where he believed Henny's house was located. He knew he'd arrived when he saw the mess. He was forced to park out on the street since there was no room in the driveway. His heart quickened when he saw someone using a flashlight inside the house. It was probably Henny, but there was a car, one in pretty good condition, parked in the driveway. It could be a burglary in progress, he thought to himself, but it would be a pretty stupid burglar if this was their procedure. He radioed what he was witnessing to Cindy, telling her it was probably nothing, but he wanted to have Benjamin on standby should the situation turn bad.

Hawkett checked his gun to make sure he had a bullet chambered. Then he quietly walked around the vehicles and other junk in the driveway and worked his way to the garage. Benjamin had told him that was the best way to get into the house. He heard the chatter of two females and saw the light of a flashlight coming his way.

"Goodness, Pearl, did you ever see such a mess? I mean I've seen pigs who . . . "

Both women came to an abrupt halt when they saw Hawkett standing in the doorway with his flashlight shining on them. He was curious what they were doing. Both women were carrying bundles of

165

clothing.

"Ladies, mind if I ask what you're doing here? Please don't tell me you're robbing the place."

"You dumb son of a . . . "

Thelma interrupted Pearl's profane insult, "Quiet Pearl, I'll handle this." Turning back to Hawkett she said, "This boy, Henny, has been helping out at Jamie Chambers' farm, our neighbor." Then Thelma felt embarrassed, "Well of course you know Jamie, our neighbor . . . I mean . . . well anyway . . . he apparently doesn't have any clean clothes to wear. I mean where is the boy's mother? Not here apparently. Just look at this awful mess. How do people live this way? Anyway, Pearl and I came to find his clothes, figuring there were probably some dirty ones lying around here we could wash, or patch up if need be. See what we could find. And that, Mr. Hawkett, is not theft, it's charity—taking care of one's neighbors." She finished her reply with a defiant look.

"Well, you probably ought to get permission from somebody before walking into their house but . . . "

"You gonna haul us in, big boy? Don't say another word, Thelma. Anything we say can be used against us in a court of law, and you saw how that went yesterday!"

"No, I'm not hauling anybody anywhere. Take your stuff and get out of here, okay?" Hawkett was clearly irritated by Pearl's behavior and tone of voice. "Did you find enough clothes for Henny, stuff that fits?"

"We didn't find much and most of it is way beyond needing a good washing, but we'll see what we can do. I intend to visit our church's second-hand store. I know we can find some real nice clothes for him that someone else has donated. I mean it's probably not our place to do this, but well, if not us, who?"

Hawkett was surprised to hear someone else moving about in the house, behind the women. Seeing a flashlight carried much lower, and realizing it was a child, he was shocked to see it was little Andrea. She was carrying a pair of boots—helping with this project of sorts. When she saw Hawkett, she stopped, dropped the boots, ran to him, and wrapped her arms around his legs.

Jamie sat in almost complete darkness. One lone candle flickered on the kitchen table. Numbly, she sipped at a glass of wine. She was thinking she should probably be drinking water to replace some of the fluids lost to tears, but she didn't really care. She played the "what if" game for a while. What if they'd not gone to the Farmers' Market in Des Moines? What if she'd been a little less short with Hawkett when they were discussing Henny, parenthood, or whatever that conversation had been about that led to him leaving? What if she'd gone to him and apologized? Then she thought . . . hell . . . apologize for what? She rolled those thoughts around for a while and got nowhere.

Then the whole self-pity thing went a step further and deeper. She was remembering the day Bud had hung himself and remembering all the hell that went with that. Remembering how she'd had to rebuild her life, pull herself up, take care of their child, their farm and now what? To have yet a second man in her life, a man she loved deeply, lost. Was it her? The kind of person she was? Too damned opinionated, close-minded, or worse, too cold? All these questions were going unanswered with no one to talk to—no shoulder to cry on.

She knew that Thelma and Pearl had planned on Andrea staying overnight with them, so there was no need to worry about her daughter. Given the mood she was in, it was much better that Andrea wasn't there to see her mother like this. She blew the candle out, went to her bed, climbed under the covers fully dressed, and cried herself to sleep.

CHAPTER 32

Benjamin walked out of June's without finishing his breakfast. He'd had only one cup of coffee, and the waitress had remarked that he obviously was upset about something. His mood clearly didn't reflect that of the townspeople—excited, getting ready for their annual rodeo parade, everybody pitching in. And his mood didn't match that of the weather either, for it looked like it was going to be another unseasonably warm, sunny day. Mother Nature had shrugged off the cold rain they'd experienced the day before.

Too many things were going wrong at once. Henny was still nowhere to be found. Roydel, likewise, had not yet been located, and Benjamin had not slept a wink all night. He'd driven around town, twice, looking for Henny, and then stayed in the office—sending Cindy home around midnight—waiting for a call.

Hawkett and Jan walked in together, both in a good mood, but knowing things were going to be tense. Hawkett had told her that Benjamin hadn't returned to his apartment during the night. They both knew he was on edge worrying about the boy.

"No sign of Henny, huh?" Hawkett got right to it. There was no use in pretending everything was sunny.

"No, haven't heard a damn word," Benjamin replied somberly.

"You want me to check his house again, take a drive around town?"

"No, I've been there once already this morning. I searched the whole place, he's not there."

"Sheriff, any word about Roydel?" Jan asked, knowing that also was eating at Benjamin and wondering if there was a connection there—worried that Henny could be in danger, or worse.

"I called again . . . I don't know . . . an hour ago I guess. They have no idea where he is," Ben replied in a tired and discouraged tone.

Jan poured a cup of coffee for herself and one for Hawkett. She handed it to him as he sat down by her desk. "So what's next, Sheriff? Do we put out a missing persons report on him?"

"Well, now that you two are here, I'm going out to check at Jamie's—make sure he's not out there somewhere. I don't know. The kid could be about anywhere—maybe in an abandoned building. I keep thinking he'll just come walking in here. I mean we've got no clear evidence that Roydel knows anybody saw him shove the body into that hole. Assuming it was Roydel, and I'm pretty damn sure it was."

"We can handle things here in town, Sheriff. I'm going to get Hawkett a scoop and bucket so he can start practicing for the parade this evening. You know we'll need someone to follow the horses and clean up their doo-doo. Don't want any fine citizens stepping in that stuff." Jan smiled as she said it, wanting to lighten the mood a little.

"Oh yeah, the rodeo parade. Darn, we have that, too. But you're okay . . . I mean you've got the reserve deputies all lined up to help with the parade route, parking, that kind of thing?"

"Sure do, Sheriff. We have a lunch meeting at noon to review their responsibilities, but I'm sure we can handle it just fine. You do what you have to do. Hawkett and I can handle the celebration and parade. Right, Hawkett?"

Hawkett was still thinking about cleaning up after the horses, wondering if she was putting him on, and pretty sure that she was. "No doubt about it," he said, "we'll keep all those cowboys and cowgirls under control. Don't worry about that."

"Alright, call me if you hear anything, okay?"

"You can count on it, Sheriff."

169

Henny awoke with a start, and, as he attempted to sit up, he hit his head. As soon as he had regained his bearings, he felt the panic return. It was dirty, dark, and dusty in the trunk of the car, keeping Henny disoriented. He was still trying to figure out what had gone wrong and how he'd come to be there. He kicked on the inside of the trunk lid a few more times and then yelled out, but all he heard was his own voice—the voice of a scared little kid who knew he was in grave danger. Henny wriggled around trying to find a comfortable position but finally gave up. He lay there, going over in his mind what had happened to him—how he'd come to be locked in the trunk of this car.

He'd beat it out of the funeral home when he saw the false teeth fly across the room and heard them crash to the floor. He knew this time, man, this time, he was in big, big trouble. He'd run out the back of the funeral home, cutting between the cars, trying to figure out where he was going to hide, when he'd spotted his best friend, Tippy, running up the alley towards him. He scooped the pup up into his arms and hugged him, wondering how the little dog had found him. Henny knew that Tippy would be in trouble too, for sneaking off the farm and into Pigmy. While trying to decide what the two of them should do and where they could hide, a hand had come from out of nowhere, grabbed the back of his shirt, and slammed him to the ground.

Henny reached up and tenderly rubbed the side of his head where he'd been struck. The force hadn't knocked him out but had dazed him so badly that he'd not fought back—had not tried to run. He remembered being drug across the parking lot, forced onto the seat of a vehicle, and covered with a blanket. He hadn't gotten a look at his attacker. Whoever it was, was strong enough to hit with a vengeance. He'd been hit many times by his mother but never that hard.

Henny remembered hearing the road sounds change from pavement to gravel, and he knew that they had left Pigmy. Twice he'd tried to sit up, and twice he'd felt something hard hit his head. After the second time he had blacked out, and, that was that, he just couldn't put it together. When he came to, he was in a trunk.

Surely no one was that mad at him for sticking the lollipop into the dead guy's mouth. Even if they had been that mad, he thought to himself, he would have been scolded for sure, but they wouldn't have locked him up.

He could tell it was nearing daylight by the tiny bit of light that was making its way through a crack in the trunk's rubber seal. Feeling the urge to pee again, and not liking it one bit, he knew he'd have to do what he'd done earlier. He could smell his urine. He felt hungry, thirsty, and scared. He turned and wedged his feet against the backside of the car seat in front of him and pushed as hard as he could, but still the thing wouldn't budge. Frustrated and feeling more alone than he'd ever felt in his life, Henny started crying softly, trying to remember the prayers he'd heard the one time his mother took him to church.

Benjamin went outside, climbed into his patrol car, and drove out of town, noticing as he did, the hustle and bustle up and down Main Street. City workers were setting up barricades, a few booths were being assembled, and a set of bleachers was being drug down the street. He wished he could stay and spend some time helping people getting ready for the event, but he had a bad feeling about Henny, and he really, really wanted to find the little guy safe somewhere. He was no longer angry or worried about scolding him for the incident in the funeral home.

It didn't take Benjamin long to get out to Jamie's farm. As he climbed out of the car, he heard a cow bellowing and was pretty sure it was her milk cow. He didn't know a lot about her farm but was fairly certain it was getting a little late in the day to be milking the cow. As he entered the barn, he saw that she was doing just that—sitting on the small milking-stool, balancing herself as she pumped milk into a bucket. Unsure if she had heard him, but certain that she hadn't seen him drive in, Benjamin shouted, "Good Morning, Jamie." Apparently he had yelled a little too loudly, as both Jamie and the cow lurched, tipping Jamie off her stool and spilling the bucket of milk.

"Oh man, I'm sorry. Didn't mean to spook everybody," Benjamin said as he helped her get up and brushed some straw off her shoulder. When she turned and glared at him, he sensed that she wasn't her normal self—that she must have had a rough night. Her hair was a mess, and she had a tired and drawn look on her face.

"Hello Benjamin," she gave him a greeting in return, but with an edge to her voice. Then bending over, she picked up the bucket and examined it. Seeing that, although the milk had been lost, the inside of the bucket was still uncontaminated, she determined she'd at least be able to finish milking without taking the bucket back to the house for washing. "I . . . well, there's no getting around it, I overslept this morning. Would probably still be asleep if I hadn't heard this damned cow bawling her head off!"

Benjamin frowned. The Jamie he knew would not be talking that way about one of her animals. "Hey, you want me to milk your cow for you?" That produced a smile from her, knowing what a joke that'd be—Benjamin trying to squat down and milk the cow.

"No, thanks. I'll get it done."

"Where's your little helper? I'm surprised she let you over-sleep."

"She spent the night with the Oldhams," she shrugged. "They love her and she loves them and from time to time I let her spend the night there. It's probably bad for her. They treat her like the Queen of Sheba and spoil the little runt." She shrugged again.

"So how are you?" Benjamin asked the question with real concern in his voice. Both of them knew what he was talking about, and both of them knew that he really cared about her. "You need a hug or anything?" Benjamin felt silly as he asked it, but it was the best he could do in the form of offering sympathy.

"No, no I'm fine. I just need to get my wits about me and quit feeling sorry for myself." She shook her head as she spoke. "I just kinda got used to having him around here. Now I guess I'm going to have to get used to him not being around here." A tear ran down her cheek, and she was regretting she'd let herself cry again. She turned, dropped the milk bucket, and went to Benjamin. Sinking her head into his shoulder, she could feel his arms wrap around her as he patted her on the back.

Benjamin had no idea what to say. He desperately wanted to find a way to take away her pain and make her smile. He wanted to tell her that he knew what Hawkett had said to Ann, but he realized that would eventually lead to Hawkett finding out that Jan had eavesdropped on his conversation with his former wife. He thought about what would happen if he betrayed Jan and the problems that that might cause down the road.

"Listen to me, Jamie. Things are going to work out between you and Hawkett just fine. Don't worry about it. This is just one of those things. This deal of Ann showing up—it's nothing."

"Yeah, well the way they were hugging and carrying on yesterday, I'd say it's a hell of a lot more than nothing." She pulled away from him as she spoke, then walked over and patted the old cow on her back.

Again, he wanted to tell her what he knew, but again he held his tongue. "Listen to me. Give him a day or two. Invite him out for supper. You two just need to talk. Things are pretty hectic right now, but wait a couple of days. Heck, I'll take care of Andrea, give her a ride in the patrol car, I don't know—something to give you two some time to talk. Okay?"

"Yeah, sure, time to talk. Thanks, Benjamin." Her thanks sounded as if she was just trying to be polite and wasn't believing a word he'd said. "So is that why you came out here this morning? To offer to milk my cow, or have you got something else going on?"

"Oh yeah," Benjamin remembered. "You haven't seen Henny this morning or last night for that matter?"

"No, why would he be out here? The last time I saw him was when I dropped him off at the courthouse late yesterday." A frown crept across her face as she once again remembered the interaction between Hawkett and his former wife on the courthouse steps.

"I know, and I appreciate you taking care of him like that. Hey just what really did happen out here? He said a sow about ate him, but you know how Henny exaggerates."

"He wasn't exaggerating," Jamie said as she relayed the facts of the story. She explained how dangerous the whole situation had been and how it might have turned out if not for Pearl's heroic efforts.

Benjamin listened to the story intently and asked Jamie several questions. He wanted her to repeat the part about Pearl actually getting into the pen to help rescue the kid. Risking her life to help rescue Henny, after the way he'd treated her in the courtroom only a few hours earlier, was quite admirable, he thought. He let the story sink in. It was changing his whole opinion of Pearl.

Jamie, seeming to have sparked a thought, walked out of the barn. She looked around the yard for Tippy. Benjamin joined her in searching for the pup, but they both came up empty.

"Well," she said, "this could be a good sign or bad sign, but the pup's not here. He might very well be wherever Henny is."

CHAPTER
33

After giving Jamie yet one more quick hug, Benjamin climbed into his patrol car. He drove out of her farmyard and headed back towards Pigmy. He was just beginning to pick up speed when he spotted the Oldham residence. He thought again of Pearl, pushed on the car's brakes, and turned his vehicle into their driveway. Both of the women were working in their garden, raking and piling up for composting, the past year's growth. And now, both were staring at him as he exited his car. Thelma had a look of apprehension and Pearl—a look of pure anger.

"How are you ladies this fine October day?" Benjamin asked with a smile as he walked towards them.

"I think we're doing just fine, Sheriff . . . "

Pearl interrupted Thelma, "Okay, got the cuffs huh? Gonna book us for breaking and entering last night are ya? Surprised your willy-nilly deputy didn't have the guts to do it then. Think he might have if I hadn't backed him down a little . . ."

Benjamin interrupted Pearl. "No, no, no. I'm not here to arrest anybody. Hawkett told me you were there looking for clothes for Henny, and I think that was a very noble thing for you to be doing. Thank you."

That seemed to confuse both of the ladies. They hadn't expected him to respond in that way. Both fell silent—thinking.

"As a matter of fact, that's why I'm out here. Have either one of you seen Henny—last night or this morning?"

"No, I've not seen him since yesterday," said Thelma. "I assume he's okay. I mean, Jamie said the injuries from the sow weren't that bad. Said she got him fixed up at the doctor's office."

Benjamin looked at Pearl, expecting some rank comment, but the old gal seemed strangely silent with a look of concern on her face. Surprisingly, Benjamin thought he saw a tear sneaking its way down her cheek as she turned and walked away.

"Oh no. Pearl, come back," Thelma was upset and began wringing her hands.

"What's wrong? Did I say something?" Benjamin asked.

"No, no. I know what's wrong. It's . . . well . . . I don't know . . . . forty years ago Pearl lost a son. He was ten years old. You know Pearl was married to my brother?" Not waiting for an answer she went on. "Anyway, they had two boys and one of them was killed when a tractor rolled over on him." Thelma shook her head. "Such a tragic loss. Sometimes, something is said and it just seems to take her back to that day, holding the crushed, lifeless little body . . . waiting for the ambulance . . . . sobbing . . ." Now Thelma was shedding tears. "Sheriff, I pray for the day that we're all in Heaven and can see that little boy again. You know I do. I pray that every day."

"I'm so sorry. I'd no intentions of upsetting you both."

"Don't worry, Sheriff. It will pass. It always does. You can't know real sorrow, if you've not known real love."

Feeling unsure of what to do, and not wanting to leave them in the state that they were in, he had a thought. "Thelma, do you know where that ticket is I gave Pearl for biking on the sidewalk? She hasn't paid it yet, has she?" He knew that she hadn't, remembering the earful he'd received from the magistrate about the commotion in her courtroom.

"No, no. It's still lying on the kitchen counter. Why do you want to pester the poor woman about it now?" Thelma asked with irritation in her voice, a side of her Benjamin had never seen.

"No, please go get the ticket for me."

Puzzled, Thelma turned and walked up the steps to her front porch and disappeared through the screen door.

"Pearl, would you please come here?" Benjamin saw her beginning to rake in the garden once again.

Thelma came out of the house carrying the ticket, and as Pearl walked back toward him, having regained her composure, she saw the ticket. He could see her anger coming back to life. "Gonna rub that in my face, aren't you. Well let me tell you . . ."

"No, please give me a minute. Okay?" Benjamin took the ticket from Thelma. He turned and faced Pearl. "Pearl Oldham, in recognition of the bravery you showed yesterday, helping save Henny Henderson's life when he was attacked by a sow, and on behalf of the people of Pigmy, Iowa, I hereby tear this ticket up and absolve you of all guilt." Benjamin tore the ticket in half and handed the pieces to her.

Pearl, caught off guard, was speechless. Benjamin could hear Thelma, off to one side, saying what a Christian thing he had done and making other comments, but Benjamin wasn't really listening to her. He was instead fascinated at how this act of forgiveness had stunned Pearl.

"Oh, well it was nothin', Sheriff." Pearl said. "I mean the boy was in trouble. I just helped Jamie a little."

"That's not the way Jamie tells it. She says . . ." then he paused, not wanting to talk about what could have happened and bring everybody down again. "Well, we're all very proud of you, Pearl, and I want to extend my utmost appreciation." Benjamin extended his hand to shake hers. Then for the first time in the several months he'd been in the farming community, Pearl did something he'd never seen her do before. She smiled at him.

Just then he could hear his cell phone ringing. Excusing himself, he pulled it from his pocket and answered it, "Yeah, it's me, what's up?"

"We just got a call from Jamie." Jan said. "She says the vet here in town just called her. He has a dog that he identified by the tag on its collar as belonging to Jamie. The vet told her that the dog is injured pretty badly. She wanted me to let you know that as soon as possible. What does she mean?"

"Damn, that dog was probably with Henny. I'll be there in a few minutes."

Henny heard a vehicle approaching. Hoping he would be rescued, he prepared to yell for help. When he heard the engine stop and the door open, he yelled out and kicked the inside of the trunk lid three times. The period of silence that followed told Henny, this wasn't help—this was his captor. He slid as far forward in the trunk as he possibly could, curling himself up, wanting to hide, and feeling helpless.

He could hear someone inserting a key into the lock of the trunk. "Listen, kid, you hear me?"

Henny didn't make a sound. He was too terrified to even breathe.

"Answer me, kid, or I'll start firing bullets into the trunk—see if that gets your attention. You still alive?"

Willing himself to reply, Henny squeaked, "Yeah, I'm still here."

"Okay, here's the deal, kid. I'm gonna open this trunk lid far enough to throw some food and water in, but that's all. You got it?"

No reply.

"I see any part of your body start coming out of the trunk, I'm slammin' the lid back down hard. You got that?"

Still no reply.

The trunk lid opened. The light was blinding to Henny. He felt something hit his knee. The trunk closed quickly, then after a few moments, opened again. This time a water bottle came flying in and the trunk lid slammed shut.

"Alright, eat that stuff, kid. It'll keep you alive for a while longer. But listen to me. You do anything stupid like try to get out of there, I'm gonna skin you alive. You want to live another day, you just lie there and be quiet. Hear me?"

Nearly a minute passed before Henny could hear anything else. He wondered what the guy was doing. Then he heard a door open and close, and he realized his captor was about to leave again. He yelled out in a hoarse voice, "Why, why am I in here? I'm sorry, I . . ."

But the engine drowned out his words as the vehicle accelerated, leaving him alone. Henny cried for a little bit, and then in the dark, he remembered the water. He felt around until he found the bottle. He removed the cap, took a little sip, and then drank thirstily—thinking he'd never tasted water so good. He felt around with his fingers until he had located a plastic container. Opening it, he felt a sandwich. Henny gobbled it up, took another drink of his water, and then rested his head on the spare tire, wondering what he should do next, why he was there, and what was going to happen to him.

Hawkett met Benjamin at the veterinarian's office, located just off the square. They were ushered into a back room by the receptionist. There, they found the vet, introducing himself as Doc Hamma, working on Tippy, lying on his side on the examination table.

"How bad is he? What happened?" Benjamin asked two questions at once.

"Well, he's going to live, that's the good news. He has some pretty severe trauma to the side of his head. Look, you can see the swelling, and his ear is badly discolored and swollen as well."

"You think he was run over?"

"No, I don't. For one thing, there are no tire marks or even tread smears, and the dog is not crushed. No broken ribs or pelvis, the kind of thing we often see in a dog run over by a vehicle. It just looks to me like he took a real hard blow to the side of the head. Maybe kicked, maybe struck with something, I don't know."

"How'd he get here?" asked Hawkett.

"Mailman dropped him off. Saw him while he was walking his route. The pup was really just down the street I guess. Out in that alley behind Temple Street. I read the name on the collar and called Jamie. Says she'll be right in. Oh, and she said the dog is deaf, wondering if that's why he'd gotten run over. Everybody's assuming the pup was run over, but again, I don't think that's the case. I think he just got struck, I don't know how or why, but looking at his head, that ear, that's my guess."

"Temple Street? Doesn't that run right behind the funeral home?" Hawkett asked.

"It sure as hell does," answered Benjamin with a grim look on his face.

CHAPTER
34

In the Sheriff's office, Jan observed Benjamin and Hawkett, both working the phones and demanding information. The tone of their voices gave her new insight into their respective personalities, and showed her a side of them she hadn't seen before. She wondered what it was going to take to repair the damage done to their relationship with the sheriff's department of the neighboring county, stemming from the verbal berating Benjamin was giving the person on the other end of the phone line. She knew that the sheriff was tired and irritable from lack of sleep, but she also knew that his real worry was Henny.

Benjamin slammed the phone down, "No leads, and not one son-of-a-bitching idea where Roydel went or what he left in. Nobody even knows what type of vehicle to be looking for." He was frowning and tapping his fingers on his desk, wanting to be doing something but not sure what.

Hawkett hung up the phone. "Okay, I convinced the DCI that this is a lot bigger problem down here, and they agreed to send somebody."

"Send somebody!" Benjamin interrupted him. "What in the hell will that do? We may have an abducted boy, maybe worse—and they're gonna send somebody?"

Hawkett interrupted now. "Listen to me, okay? We've notified all the adjoining counties in Iowa and Missouri. We've notified the Highway Patrol, the State DCI, and the FBI. That's the first step. Get people thinking about Roydel. Somebody will see something, hear something, I don't know. But it's only a matter of time 'til we get Roydel."

"Okay, okay, I know. Calm down and do my job," Benjamin said. "What else do we need to be doing here in Taylor County? Right now, where should we be searching?"

"Well, we probably should go out and look around Roydel's trailer, search the buildings out there," Jan said. "I really, really doubt he'd go back there, but, you know, the guy's a criminal and criminals do stupid things."

"Yeah, I can't believe he'd go back there again. I mean, after last time . . . " Benjamin was having a flashback of Roydel racing at him with his car and how he had had to fire his gun. He reached down and rubbed his sore knee. Apparently it wasn't much of an injury, unless the pain pills he was taking were a heck of a lot stronger than he realized. "Hawkett, can you do that? Run out to Roydel's place and look around? I just know he, or rather, they I guess, won't go there. Still somebody should look.

"Yeah, sure, I'll run right out. We've got no search warrant. You want one?"

"No, unless you see something right away, then back out of there and call me. I'll get the search warrant and bring the troops."

"Gotcha."

"Jan, you're going to meet with the county volunteer deputies over lunch," Benjamin was looking at the clock. "Well hell, it'll be noon in ten minutes. You haven't met with them already, have you?" he asked.

"No, I'd better get going. We're meeting in the back room of June's Restaurant. The county will buy their lunch the way we do every time they meet. You okay with that?"

"Oh yeah, yeah. I mean them being volunteers and all. But listen, bring them up to speed on things with Henny being missing, okay? Tell them we may have to pull them off this celebration thing to help look for him."

"Consider it done, Sheriff," Jan said.

She was gathering her things and getting ready to leave for the meeting, when Benjamin stopped her. "Listen, one more thing. The Sheriff's Department always has a car in the parade right?"

"Yeah, every year. We usually drive our best vehicle, which would be yours. Somebody needs to make sure it's washed before the parade. You want me to do that?"

"If you have time. You'll probably be the one driving it. We can trade cars if I need a set of wheels. But listen. If by parade time . . . what . . . six o'clock . . . if we haven't found Henny, I want you to be doing a broadcast over the car's loud speaker during the parade—asking for help. We'll come up with what we're going to say later this afternoon, but there could be a couple of thousand people around town, especially at the parade, and that'd be a good way to get more help."

"I agree, Sheriff. We maybe can talk about that later. Hopefully it won't be necessary. Hopefully the boy will show up, but either way, I've got to get going."

Hawkett stood up, still looking at the notes on the desk he'd been using, then turned to Benjamin. "Guess I'll head out to Roydel's."

They could hear Jan's voice out in the hall, "Right in there."

Hal Dallis came walking into the office. Benjamin's first thought was, "What the hell does this guy want?" He didn't want to deal with Hal, remembering the bad first impression he'd made on Benjamin in their initial interview. Then he remembered their phone conversation and asking Hal to stop in when he was in town for the parade. Hal nodded, and Benjamin turned to Hawkett, "This is the farm manager who's in charge of renting out about half of the farmland in southern Iowa." He smiled at Hal as he said it.

"Glad to meet you, Hal," Hawkett said as he reached out to shake hands with Hal. "Is what the Sheriff says true? You the man who controls the land? Hey that almost rhymes. Makes a good slogan for your company."

"Yeah, yeah, real funny. But no, I'm just a small time guy. I manage less than twenty thousand acres, nothing like the really big firms take care of."

"All of it in Taylor County?" Hawkett asked.

"Oh no. Those farms are located in six different counties, but a good share of it's in Taylor County. I mean it's no secret that I represent a really big investor who has over three thousand acres of farmland in this county alone."

"Does this investor own farmland that you manage in any other counties?" Hawkett was intrigued by this whole farm ownership/farm management thing.

"Yes, this investor owns . . . oh, let me think . . . probably almost eight thousand acres spread over three adjoining counties."

"Man," Hawkett was attempting to do the math in his head. "And eight thousand times two hundred and twenty five dollars an acre rent paid by the farmers, what's that, nearly two million dollars of income."

"Yeah, but first, for the record, we're not renting any land over two hundred dollars an acre—trying to hold down the cost for our clients. And secondly, just try to imagine the dollars of farm payments, land improvement, and taxes my clients are pumping into southern Iowa. I mean, you think about it, it's a massive flood of economic development dollars coming into your area."

"Yeah," Benjamin tried to keep a note of irritation out of his voice. He was wanting to be rid of his guest, as he was still not sure he cared much for him. "Well again, what can we do for you? We're not looking for any farmland to rent . . . "

"Yeah, well first of all, I came down here to drive my pickup in your parade, throw a little candy out to the crowd, try and generate some good public relations for our company. Having one of our farmers killed on a property we manage is not good advertising, if you know what I mean."

"Yeah, sure, we understand," Benjamin said.

"Anyway, while I was here, I thought I'd go out and fill in that hole that you guys dug the murdered guy out of."

"Carl Smith," Benjamin interjected. He felt as though the deceased deserved some respect as opposed to being referred to as "the murdered guy".

"Yeah," Hal replied with a slight irritation in his voice. "Yeah, Carl. Anyway, sooner or later, somebody's going to run into that hole. Somebody out driving around on their ATV or some kids tearing around, I don't know. People have been messing around that site. Anyway, I was wondering if it was okay if I took the company's backhoe and filled that damned hole in?"

"Well . . ." Benjamin started to reply, not really having thought about it one way or the other. "Well, I suppose it would be okay to fill the hole, clean things up out there. It is a crime scene, but we destroyed any plausible evidence the night we dug Carl up. Too many people reacting too fast. There's probably no more evidence to be gained. Yeah, I think it'd be okay for you to fill in the hole."

"About the backhoe," Hawkett interrupted them. "Do all farm management firms furnish those things for their clients? I mean didn't somebody say it was used by your clients to . . .what . . . fix terraces, dig up broken tile lines, that kind of thing?"

"Yeah, that's right. We actually have two of them. The farmers who use them have to sign a disclaimer and furnish their own fuel. But, no, I don't know of other firms loaning them out like we do. I do think it's one of the better ideas Iowa LandCo came up with. I mean, when a terrace gets washed out, or a tile line gets plugged, it can take us weeks to get a contractor there to fix it. Most of these farmers will do it as soon as they can, and it's been a terrific selling point for letting the company manage people's farms."

"And you guys don't rent any land for over two hundred dollars an acre, huh? Tell me, Hal, how high are some of the competitors renting out land?"

"Well, I can't confirm it, but I've heard of some of these guys getting up to three hundred dollars an acre. Can you believe it? I don't know. We've held the line so far, but if my investors start hearing of these kinds of prices, they're going to be after me to raise rents too." Hal was shaking his head as if to say it was all beyond his control.

Benjamin had had enough of this chit-chat. They had a missing boy to find. "Well, go ahead, fill in the hole, get your backhoe out of there, and hey, enjoy the parade, okay?"

Henny lay there thinking about how uncomfortable he was and that it was time to quit feeling sorry for himself and do something. He decided to try and move some of the junk lying on the floor of the trunk, slide it over to the side and out of his way, and carve out a smooth place to lie flat.

There was some light filtering through the cracks of the trunk lid, but it was still dark, and he had to rely on feel. He got hold of a couple of wood blocks, something that felt greasy, the trash from his sandwich, and the empty water bottle. He shoved them over into the corner by one of the tail lights. Then he took off his sweatshirt to use it

183

for a pillow.

He felt along the bottom of the trunk one more time for foreign objects before lying down and cried out when his hand struck a sharp object. He carefully picked it up. As he felt it, he tried to identify what it was. It felt like a knife blade without a handle and suddenly his hopes soared.

He couldn't kick his way through the back seat of the car, but maybe he could hack his way through with the knife blade. Using his sweatshirt as a handle, he gripped the knife and went to work, hacking through the material that made up the back seat of the car.

CHAPTER 35

Roydel woke with a start, struggling to gather his senses and remember where he was and what he was doing. Staring up at the ceiling, he was only able to see out of one eye. That really brought things into focus for him. Yeah, he thought, that's funny. One eye. Focus. He'd have to tell Erlene that one.

Then that got him to thinking, what if he had his .22 and was about to shoot a nice fat red squirrel setting up in an oak tree? How would that work if a guy only had one eye? Trying to imagine himself peeking down the barrel. Would having only his right eye cause him to shoot to the left of the target? Would he have to compensate? Damn. He was getting a headache trying to figure it out. Maybe it'd be better to just use a shotgun and pick out a few pellets when he was eating the squirrel.

Feeling the need to take a leak, he gingerly rolled over to his side and tried to see where Erlene was. He would need her to help him get to the bathroom. Well, he thought, he'd been able to hit the toilet every time, that was probably a good sign.

As he rolled over, he gasped. Surprised to see two kids standing there, staring at him, not saying a word.

"What're you kids doin'? Shouldn't you be in school or somethin'?"

"Momma home-schools us," the girl said. Although she was quite thin, she was a cute little thing. She was not as homely as her younger brother, who Roydel thought, clearly had been eating way too many cheeseburgers and fries. The kid was pretty darned plump.

"Home-school, you say? How's that go? You don't get on the bus or nothin'? Just roll out of bed and ma says, 'Okay class, today we're goin' to study elephants, do some math, light up a Bunsen burner . . .' Huh?"

Well hell, Roydel thought, these people were already chemists. Thinking of the combination of drugs they put together, getting their meth manufactured. These kids probably had quite an advantage over regular school kids, in the chemistry part anyway. But boy, they could sure use some clean clothes.

"What happened to your eye, mister?" Both kids stared at him with unpleasant looks on their faces, and suddenly Roydel felt very self-conscious and irritable.

"Hey, why don't you little home-schoolers go find your momma and learn something about respect, okay? Be a good English assignment for you. Both of you can write a thousand word paper about respect."

Neither of the children replied, but just stood there staring at him.

"Hey, get out of here. Find Erlene. Tell her that her patient is needing some assistance pretty quick, okay? You two do know Erlene, right? She's that gal that brought me here. Where the hell is she at anyway?"

The little girl spoke again, "She's smokin' with Mom."

"Smokin' what? It'd better be nothin' stronger than weed." Roydel repeated his question, "I said, smokin' what?" The tone of Roydel's voice was turning angry and the kids were sensing it.

"She's got her pipe, ya know . . ."

"Pipe? Girl, you better hope she's smoking tobacco in that pipe or else . . ."

By then he was talking to their fleeting backs. The two kids had beat it out of there, having evidently learned in their home-schooling— there was a time to get out of the room fast, and that's just what they

186

did.

He lay there for a while, got himself turned over on his other side, and stared out a dirty window. He thought to himself, as he repeatedly had for the last twenty-four hours, what a dump the place was. But, he'd not known where else to hide quickly, so, lying in the back of Erlene's stolen mini van, he'd directed her to drive him to his meth supplier's place just over the Missouri line.

They'd offered the man five hundred dollars to put them up for a couple of days—no questions asked. They'd told him, "it was the least he could do, them bein' business partners as such . . ." The meth-head had stood there, staring at Roydel's face, trying to act as if he was considering their request, acting as if he even had the ability to think coherently. Roydel had thought that he was going to have to use the spare gun Erlene had found hidden at his place and put it up alongside the guy's head before asking him again. But no, that'd not been necessary.

Erlene had peeled the five hundred out of her purse and held it out in front of her, and the guy had said, "Okay, two days, no more," then snatched the bills out of her hand and headed back out behind his house somewhere.

Roydel heard footsteps coming up the stairs. "Erlene, that you?"

"Comin' baby."

She walked in, gave him a lazy smile and said, "How you doin', baby? Need some more pain pills. We got plenty, don't worry. This place here is a regular drug store," laughing as she said it.

Roydel watched her moving about the room, quicker than her normal self. "Erlene, honey, please tell me you've not taken up smoking meth, because if you have, I'm afraid I'm gonna have to leave you right here. If you're smokin' that crap, you belong right here with these losers who are makin' it. Please tell me you're not."

She glanced at him, turned away, and quickly walked over to the window. She looked out and said, "Hey, I'm hitting it a little, Roydel, but it's no big deal. I've got it under control. I just need some to take the edge off you know."

"Erlene. Hey look at me, woman!" That got her attention as she came back over, and sat down in the folding chair by his bed. She kept moving her hands up and down, touching her face, her hair, and he knew she was high on meth. He'd seen it so many times. "Erlene, there is no such thing as little when you're talking about this shit. Man, who got you started on this stuff? How long's this been goin' on?"

"I don't know. After I left with that guy . . . you know, Eddy. Eddy used it all the time. I started trying a little, you know?"

"Eddy, who the hell is Eddy? Is that the dumb-ass trucker you ran off with?"

"Yeah," her head bobbed up and down an excessive number of times as she felt the drugs bounce in her system.

Roydel stared at her with his one good eye, feeling the Nuxton rage come upon him, thinking he needed to hit somethin' and it probably ought to be Erlene. He needed to knock some sense into the woman. "Where's your boy, Eddy, now? He dump you off at a truckstop? Got tired of you? Your new-found hobby too expensive to support for the both of you?"

"Roydel, you ought not talk to me like that. I mean I came runnin' when I heard you was hurt, didn't I? Made myself into a wanted felon now, helpin' you break out of that hospital, bringin' you here?"

"I got a feelin', Erlene, you didn't come runnin' to help me. Hell, you was probably already coming back to me 'cause you was thrown out by your last boyfriend. Needed someone to finance your new habit. You just happen to show up when I was in a corner. Needed the help."

"Roydel, you was always my man, you know that. All the way back to grade school, you was always the one . . ."

"Shut-up, Erlene. Help me get to the bathroom, woman. See if you can find any soap around this place so I can wash up a bit. We got a couple of things to do, then we're headin' for Arkansas."

"Are you sure this is what you want to do—lead the colt? I mean most kids your age will be riding their bikes in the parade. We could get yours out and decorate it, hang some streamers on it, some balloons maybe?"

"No, Mom, I want to lead Frisky in the parade. Okay?" Andrea was annoyed that her mother kept challenging her on this issue.

"Okay, but I'm going to have to walk along beside you, just to be safe you know. Frisky's a good colt, but he might get spooked. You never know."

"No, Mom. I can lead him by myself."

"No, the deal is, if you want to lead Frisky in the parade today, you're going to have to let me walk alongside. I'll try to stay a little ways away, but I'm going to be there, just in case. Deal?"

"Alright," again she responded with an annoyed tone in her voice.

Jamie stepped back and inspected the colt. She liked what she saw. His hair coat had a nice healthy shine, and his mane was brushed out. He *should* look good, she thought. He'd come from a good pedigree and had been fed and handled properly. Then her thoughts drifted to another horse she'd owned and ridden for years. It had given its life to save her daughter, not three months ago. She thought of the incident, her riding the horse that way, and what she'd had to do.

Damn, she did not want to go there and told herself—that's enough of that. She reached down and picked up each of the colt's legs to inspect the hooves. Yep, the colt was in fine condition and would look good in the parade. Too bad he was too young to be ridden yet. She'd rather lead Frisky with Andrea riding—maybe have some cute outfit on her daughter, something matching the colt. That'd be fun, but it would have to wait until next year's parade.

"Okay, we've got to get moving, Andrea. There's a lot to be done before we head into town for the parade, and you've got to do your share, or else . . . well you know . . ."

"Yeah, yeah, I know. We don't get to go. You want me to gather the eggs and feed the chickens. What else?"

"Put Frisky back in his stall for now, but be careful, okay? Give him one slice of hay, and make sure he has some water too."

"Sure, Mom."

Andrea took Frisky's lead rope from Jamie and started leading the colt towards the barn, then stopped. She turned and looked at her mother. "Mom, what do we do if we see Hawkett?"

"What do you mean, what do we do?"

"I mean, is it okay if I talk to him?"

"Yeah sure, Andrea. That's fine. Why wouldn't it be okay to talk to him?"

"Well, you know, he's like my friend and you hate his guts now."

"Andrea, I do not hate Adam Hawkett's guts. Where did you get that idea?"

"Well, he was living with us, and he's my best friend in the whole world, and now you won't let him live here no more, and now I'm never gonna have him for my dad anymore in my whole life."

Jamie was speechless. She stood there watching her daughter hold the colt. Andrea had begun to cry a little as she turned back toward the barn and began leading the colt again.

"Andrea, stop." Jamie caught up with her daughter and gently took the lead rope away from her. "Listen to me. I don't hate Hawkett. It's just that he and I don't share some of the same values. Do you remember what values are? What I told you?"

"Yeah, Mom. Being honest, treating people with respect . . ."

"That's right, kiddo. Well, I mean . . ." She thought to herself, how do I explain this to a kid? "I think that if a man and woman are in love, they should get married. You understand, don't you?"

"Yeah, and if you guys would get married then we could be a family again and . . ."

Jamie interrupted her, "That's the problem, Andrea. Adam doesn't want to get married. He just wants to live here—be a part of us but not really a part of us. You understand that?" Jamie wanted to say, be a part of us like when you were born and your daddy lived here as my husband, but she knew that would bring up questions of the suicide and complicate the whole issue. "You know his first wife came back here, and I'm not sure he's not still in love with her, so . . ." she stopped. How could she explain this all to a five year-old when she didn't even understand it herself? "Listen, quit worrying about it. You know I love you more than anything else in the world, right?"

"Sure, Mom." The tears seemed to be drying as Jamie knelt down, still holding the colt's lead rope, and felt him nuzzle the back of her head as she hugged Andrea close to her. "Go finish your chores, little one. We have a parade to get to."

Hawkett had been all over Roydel's little paradise. He'd searched the trailer house twice, along with all the other buildings. He'd found absolutely no trace of Roydel or his girlfriend. This was no big surprise. The crime scene tape was still draped across the driveway. Roydel's car was still in the ditch where he'd wrecked it. Hawkett walked back to the patrol pickup, then stopped and surveyed the scene, wondering what he might have missed. Something was bothering him, but what?

It was the car. The trunk lid was open. They'd searched it the night of the confrontation, after sending Roydel off in the ambulance, but hadn't they left the trunk lid closed? He could have sworn that he had personally slammed the lid down, after looking inside the trunk, and stuck the keys back into the ignition. Good place for the keys, he'd thought. Nobody was going to drive off in a car that had the front end smashed in.

He ducked under the crime scene tape again and walked back to the wrecked car. Another small mystery became apparent. Not only was the trunk lid open, but there was some garbage inside—an empty plastic water bottle and some other debris, that would have been bagged up as evidence if it had been there before.

As he leaned down he thought that he could smell urine. Hawkett shook his head. It was probably kids getting their kicks out of messing around with the car, he thought. But, would they urinate in the trunk? Man, kids these days—just no respect for anything.

CHAPTER
36

Henny gave up. He'd been hacking on the back of the car seat for almost an hour, stirring up dust and foam particles, making the air in the trunk hard to breathe. He'd managed to break through the seat, but there was something on the other side, and he was pretty sure it was chunks of concrete piled in the seat. Now he knew why he hadn't been able to kick through the seat and why he probably wouldn't be able to cut through it either. He lay silently, covering his mouth and nose with his hand, trying to keep the dust out of his lungs. His laboring had caused him to become very thirsty but his water bottle was empty.

After a bit, he fell asleep and dreamed. He was dreaming of being at Jamie's farm—helping her feed her sheep. Then the dream moved to her house and he was sitting at her table, eating mashed potatoes with gravy and taking big drinks of cold milk. Jamie was telling him he could drink all the milk he wanted and never stop. Then for some reason, someone started pounding on the table and yelling at him. He woke with a start.

"Hey kid, say something. You okay? Answer me or I'm gonna

start shootin' bullets into the trunk. Hurry up!"

"Yeah, I'm here," his voice croaked. "I need some water, I'm thirsty," he said, then added, "please."

There was a moment of silence, and then he heard a key going into the lock. Henny was thinking, thank God, I'm going to get out of here. But the trunk didn't open.

"Listen to me, kid. You know what insurance is?"

Henny had no idea what he was talking about.

"Answer me kid. You know what insurance is?"

"No."

"You don't? Well hell. Anyway kid, what you are is insurance. If things don't work out for me, I may have to use your life for insurance. Otherwise I would have shot you already, you understand?"

Henny didn't answer, then jumped as he heard the guy's hand slap the outside of the trunk. "Do I understand what?"

"Oh damn. All right kid. Here's what you need to know to stay alive. I'm gonna open this trunk lid and let you out. But you better keep your eyes shut, you hear? Or I'm gonna shoot you dead right there in that trunk. You understand?"

"Yeah, sure. I understand."

"Okay, here goes." Slowly the lid started to open, and before he shut his eyes completely, Henny looked down and saw the guy's feet. He saw his shoes and remembered them vividly. They were the same shoes he'd seen on the guy who shoved the body into the hole only a few nights earlier. Trembling with fear, then succumbing to panic, Henny fainted.

Benjamin stood on the steps of the courthouse, watching as the town filled with people. Vendors were igniting their grills and the smell of the smoke was a delicious aroma on a beautiful fall afternoon. People were unloading horses to ride in the parade and a steady stream of antique cars and tractors were being driven or hauled into town. Some small amusement rides were being set up for the kids, along with a dunk tank to be used to raise money for the fire department. Band members were tuning their horns. It looked like a great time to be a member of this community.

Still, he continued to worry about Henny, and his thoughts were

193

filled with dread. He sighed, wishing things were different. Wishing for just a moment that he wasn't the sheriff and there wasn't a missing boy to worry about. He wished that he could enjoy the beautiful fall day, the town festival, and walk among the people, shaking hands and tasting their wares. He wished he could watch the parade, maybe even take a few pictures on his camera. Then, bringing himself back into focus, he remembered who he was and what needed to be done, what he'd always done—his lot in life.

"Sheriff, we just had a call from someone driving into town from the south, coming up the highway. Said they think they saw a body floating in the river by the bridge," Jan's voice was choking with emotion.

"Oh no, no. Where's Hawkett?"

"Here. Let's go," Hawkett hustled out the door past Jan. "We've got to take Jan's car, she's going to use yours for the parade. Okay, Jan?"

"Sure, sure, get going. Here are the keys. Call me the minute you know, please."

They left town at a high rate of speed, with lights flashing and the siren blaring. They reached the river bridge in only a few minutes. Both men jumped out of the car and rushed to the side of the bridge. Seeing nothing, they crossed to the other side.

"There, against the piling. Something's there, what is it?"

Benjamin was praying to himself as they worked their way down the steep embankment, and thanking God when he could tell for sure that the object was not human. It was a dead deer floating in the water, wedged amongst the debris with a broken arrow shaft protruding from its side.

"Okay, false alarm. We'll call the game warden and have him take care of this corpse. I have no idea what they do with them."

Benjamin called Jan on his radio upon arriving at the car and could hear the relief in her voice. She thanked him twice for letting her know. He asked her to call the game warden and turn the problem over to him. They drove back into town. Both men were feeling great relief that it hadn't been Henny's body in the water, but also anxiety, knowing that they'd wasted time in this trip and the boy still hadn't been accounted for.

Coming out of another dream, Henny was completely disoriented. He had no idea where he was. Still in the trunk? Things felt different. It was darker and much smaller than the trunk and much colder. It felt like he was lying on a curved metal surface. In a panic, he waved his arms and legs about, trying to define the boundaries of his space, trying to figure out where he was.

He could see a small ray of light, and, with some effort, contorted his body so that his head was nearer to it. He investigated the hole. It was about two inches in diameter and appeared to go straight up, but to where? Feeling panic, he realized where he was. He was buried underground in a metal barrel and the opening was a pipe that went above ground so he wouldn't suffocate.

Overcome with terror, Henny began to scream into the pipe. Hearing his hoarse voice crying out, he realized he was yelling to no one.

Never had he felt so desperate, so alone. Henny started shaking. He wrapped his arms around himself and curled up into the fetal position. Feeling claustrophobic and breathing hard, he stretched out his legs and kicked at the top of the barrel a couple of times, but panicked when dirt started spilling in through the jagged hole around the air pipe. He curled up and tried to calm himself, wondering over and over, who was doing this and why were they doing it to him. Then he remembered the feet, the shoes—that he was a witness.

Jamie stood beside her pickup. She looked in the side-view mirror, realizing that she was more worried about her own appearance than that of her daughter and the colt who were to be in the parade. She felt insecure and didn't like it one bit. She knew it was all about Hawkett's former wife and how she looked. She started to roll these thoughts around her head and then stopped—thinking enough was enough. No more debating with herself and getting all worked up. It was simple. She was deeply in love with Adam Hawkett, wanted to spend the rest of her life with him, and wanted him to be Andrea's father.

All right, maybe they didn't have to be married. Maybe they could figure it out some other way. Hell, she thought, thousands and thousands of couples did. Okay, then what was she going to say to him if they met on the street during the parade? She thought about that for a few moments, but came up blank. She'd just like to walk up to the guy, wrap her arms around him, tell him she loved him and let it happen. Or not . . . visualizing herself on Main Street in Pigmy, hugging a guy in front of her neighbors, and then having him say to her, "Sorry, Jamie, but it's Ann you know, she's come back into my life . . ."

"Mom," Andrea interrupted her mother's daydreaming. "The people called again about Tippy. They want to know when are we going to pick him up. The lady said to tell you they're going to shut down for the parade so we better hurry up or else they'll keep him all night. I think she said something about that would cost you more money. Okay?"

"Oh yeah, the vet's office. Sure, we'd better get going. You got your things, your allowance—just in case you want to ride some of the rides or anything?"

"Yep, got it all, Mom. Can't wait to get on the air-slide."

"Okay, load up, kiddo. Let's get into town, pick up Tippy, and get lined up for the parade."

The veterinarian gave Jamie his theory about Tippy's injuries, still believing that the pup had been struck by some object or maybe kicked in the side of the head. They were upset, but thankful they had the pup back, and it appeared he'd heal from the injuries. Jamie gathered him up in her arms and carried him to their pickup parked behind the vet clinic. People were lining up for the parade less than a block away so it seemed like a good place to leave the trailer, and the vet was happy to let her park there.

They unloaded the colt and brushed him a little. Jamie handed Andrea his lead rope and started walking with the pair towards the other parade participants. They'd not gone ten yards when Tippy, sitting up in the seat of the pickup and watching them walk away, lifted his head and began to howl in distress. He was making quite a racket, so Jamie turned around. She took the lead rope from Andrea, led the colt back to the side of the pickup, opened the door, and tried to calm the pup.

After a short while, Tippy, satisfied that they were back, lay down on the seat again. Jamie closed the door and started to lead the colt away, but sure enough, Tippy had his front paws up on the steering wheel and was once again howling at the top of his lungs.

Now what? She couldn't take him back into the vet clinic. They were locking up as she'd left with Tippy. There was no time to take him home, and she hated to leave the little guy out there anyway—locked in a pen—howling. She was wondering who she could leave him with when, just on cue, the Oldhams came driving up the street in Thelma's large Oldsmobile. Jamie flagged them down and explained her dilemma.

Thelma didn't respond right away. Looking at the pup, she wondered just what they were going to do. They had planned on sitting in their special spot right in front of the drug store. She had wanted to hurry up and get their lawn chairs there before anybody got their spot. But Pearl—bless her heart, thought Jamie—jumped out of the car, hustled around to their pickup, and picked up the pup. She assured Jamie she'd look after him and told her not to worry, but to get going, as the parade was forming.

CHAPTER
37

Benjamin and Hawkett were standing by Jan's patrol car, getting ready to walk into the courthouse, when they became intrigued by a man and a woman unloading a large number of dogs from a trailer. The sign on the side of the trailer said, THE BAKER'S TWENTY DOG HITCH. The couple was busy hooking the Huskies together in order to pull a miniature covered wagon. The two men were amazed at how well the dogs were behaving and continued to watch the phenomenon, when Benjamin's cell phone rang and pulled them out of their trance.

He retrieved his cell phone from his pocket and, seeing it was Jan, answered it. "What's up?"

"We've got a guy here, says he's a courier delivering information from the State's DCI. Says you have to sign for it. I can't."

"Oh yeah, that'd be those cell phone records from Carl Smith's and Roydel's phones. About time. Yeah, I'll be right in. We're just right out here on the sidewalk."

Both men walked into the courthouse and down the steps to the Sheriff's Office, and there found the courier. Benjamin, after having produced identity, was allowed to sign for the documents. He took them and handed them to Jan, who quickly opened the envelope and started studying the papers.

"Okay, here's Carl Smith's cell phone records for the two days before his body was found." Jan said. "And here's Roydel's from the phone we confiscated at the time of his arrest. Hawk, you want to take Roydel's? Here's a highlighter. Identify any special calls. I don't know, maybe they're all special. This is pretty neat; they've identified the name of every person calling or being called and from what tower the call was relayed. It gives you some idea where people were. Wow!"

Hawkett pulled a chair up next to her desk and sat across from Jan. After a quick scan of the list of people that had communicated with Roydel's phone, he was immediately surprised. "Okay, what in the hell would Roydel be doing talking to Hal Dallis late at night—I mean near midnight—just last Thursday. Let's see. Yeah . . . and then again Sunday afternoon . . . at 3:35. That call lasted just over a minute. What the hell would those two be talking about?"

"Well," said Benjamin, "we know that Roydel's done some trucking for Carl Smith in the past. I don't know, could there be some connection there, maybe the backhoe? I suppose Roydel could run the backhoe. Maybe ran it for Carl sometime in the past. I don't know," Benjamin shook his head. "Better visit with Hal and find out, probably nothing, but still we need to know."

"I've got a call on my list here," said Jan. "Let's see, Carl Smith, on the day he died, talked to Hal, too." She looked up at Benjamin, a look of concern on her face.

Benjamin shrugged, "Again, could be explained easily enough. I mean, there's the connection of the backhoe. Maybe some other farmer needed it. And I think he told me they get together a couple of times a year to discuss cash rents, lease terms, that kind of thing. I mean it's what a farm manager does—talks to his farmers, right?"

"Yeah, but still, we got Hal talking to the murder victim the day he was murdered, and we got Hal talking to the guy we figure murdered Carl—a little over a day after we find Carl buried? Yeah, maybe it's nothing, but like you say, Hal needs to kind of fill in the blanks here for us."

"Well, Hal is in town now, we know that. He was washing his company pickup at the carwash when we went by on our way back into town. Getting ready for the parade I suppose," Hawkett said.

"Yeah, we'll visit with him before the day is out, maybe catch up with him right after the parade," Benjamin replied. "Pretty hard to imagine he's up to much mischief if he's brazen enough to drive through town in the parade."

"You guys got any more names you can give me from that information?" Benjamin asked. Neither person replied, still intently studying the phone records. "Jan, you've got to get going, the parade is going to start in just a little bit. We need your smiling face driving my shiny car to put forth our best image. And please don't forget to broadcast that we're looking for Henny, a couple of times during the route, okay?"

"Don't worry, Sheriff, I will," she replied without looking up, still studying phone numbers. "There was only one other number on the sheet that they were unable to identify. The contact is listed as 'Sweet Thing' in Roydel's cell-phone directory, but the notation says that the DCI was unable to determine who that person was."

"Sweet Thing?" Hawkett said, "That would be Roydel's girl-friend, Erlene, no doubt."

"Give me her phone number," Benjamin said, and as Jan read the number off, Benjamin punched it in his cell phone.

Roydel was feeling just pretty darn good, sitting out in the warm sun on a picnic table at a rest stop along the interstate. They were taking a break from their hard drive south, less than a hundred miles from Pine Bluff, Arkansas, where Roydel had a friend who'd put them up—no questions asked. He was feeling pretty good about Erlene, the way she was helping him, but feeling bad about some of the hard things he'd said to her about smoking meth.

Still, when he needed her, she'd come through, got his ass out of that hospital and the woman had had enough sense to locate pain-killers and antibiotics to carry him through. She'd followed his directions perfectly, returning to his trailer and finding his backup gun and hidden stash of money in an envelope—over twenty thousand dollars. She could have run with the money and she hadn't. So now he was a long way from Taylor County and was feeling pretty good, riding high on the hydrocodone pills Erlene had stolen from the hospital. He was even learning how to appreciate the world with the handicap of only one eye.

Erlene changed the bandages for him a couple times a day, and damn if she wasn't getting pretty good at it. He'd watched her face closely, and she never even changed expressions while looking at the mangled side of his face. She'd even said that he was going to look pretty "bad ass" when everything healed up. Roydel imagined himself walking into a bar, people turning to look at the one eye, wondering what that "mean sumbitch" did to let that happen and all the stories he could make up.

He was thinking to himself, this could be fun, the new Roydel Nuxton. He thought of the little "groupie chicks" it might turn on, seeing "Old One-Eye" or better yet, he could get himself a patch to put over the eye—kinda like that cowboy from the movies. What was his name? Rooster, yeah Rooster Cogburn—the guy John Wayne played. He may even get himself a cowboy hat, tilt it down over the scarred side of his face, then casually lift it to get the shock value. He smiled to himself as he imagined it.

He took a long drink from the cold can of root beer Erlene had pulled out of the cooler for him. He watched the trucks and cars fly down the interstate—everybody in a hurry to get somewhere. Erlene, typical for Erlene, was in no hurry. She'd been in the restroom for going on twenty minutes. She was probably fixing herself up. The woman liked to keep up her appearances for her man. Roydel liked that. He thought to himself, once they got to Pine Bluff, he'd take her out to a nice restaurant, then go somewhere and buy her some new clothes—take care of her for taking care of him.

He frowned. The one dark spot on the horizon was her newfound love of meth. But surely he could help her get past that bad shit. There had to be a way. He might have to lock her up in a basement for a month, not wanting to do it, but knowing it was for her own good. And, he thought, he had to be a realist. She might not be able to beat the need for the drug. If that turned out to be the case, he would have to dump her somewhere, knowing how fast she'd go downhill and what a liability she'd be. There was just no future for a meth-head.

He hoped it didn't come to that. He thought grimly of what she might tell the authorities if he did dump her, and realized, if worse came to worse, he might have to put a bullet in her and dump her somewhere in deep water. He shook his head. He really shouldn't put the worst possible view on things when they were currently going so well. He was interrupted in his thoughts by Erlene's cell phone ringing in his pocket.

201

He had forgotten that she'd even given it to him.

Roydel pulled the phone out, wondering who in the world would be calling her. Erlene had sworn that nobody in the world had the number but him. Well he might as well find out, he thought to himself. It was probably some supplier wanting to sell her some product, and he'd sure as hell put an end to that. "Yeah, hello."

The voice on the other end sounded familiar, but he couldn't quite place it. "Yes, hello. Uh . . . I believe I have called Erlene Bass's phone number. Am I correct?"

"That depends on who you are, and why you're callin'."

"I'm Sheriff Benjamin Willoughby, calling from Pigmy. Is this Roydel? Sure sounds like you, Roydel."

Damn, he thought to himself, wishing he hadn't answered the phone. What to do now? He didn't want to just hang up and let the sheriff think he was rattled. Well hell, he could handle this. He was a cool guy. "Yeah, Sheriff, it's me, your one-eyed friend. How's things in Pigmy? They had their parade yet? Believe I'm gonna have to miss it this year. Sorry if you were calling me to see if I'd ride in the prison wagon through the parade, let angry citizens throw rocks at me," Roydel smiled to himself as he made it up on the fly. He thought it was pretty clever and would no doubt piss off the sheriff.

"Well actually, Roydel, we'd rather have you as a guest in one of our jail cells here—skip the parade entirely. Where you at? When are you coming in to see us? Be better for you, Roydel, to turn yourself in. You know we'll find you sooner or later. Turn yourself in, and I'll try to help you plea bargain down your sentence."

"Ha! Sorry, Sheriff, but I'm a long, long ways from Taylor County. Pretty soon we're going to be visiting my friends in Toronto, and I promise you, you're never gonna find us up here. Millions of acres of timber and lakes—old Roydel can live off the land forever, you know." Roydel was thinking to himself how clever he was. It must be the pain pills—making stories up like this on the go—throwing the law off in the wrong direction.

"I don't doubt it for a minute, Roydel. But still we'll find you someday. Listen, I need some information right now, and you need to give it to me. People up here are worried sick about the boy. We need to know he's all right, or . . . well, we need to know where he is."

"Boy! What boy are you talkin' about?"

"Don't play games with me, Roydel. I'm talking about Henny. You know, the kid that saw you shoving Carl Smith into that hole. What'd you do to him, Roydel?"

Roydel was hearing a different tone in the sheriff's voice, and remembered what a mean-ass he could be. "Sheriff Benjamin . . . whatever . . . can't remember your last name. You listen to me, okay? I never did anything to any kid, and I never shoved Carl into that hole, you understand? You may have me for the shootin' at the convenience store at Clarinda, but that's it, you understand?" Roydel paused, building up a head of steam, "And listen to me Sheriff Ben-ja-min, when I get done healin' up a bit, I'm gonna come git you, you can count on it. You hear me?"

There was no immediate reply from the cell phone, and Roydel held it in front of his face, trying to see with his one eye if they were still connected. He watched the battery indicator make one last feeble warning, and the phone went dead.

Kid? What kid? Roydel thought to himself. What in the hell were they trying to pin on him now? He reached into his duffle bag, lying next to him, looking to see if Erlene might have stolen an extra battery for the phone. He'd give her a good chewin' if not—try to teach the woman how to do things correctly. He moved the envelope out of the way and was alarmed that it felt a little lighter than before. He grabbed the envelope and opened it, doing a quick count. He felt rage coming on Half the money was gone—nearly ten thousand dollars in cash, missing.

So what was the deal? His gun was there, his clothes, the dead cell phone. He looked up, scanning the area, and wondered where Erlene was and what she had to say for herself about the money. It'd better be pretty damn good or she was going to get a little black and blue.

As he glanced around, he just barely caught the back of Erlene's van, pulling onto the interstate and heading south without him.

CHAPTER
38

"Well damn," Benjamin said as he looked at his cell phone. "Either he hung up on me or his phone went dead. Or, I suppose it could be we just lost a signal. Maybe Roydel drove into a valley or something. I don't know." He rang the number again, and then two more times, and each time the call went right to voicemail, a generic voice asking him to leave a message. On the last try he did leave a message, "Roydel, call me."

"You sure it was Roydel?" Hawkett asked.

"Yeah, no doubt in my mind," Benjamin was still staring at his cell phone, wanting in the worst way to figure out how to talk to Roydel on it again—ask more questions. "Okay, he either can't or is refusing to talk to me."

"What did he say about Henny?"

"He said he didn't touch Carl Smith and said he had nothing to do with 'any missing kid'."

"You believe him?" asked Hawkett.

"Well . . .yeah. I mean the guy's probably a professional liar, but

I don't know, the way he came right back at me . . . yeah, it sounded like he didn't murder Carl."

"Then who? That would only leave Hal Dallis or Carl's wife, Emily, or maybe the pair of them. Unless we've got someone completely unknown in on this."

"Well yeah, and of course there's Josh Flora. I'm thinking he's a pretty unlikely candidate. Well, hell, none of them really seem likely," said Benjamin.

"Well the only loose end we have to work with now are these cell phone records, and they indicate we should talk to Hal Dallis. Maybe nothing there, but still, we need to visit with him."

"I agree completely. Let's see. Jan took off for the parade while I was on the phone, didn't she. Okay, then let's leave Cindy here to keep an eye on things, handle calls, and let's you and me head out into the street here, see the parade, find Hal, and have a talk with him."

The two men left the courthouse, watching the growing number of people filling up the town of Pigmy. The sidewalks were loaded with happy people—walking, looking, parking their lawn chairs—everybody jockeying for the best possible position to watch the parade.

"Hey, look there. See that group of people grilling burgers down the street?"

"Yeah," Hawkett replied.

"The taller guy on this end, a little younger than the rest of them, that's Josh Flora. We may have to visit with him before the day's over as well."

Benjamin asked Hawkett to head south a couple of blocks, as he would go north about the same distance—both of them on foot, but staying in touch with their hand-held radios.

Hawkett could just feel the energy and excitement in the air—people laughing, children bouncing around, musical instruments playing as the band came marching up the street. The band was followed by the local military reserve officers carrying a United States flag, and as they passed the crowd, a momentary hush came over everyone as they stood. Men took off their caps and many people put their hands over their hearts. Hawkett felt an immediate sense of pride to be working among people like this, glad to see them enjoying being together as a community at an event such as this one. He watched as Jan drove past in the Taylor County Sheriff's car with the lights flashing, and, every once in a while, she'd hit the siren. She spotted him and waved.

After Jan came the kids, riding their decorated bikes, pulling wagons, leading dogs—some dressed up in costumes. Hawkett smiled, and then he saw a lady walking with a youngster leading a young horse. He knew from a block away who it was. He felt his heart start to race, wondering what to do, playing it out in his mind. Should he just wave, be cool, try to stay neutral? Or should he walk away now, avoid the confrontation, and not risk upsetting the two people coming right toward him. Suddenly they were there, not ten yards away—Jamie, as beautiful as ever helping Andrea lead the colt along. They were smiling and waving at the crowd.

"Hey!" he surprised himself, shouting at them. Both females turned and looked right in his direction. Their smiles were replaced by looks of surprise, both sets of brown eyes were locked on him. Not knowing what to say, he smiled and waved, feeling horribly inadequate, and feeling as though he should have kept quiet.

Jamie stared at him as she stood there in the middle of the street petting the colt's head, and he thought she was going to say something. He was thinking—please say something, smile, anything. But then she felt the pressure of other people coming up behind them as the parade started to bunch up a little. She looked at him again and then headed off leading the colt. Andrea, waving as they left, turned her head and watched him as they walked on up the street.

What to think of that, he wondered, continuing to watch them until they were around the corner and out of his sight. He stood there in a trance, not noticing the people and cars going by, but instead thinking about the two people that meant everything to him.

Suddenly his trance was broken when a familiar pickup passed in front of him with "Iowa LandCo" written on the door and a phone number below the name. Hawkett recognized Hal waving at the crowd, throwing handfuls of candy to the kids on the sidewalk. This wasn't the place to stop him, but at least they knew where he was, and Benjamin was waiting towards the end of the parade. Hawkett was considering calling Benjamin on the radio, but instead he cut across the block and started walking to where the parade ended. He saw the telephone number again on the side of Hal's pickup and, just on a whim, pulled his cell phone out of his pocket and dialed the number.

After three rings a woman answered. "Hello, this is the Dallis residence, can I help you?"

"Oh, I'm sorry, I thought I was calling the offices of a firm called Iowa LandCo. I must have dialed the wrong number," thinking as he said it that it really didn't make sense.

"Oh, no, you want to talk to my husband Hal. He's not here right now. Would you like to leave a message?"

"No, my call was just actually . . . Well I was hoping to speak to one of the other staff members of Iowa LandCo. I had some questions to . . ."

She laughed into the receiver. "No, there is no other staff. Hal is Iowa LandCo. He's a one-man show. I know, funny isn't it? I mean the name sounds like this big outfit, but Hal likes it."

"You mean your husband, Hal, is the only person involved with Iowa LandCo Management? There are no other people, no other farm managers, no secretaries, just Hal?"

"Yes, I believe that's what I said," Hal's wife's tone was getting a little less friendly. "Now, could you tell me who you are and I'll have Hal call you back."

"Well actually, I'm here in Pigmy. I'm a deputy sheriff, and . . . well . . . Hal just went by me in the parade," Hawkett paused, thinking to himself how stupid that had sounded.

"Wait, is there some problem? I mean if you know where Hal is why did you call here?" She asked with a hint of nervousness in her voice.

"No, no problem, er . . . uh . . ."

She interrupted him, "We got that other thing all cleared up. Nobody filed charges. I hope you're not trying to stir things up again."

"What thing did you get cleaned up, I'm sorry but I don't quite understand . . ."

Mrs. Dallis interrupted him again. "Hey, I don't think I want to say any more. You want to talk to Hal, you go talk to Hal." Hawkett heard the phone slam down on a receiver.

Hawkett wondered what the heck that was all about. He became lost in thought as he tried to remember things Hal had said. Something about trying to hold down the cash rents, seeming to imply that there were other people working for Iowa LandCo. And the confusion about whether the cash rent was two-hundred dollars or two twenty-five? After all, twenty-five isn't much money, but when you multiply it times several thousand acres . . .

Hawkett, suddenly felt a coldness come over him. He had more questions that he needed answers to as he started moving up the street, wanting to find Hal and get some clarification on a few things right away.

Halfway up the block, in the middle of Main Street, Hawkett had to detour around a group of men and women. They were cooking hamburgers on a large portable grill, mounted on wheels and hooked to a pickup. It smelled delicious. Hawkett was wishing he had time to stop and buy one but figured he'd better keep moving when he practically ran into Josh Flora, wearing a cap and apron that said Taylor County Cattlemen on them.

"What?" Josh asked.

"No nothing, sorry. Just trying to work my way through the crowd. Sorry."

Hawkett started to move around Josh, then stopped, "Hey, Josh. Answer a stupid question for me, will you?"

"What?"

"We keep having these discussions about people wanting to rent the farm that Carl Smith was found on. You know . . . uh . . .buried. Anyway, I believe you used to farm it?"

"Yeah?"

Hawkett thought, this Josh is a man of few words. "Anyway, we always have this stupid question come up. Was it renting for two-hundred an acre or two twenty-five? I mean I know it sounds like a trivial . . ."

Josh interrupted him, "Hell, I offered him two hundred—even put it in writing, but he said the land owner he represented had to have two hundred twenty-five. And that's not all. To seal the deal, they wanted twenty-five dollars an acre right there on the spot—in cash. You ever heard of such a thing? The farm manager . . . what's his name? Dallis . . . yeah, Dallis . . . agreed with me. Said, yeah it was strange, but his client who owned the farm didn't really trust banks that much and liked to see a little money in cash up front, to let him know you were serious."

"Cash? You mean pay twenty-five dollars an acre times . . .what? Two hundred and forty acres, something like that. Must be over six thousand dollars. Wow!"

"Yeah, but think if it's for all the land Hal was renting out for his client. Twenty-five dollars an acre times several thousand acres, man, that really adds up!"

Hawkett watched the burgers sizzle on the grill. Feeling his stomach growling as he said, "But apparently Carl Smith agreed to the deal. Carl must have been willing to deal that way?"

"Well, I heard he was doing it, but not liking it. I mean, you have to wonder what the landowner was really doing, taking that much money in cash. What he was probably trying to do was hide it from the IRS, not pay taxes on it, the greedy bastard."

"Yeah well, thanks for the information, Josh. Hey, hand me one of those burgers. Man, they smell delicious. How much I owe you?"

Hawkett bit into a sandwich that was absolutely delicious as he continued up the street, thinking about Hal Dallis, the one-man real estate manager of Iowa LandCo. He thought about Hal representing a client who wanted part of his rent paid in cash. Thinking along the lines of what Josh had said, there was something a little fishy there, probably some sort of tax evasion deal. He thought about how many thousands of dollars Carl would have to deal with in cash if he actually did do business that way. Hawkett remembered how Benjamin had mentioned the safe at the Smith residence and Emily's comments about the large amounts of cash her husband had kept around.

As Hawkett finished his hamburger, he was feeling some anger building. He was thinking about a landowner living in some state far away, buying farms in Taylor County and charging the local farmers quite a bit of money to rent the ground. Then using it as a way to hide some of the income from the IRS. Well if that was the case, he'd follow up on this and get to the bottom of it—cause a little trouble for this investor with the IRS.

Then Hawkett came to a complete stop as a thought hit him. He began to realize that the undeclared cash would only be a problem for the investor if he knew about it. Two hundred dollars or two hundred twenty-five? Hal was probably doing this on his own and skimming the money right off the top—forgetting to mention it to anybody. Man, Hawkett thought, now we do have a motive for murder. Twenty-five dollars an acre times several thousand acres? Yeah, that kind of money could end up getting someone murdered.

CHAPTER
39

Thelma laughed out loud. The twenty-dog hitch was going by them in the parade and she'd never seen anything quite like it, all those Huskies hooked together, pulling that little covered wagon. She turned to say something to Pearl who appeared uncharacteristically calm and had been that way since talking to the Sheriff earlier that day. Well yes, thought Thelma, the Lord had intervened here. He'd seen Pearl's anger and frustration over the way life had turned out for her, losing a child like she had, losing her husband, having to live with her sister-in-law. Maybe this would be a turning point. There was always hope that things would get better, thought Thelma.

She was still watching Pearl, who was smiling and watching the parade while petting the little injured dog lying on her lap. The little dog must be feeling pretty tough, thought Thelma. It hadn't even moved when the large group of dogs went by pulling the wagon. He was probably drugged out on pain medication as he sure didn't act like the same little mutt she'd seen playing at Jamie's farm.

"Hey, it's me," Hawkett said into his hand-held radio. "Hal Dallis is coming your way. Find a place at the end of the parade to get him off by himself. Be careful, I've got a really bad feeling about that guy. Put him in cuffs if you have to. I'm heading that way."

Surprised, Benjamin replied, "Cuffs? What? You find something out? Is he our guy? What?" He was talking into his radio and hoping Hawkett could hear over the crowd noise.

"I'll tell you when I get there. Just be careful and get him cornered." Hawkett trotted down an alley and headed at an angle to the parade route, trying to catch up with Hal and get some answers.

Hal jerked his pickup out of the parade, nearly running over a teenager, then drove up an alley and parked. "Now tell me again," he commanded, talking into his cell phone. "Who called you?"

"He said he was a deputy, said he was in Pigmy, and he just saw you go by in the parade. I know what you're doing in the parade, but what does that have to do with a deputy calling our home, asking me questions about the other people who worked at Iowa LandCo?"

"He asked you that? Why?"

"Hal, how in the heck am I supposed to know? You tell me." She paused waiting for a response, visualizing him sitting in his pickup. "Hal, it's got nothing to do with that other deal? You're not being accused of stealing any money from any of your clients? Hal please tell me that . . ."

"No, no it's nothing like that . . . uh . . . I got a couple of unpaid parking tickets he probably wants me to take care of. You know how these local cops are. Everything's a big deal with them. I'll find him and take care of this, okay? Talk to you later."

Hal, hearing his wife start to say something, pushed the end button on his phone. He got out of his pickup and looked up and down the street. Yeah, there he was. He could see Hawkett working his way through the crowd of people on the other side, but then lost track of him in the group of cattle producers grilling their burgers. Hal moved over a little and could see Hawkett engaged in conversation with that "shit head", Josh Flora. This can't be good, he thought. Then he heard someone say, "Excuse me, sir, but could you move a little? We're trying to watch the parade."

Annoyed at that, Hal turned to see two elderly women sitting in their lawn chairs, one of them was holding a dog. He wanted to think of a really good comeback and put them in their place, but was surprised to see the dog sit up and growl at him with its neck hair standing up. The dog was small, he thought, but those teeth bared like that . . . Then he remembered. He'd had another run-in with that dog. He thought it was dead. As he turned and headed back towards his pickup, he could hear the dog barking. He knew he'd better get out of there.

"Easy pup. What was that all about, Pearl? You suppose it's the drugs? Maybe they're wearing off. Suppose we ought to get hold of Jamie?"

But Pearl wasn't listening. She was watching Hal walk away and not liking his attitude or the look he'd given them. She was wondering what had possessed Tippy, a dog that was deaf, to act the way that he had—growling and trying to get at the guy. The dog must have smelled something—smelled that guy and thought of something bad—and Pearl knew something wasn't right. No sir. This guy was up to something bad and she needed to tell the sheriff or his deputy. But where the hell were they, she wondered as she watched Hal turn to go down the alley.

"Here, Thelma, take this pup," Pearl said as she arose and shoved the dog onto Thelma's lap.

"What are you doing, Pearl? Come back here. Pearl, you hear me!" Thelma watched her sister-in-law hustle down the street, peek into the alley, and then disappear.

Pearl didn't have to go very far. She could see Hal standing by his pickup about halfway down the alley, and she ducked just as he looked around—sure he was up to something. She moved a little bit closer, using a trash dumpster as cover. She was trying to get near him, and find out what he was up to. Pearl gasped quietly, watching Hal take a duffle bag out of the bed of the pickup and then pull a handgun out of it. She ducked her head as he looked around again, but was pretty sure he had seen her that time. She stretched up carefully, watching Hal get back into the truck with his gun, knowing that the situation was really bad. Somebody was going to get hurt, and she had to do something.

She watched as Hal drove out the other end of the alley, then turned and ran back to the street in a panic. She was looking for the sheriff or one of the deputies—somebody to help—knowing she had to do something. She looked up the street again. This time, she saw Hal pull up to the stop sign, then cut right through the parade and drive away. All right, dammit, at least she'd follow the bastard, be able to tell the sheriff which way he went—maybe even where he went—something to help out.

Pearl turned and walked quickly to the first pickup she saw. Glancing inside, she saw that it was an automatic and that the keys were in the ignition. She yanked the door open, turned the key, and heard the motor come to life. Seeing a break in the parade, she gunned the pickup out into the street. She could hear people yelling behind her, but she didn't care. She accelerated up Main Street and turned in the direction Hal had gone—pulling the cattlemen's grill behind her—still hooked to the "borrowed" pickup. Smoke was pouring out of it, as burgers and hot charcoal flew onto the street.

Benjamin and Hawkett were already in Benjamin's patrol car flying out of Pigmy. By the time Hawkett had found Benjamin and had learned that Hal hadn't made it through the parade route, things started happening pretty quickly. The two of them had compared notes and determined that Hal was their guy. But where was Henny?

"Oh hell," Benjamin had said. "He wanted to know if he could fill that hole back in, the one that Carl was buried in. You don't suppose . . ." They had spotted Jan and told her what was going on as they ran toward the car. They had told her to arrest Hal on the spot if she saw him. Then they were off, Benjamin praying all the way out of Pigmy.

They arrived at the Dickenson farm in short order and drove right to the spot where they'd found Carl Smith buried the previous Friday night. Driving closer they could tell the hole had been filled in. They got out of the car and as they walked towards it, both men were hoping and praying that another body wasn't buried in that same hole. They reasoned that no one would ever suspect that could happen—the same murderer planting two bodies in the same hole—who would ever suspect such a thing? Not three steps from the patrol car, they both saw the white plastic pipe sticking up out of the fresh dirt.

"Why? Did he use that to mark the hole? Why would he do that?" Benjamin asked.

Hawkett dropped down on his knees and examined the pipe. "I know I'm jumping to conclusions here, but there is a chance this is an air vent, trying to keep someone alive. Maybe . . . I don't know."

"You think Henny could be buried down there? What . . . breathing air through that pipe? The dirt would crush him, there's no way . . ." Benjamin was asking, looking, feeling his heart pound and his hands tremble.

"We're gonna have to find out right now. You know how to run that backhoe?" Hawkett asked. He knew the answer to that and was hoping it was similar to the tractor that he'd used at Jamie's farm.

"Hell no! Maybe we'd better get the rescue squad out here, find some farmer, somebody who can run the damn thing."

"There may not be time. The kid's probably not there, but we're going to find out." Hawkett climbed into the cab of the backhoe, surprised to see the keys still in the ignition, and started the motor. Hearing the motor running, Hawkett started moving the hydraulic levers back and forth, trying to get a feel for which levers moved which arms, and pretty quickly he felt he could handle it. He shifted the backhoe into gear with some jerking and drove it over to the dirt pile where Benjamin was on his knees, attempting to yell down the pipe.

Once Hawkett had raised the dirt scoop up and over the pile, Benjamin got up and moved out of the way, rushing around to the side of the cab. "You sure you can do this? Don't cut him in half. Be careful, you hear me?"

But Hawkett wasn't paying any attention to Benjamin. He had his hands full running the machine. He was tense and nervous, wondering what they might find and hoping it would be nothing but dirt.

Hawkett worked dirt out of the hole, taking small scoopfuls and dumping them off to the side. Benjamin, having made the decision that it was better to be safe than sorry, called Jan and told her to get the EMTs on the way and the fire department too. He didn't know what was going to happen in the minutes that followed or what they were up against and hoped that this was all foolishness. But if it was, why the pipe?

Hawkett yelled out of the cab, "See anything yet? Climb down in there, poke around a little, feel that pipe."

Benjamin sat down on the edge of the hole and slid himself into it, dropping about four feet. He got down on his knees, but as he carefully shook the pipe, he felt it come loose. He watched in panic as dirt rushed in around the opening. If it was an air hole, he'd just destroyed it.

He pulled himself up and out of the hole and yelled to Hawkett, "Hurry up. It felt like another couple of feet, but I pulled out the pipe!"

Hawkett had already started working deeper into the hole, wishing that he was experienced with the machine and praying he didn't cut anybody in half. If he was in the hole, there had to be some sort of container to protect the boy, he thought. Then he hit something solid.

With the bucket lifted and the engine off, he grabbed a shovel hanging on the side of the backhoe. Down into the hole he went. Benjamin was yelling questions, but Hawkett knew there was no time for talking. He threw dirt up and out of the hole, poking the shovel into the dirt, feeling for resistance. The dirt, having been handled repeatedly, was loose and easy to move, and it didn't take Hawkett long to realize he was digging towards a metal barrel. Knowing that Henny was probably inside the barrel, he felt an even greater sense of urgency. He dug faster, hearing Benjamin, who could then see the barrel, yell into his radio.

In minutes that seemed to last forever, Hawkett had discovered that one end of the barrel had a lid on it, and once on his knees, he began to dig with his hands. Prying the lid open, he could see the small boy's head. Henny's eyes were closed and a horrible feeling came over Hawkett. He looked up and yelled at Benjamin, "He's here, but I don't know if he's alive. Can you get down here and help me get him out of this barrel?"

Benjamin moved quickly as he dropped down on the side of the hole and clumsily slid into it. His right foot landed hard, on the back of Hawkett's calf. Hawkett let out an exclamation of pain but didn't look up.

With enough dirt shoved away, Hawkett was able to reach his arms into the barrel. He grabbed for Henny's wrist. "Alright, there's a pulse!" Hawkett felt overcome with emotion, half anger and half relief, but knew the pulse was weak and the situation—desperate.

After another minute had passed, the two had shoved enough dirt to one side of the hole that they were able to pull the little guy out— still unconscious. "Suppose we should move him, get him up out of this hole?" Hawkett asked as he brushed dirt off of Henny's face.

"Yeah, I don't think he's going to have anything broken, but we need to get him up out of this hole, get some more air, and start working on his chest if he quits breathing. You climb up out of here. I don't think I can. I'll hand him up to you."

Hawkett was up and out of the hole in no time. He turned to grab Henny below his armpits. Benjamin grunted as he gave it everything he had to lift the boy as high above his head as he could.

CHAPTER

40

Benjamin was on his knees on the ground beside Hawkett. Both of them were watching the little boy's breathing and were prepared to start working on his chest if he quit breathing again—not knowing what they were up against. Internal injuries? Shock?

They were talking to each other in broken bits of conversation. Benjamin was caught between two emotions. He was scared, like he'd never been in his life. Praying and telling God he could have his life if he'd save the boy's, and thinking in the same breath what he was going to do to Hal Dallis when he got his hands on him. There wouldn't need to be a trial. Justice would be taken care of quickly. Benjamin didn't care what the consequences might be—just knowing rage and anger like he'd never felt them before, and knowing what he was going to do.

"Where in the hell are the EMTs? Didn't you say you called in?" Hawkett asked.

"Yeah, I did. I don't know, I suppose half of them are doing something in the parade. I'll call Jan again . . ." He stopped. Glancing over his shoulder, he could see a vehicle coming down the road towards them, slowing for the turn. "That's probably them."

"Damn, did he stop breathing again?" Hawkett began shaking Henny, putting his hands on the boy's chest, then leaning down toward his mouth and listening. "No, I think he's breathing, but boy is it shallow. How's his pulse?"

Benjamin was holding Henny's wrist. "It's there. I have trouble finding it, but it's there."

Hawkett reached down and lifted Henny's eyelids, checking to see if his pupils were dilated. He started to say something to Benjamin but was interrupted by him.

"Son-of-a-bitch!" Hawkett watched Benjamin stumble as he tried to get up too quickly, then turned to see a pickup pulling up beside them with the words "Iowa LandCo" on the door.

Hawkett regretted that his gun was back at the office. He hadn't wanted to wear it during the parade. He stared at Hal Dallis who was already out of his pickup and walking right towards them, a handgun at his side that looked like it could do the job, and Benjamin, acting like he didn't know better, was heading right at Hal, yelling obscenities as he did.

"Ben!" Hawkett yelled. He heard a gunshot and then another, and saw Benjamin go down just as he was lunging for Hal's leg, but falling short of the mark.

Hawkett patted Henny on the chest—saying goodbye to the little guy. He knew that they were all going to die right there. He stood up and faced Hal, a man who had shot at least two men already.

Hal was staring down at Benjamin—still trying to get up, crawling toward him. He pointed his gun at Benjamin's head—ready to finish the job.

"Stop! For God's sake, stop!" Hawkett yelled. His voice broke as he walked directly towards Hal—getting ready to die beside his partner.

Suddenly the men heard a banging and rattling noise, and turned to see what the ruckus was. Pearl came flying up the road and turned into the field. The grill finally broke away from the pickup's hitch and rolled into the county ditch spewing out hot coals as it did. Smoke began billowing out of the grass.

Hawkett moved fast, having just the split second of distraction that Pearl had caused, and dove into Dallis, going for the gun first. He

217

heard it go off as he forced it to the ground. Then following his momentum, he drove Hal backwards. Getting a couple of hard blows into the guy's face, he saw blood splattering out of his nose as both men fell to the ground. Hawkett scrambled to get on top of Hal and pinned him to the ground. Then, raging with anger and his adrenaline pumping, Hawkett repeatedly pounded him in the face, his knuckles cracking.

"Stop!" Pearl screamed as she knelt on the ground beside Benjamin. "He's done. Get over here. I can't stop all this bleeding by myself!"

Time seemed to have come to a complete stop. Hawkett felt as if he were in a dream, seeing people rushing around everywhere. Man, half of Pigmy must be here, he thought. Medical professionals were surrounding Benjamin and tubes were already sticking out of him. Flashing lights were lighting up the darkening evening sky. It was a surreal setting, even to a hardened lawman.

Hawkett was thankful that Jan had arrived. She was totally in control of the situation, barking out orders, lending a hand, and glancing at Benjamin's motionless body with a worried look on her face, as she talked into her radio.

At one point he thought he heard someone say that the boy would be okay, as they lifted him into the back of an ambulance. Then he heard somebody else say, "but the sheriff . . ." before their words were drowned out. Hawkett, in an attempt to shut that thought out, instead turned his thinking to the past, remembering the years they'd had together. Benjamin was more like a father to him than a partner, and he began to wonder what life would be like without him, when he heard . . .

"You sure you're okay, Hawkett?" Jan was looking at him with a concerned expression on her face.

"Yeah, sure. Yeah, I'm fine. What are they saying about Benjamin?"

"Well, he's still alive," her voice choked with emotion, "but he's just lost so much blood. They've got him ready to go. They're heading to the Clarinda Hospital, probably Life Flight from there if . . ." She didn't finish her statement, but instead covered her eyes for a minute. "Listen, the guys from Page County have got Hal in custody. You want to ride with me? Go to the hospital . . . you know . . . be there—one way or the other?" Again her voice broke.

"Yeah, let's go."

218

So there he sat, dirty, bloody and mentally drained. Nearly two hours had gone by. Life Flight was in the air, heading for Clarinda, but still, the doctors and nurses were unable to get Benjamin stabilized for the trip. People were running in and out of the emergency ward, needing this and that. The only item Hawkett recognized was more blood.

Waiting, waiting . . . He knew that was all he could do and it was a helpless feeling. He'd played the regret game for a while, thinking about what he should have known, what he should have done, how unprofessionally two professionals had handled this situation.

Well, Benjamin would be happy to know that Henny was going to be okay, physically anyway, thought Hawkett. He was wondering what had been done to the boy, how much trauma he had suffered mentally, how that might screw up his life. Hawkett continued to think about Henny, remembering the scene that he'd heard about in the funeral home, smiling to himself as he visualized Benjamin throwing the dentures across the room.

He smiled, thinking that he'd better hold onto that memory, because at any moment, someone would come out of that room and tell him what he didn't want to hear. Nervously, he stood up and walked over to the window where he could watch the staff adjusting tubes, checking monitors, talking to each other. Unable to hear what they were saying, he wondered what they'd do if he just walked through the swinging doors and touched his old friend. He wondered what he'd say if Benjamin opened his eyes and looked at him . . . then Hawkett jumped as he felt a hand on his shoulder.

Turning around, he saw Jamie. He grabbed her and wrapped his arms around her.

"How's he doing?" Jamie asked, looking up at him.

"Not good, but he's still alive. I keep worrying that someone will come out and say, 'We're sorry but we did everything we could.'" Hawkett stopped himself, unable to go on.

"We've been praying for him, Adam. That's all we can do now."

"Yeah, thanks. Where's Andrea? Is she here or did you have to leave her someplace?"

"No, she's right down the hall, sitting by the nurse's station. They won't let any children in here. I had to lie and tell them I was a relative or I wouldn't have made it this far. I feel bad about doing that, but . . ." she said shrugging, "I wanted to be here."

"Yeah, well thanks for coming. I'm sorry about the way things have worked out. I mean . . . we've got to talk . . . I mean, if you want to talk. Hell I don't know, I just . . . "

"Yes, Adam, I want to talk. We'll find time for that when the time's right. I'm sorry. I was too pushy, trying to project this dream I had. You know—taking too much for granted, maybe asking too much of you."

She looked up into his eyes again, trying to find something, but what? Hawkett, feeling another opportunity to make things right and get back on track, but then again feeling so wrung out and not knowing just what to say, fell silent. Just having her there, eased his pain.

Jamie broke the silence. "Well, I'm going to go back and get Andrea, maybe get something to eat, then go home and take care of the animals. Are you gonna be okay, Adam?"

"Yeah sure, I'm fine. Just, you know, hoping and hoping." He nodded back over his shoulder toward the emergency room.

"Yeah, well keep me informed, either way, okay? We'll be praying."

She turned and began to walk away, and Hawkett thought, no, now is the time. He called out to her, "Jamie!"

Startled she turned to look at him, both of them aware that he'd attracted the attention of everyone in the hall. People came to a halt, stopping to see what was going on. Hawkett didn't care. He walked towards her. "I don't know, am I supposed to drop down on one knee or what?" He tried to keep the emotion out of his voice, but was feeling it so strongly that he didn't care what he said or how he looked. He just wanted to convey his message to her.

"Jamie, I want to marry you. Line up the minister, pick a date, I don't care. But if you'll have me, I want to spend the rest of my life with you." As Hawkett said this, a little girl came running down the hall towards them and grabbed the two adults, who were now holding onto each other.

Two nurses were holding the doors open to the emergency room, getting ready to move Benjamin. They stood still, watching the marriage proposal take place right in front of their eyes. Inside the emergency room, an attending nurse reached across Benjamin's stomach and was surprised to feel his hand take hold of hers and squeeze it gently. She wondered if that was actually a smile she saw on her patient's face.

If you enjoyed this book, be sure to read *The Iowa Farmer's Wife*, another book by author Bill Beaman and prequel to *Second Chances*.

The Iowa Farmer's Wife is a gripping story, a page-turning mystery about a murder that takes place in the rolling hills of southwest Iowa. Bill Beaman intrigues his readers by planting a horrific homicide smack dab in the middle of the heartland.

When a rural banker is brutally murdered, two DCI detectives travel to the scene of the crime to investigate. Little do these "city boys" know what their trip into the country will entail. The plot thickens as the investigation revolves around a young widow and her struggle to hold onto her farm.

To learn more about the author, Bill Beaman, and to order copies of his books, visit:

WWW.THEIOWAFARMER.COM